False Start

by

Sasha
MARSHALL

Copyright © 2021 by Sasha Marshall

Published in the United States of America.

All rights reserved.

Cover Design: Sasha Marshall

Interior Design: Nola Marie

Proofreading: Dane Marshall

Photo/Art Credits:

Creative Fabrica: PIG.design, A design, Regulrcrative

This is a work of fiction. Names, characters, places, and incidents are either the products of the author's imagination or are used fictitiously. Any resemblance to actual persons (living or dead), events or locations is entirely coincidental.

All rights reserved. No part of this book may be reproduced in any form or by any electronic or mechanical means, including information storage and retrieval systems, without permission in writing from the publisher, except by a reviewer, who may quote brief passages in a review.

CONTENTS

Chapter One	3
Chapter Two	14
Chapter Three	20
Chapter Four	27
Chapter Five	35
Chapter Six	41
Chapter Seven	48
Chapter Eight	54
Chapter Nine	63
Chapter Ten	71
Chapter Eleven	79
Chapter Twelve	89
Chapter Thirteen	96
Chapter Fourteen	102
Chapter Fifteen	110
Chapter Sixteen	117
Chapter Seventeen	124
Chapter Eighteen	131
Chapter Nineteen	137
Chapter Twenty	145
Chapter Twenty-One	155
Chapter Twenty-Two	162
Chapter Twenty-Three	169
Chapter Twenty-Four	176

Chapter Twenty-Five 182

Chapter Twenty-Six 190

Chapter Twenty-Seven 198

Chapter Twenty-Eight 208

Chapter Twenty-Nine 214

Chapter Thirty 222

Chapter Thirty-One 229

Chapter Thirty-Two 235

Chapter Thirty-Three 242

Chapter Thirty-Four 247

Chapter Thirty-Five 254

Chapter Thirty-Six 258

Epilogue 264

Acknowledgments 271

About the Author 273

For Derek & Olaf

Thank you for making this book all it could be. It needed the heart of a football fan and his feline companion.

CHAPTER ONE

NOW

I'M OGLING MY AQUA Man calendar and the stud on the cover photograph above my sister's blonde head while listening to her rant about the mediocre sex she's been having with a guy named Dave. Out of the blue, an old, familiar smell wafts into my office. Goosebumps erupt on the surface of my skin and heat curls in my belly. My fingers tighten around the arms of my office chair, and my toes leave imprints in the soles of my shoes. I leap to my feet, cross my office in five swift strides, and stick my blonde head into the hall only to discover the back side of the source of the scent. I'd know that juicy ass anywhere because my hands have intimately touched it for years.

Zina sticks her head out to see what interrupted our conversation. "Ah, hell. What's he doing here?"

"I don't know, let's go find out.".

At the end of the hall, he takes a right toward the coach's offices. We speed walk down the hall, pause before we turn the corner, and wait to see where he goes. The door to the head coach's office opens, and Otto Bullock steps out with a smile on his face. He loudly greets his guest by excitedly shaking his hand. Otto is my godfather and apparently a freaking traitor! As the two men step through the office, I use hand signals to indicate we should move. Zina nods in understanding before we creep down the hall like two teenagers sneaking out for the night.

Zina is my sister and partner in crime. We're only eleven months apart, so we're pretty close… and nosey, which is how we end up leaning against the door to Head Coach Otto Bullock's office with our ears pressed flat against the piece of wood. We're doing this because my ex-husband just walked inside said office.

I should've known to trust my gut feeling this morning when I woke up with dread in my belly. It's no coincidence that my otherwise unexplained anxiety and his appearance are linked. The man gives me heartburn… and lots of really great orgasms. God, he always got that right, but it wasn't enough to hold me and my college sweetheart together when things got tough.

Except… the sex. Lord. Have. Mercy. He is a god in the sack, and he uses his sexual prowess to make me do stupid things like sleep with him anytime we're in the same city. And that happens a good bit because I'm a weak woman.

It's common knowledge that the New Orleans Voodoo football team has a critical quarterback issue at the moment–our last quarterback retired, and the backup QB asked to be traded to North Carolina. It doesn't escape me that my ex is a quarterback, but he has a successful career in Los Angeles with the Spartans. He's a free agent this year, but the city loves him, and at age 28, he's still performing at the top. He took his team to the Superbowl last season against New England. They lost, but he still made it there, which is no easy feat in professional football. There's no reason for him to leave his team.

"Stop breathing so loud," I whisper to Zina. Every time I think I can make out what the two men are saying, Zina starts breathing like Darth Vader.

"They said your name!" she whisper-yells.

"Shhh, I can't hear!" I whisper-shout back.

A deep male voice sneaks up and scares the crap out of me and makes my sister scream in terror. Shit. Our cover is blown now. "Who unleashed the Hell sisters?" Assistant Coach Jed Jones asks. He flinches every time he sees us together, because we're known for giving all the guys hell. Just last year, we crashed his wedding and replaced all the expensive wine with blackberry moonshine. I've never seen so many people vomit in formal attire. How were we to know the guests couldn't handle their liquor? Surprisingly, Jed wasn't upset because he said it was the only time he's actually liked his new mother-in-law. Apparently, she's a frisky cougar on the dance floor when she gets her shine on.

Before I can back away from the office door, it's wrenched open, and I fall forward into the hairiest chest I've ever seen peeking through an unbuttoned polo. I eat a mouthful of Coach Otto's gray strands and cough them back out. Crap. I'm going to have to pick these off my tongue individually.

"Hey, Coach," I say, smiling and spitting out a few more hairs. I try my best to act casual and must epically fail because Coach is frowning at me like I've lost my mind. A hair tickles the back of my throat and makes me gag. Ugh.

"Zhanna, are you alright?" Coach arches a curious brow.

Other than choking to death on his fur, just freaking swell. "Yes, sir."

He uses his thumb to point behind him where my ex sits. "I guess you want to talk to this guy. Come in so we can chat."

Not particularly.

Following him through the door, I find Bryant seated on the left side of the massive office on a large, tufted leather couch. While Coach turns around to shut the door, I notice Bryant's wearing a Voodoo team polo in the beautiful black and gold colors, so I flip him the bird to let him know how I feel about it. He leans his gorgeous head back as a deep, hearty laugh escapes him. It's a good laugh that makes me remember the good times between us. I almost laugh with him until I remember I don't like him. I cut that shit out.

Pale green eyes meet my hazels, and my heart comes to a skittering halt. I momentarily forget how to breathe. He's quite the work of art standing at 6'5 and looking like every girl's wet dream. He weighs in at 240 pounds with a tight, muscular body covered in black ink. His long chocolate-colored hair with caramel sun streaks is pulled back into a man bun. If he weren't dressed in gray dress slacks that showcase an ass you can pop a quarter off of and a polo showing off his corded arms, he would look like he just rolled his stupidly pretty ass out of bed. The week old-beard rounds out the complete package of one sexy beast.

Finally, he stands like a gentleman. "Zhanna, you're as beautiful as ever." He leans in to hug me and lays a sweet kiss on my forehead, whispering, "I miss you."

He's been telling me that every time he's seen me for the past two years. He didn't seem to miss me when his dick was in another woman's mouth. I can only assume he's trying to get into my panties, which isn't hard to do. I'm ashamed. I pull out of the embrace as soon as it's acceptable and smooth my pencil skirt out before I take a seat on the couch beside him. I cross my legs and wait for Coach to take a seat behind his desk.

"I'm going to be frank with you, sweetheart. I know you and Hudson have history, but we need him on this team just like we need you on the team taking care of and rehabbing the injured. I'm hoping the two of you will get along fine by being the consummate professionals I know you to be," Coach begins, laying down the law.

We'll get along just fine alright–like a house on fire.

"Zhanna, you and Zina have a special place in my heart. You may not see the intelligence of my decision to trade for your husband, but I made the same decision your dad would've made if he were still head coach."

"Ex-husband," I gently remind him.

He has to go and bring up my dad, may his soul rest in peace, but he's right. When my dad was head coach of the Voodoo, he would've fought over the chance for Bryant to play for him. He loved a shotgun quarterback. Given the predicament the team is in now, I would also make the same decision. It doesn't mean I have to like it one bit.

"So, what you're saying is Bryant is our new quarterback?" I ask, further clarifying matters.

"Yes, baby," Bryant answers.

I pat him on the leg in a condescending manner. "Shhh, the adults are talking."

Coach arches a brow at my rudeness. "Yes," he says, "Bryant is our new starting quarterback."

"Is the ink dry?" I ask, holding my breath.

Bryant blows out a breath of exasperation. "Christ, woman."

Coach humors me. "Yes."

"Did you forget that I was arrested and sent to jail for trying to murder him?"

True story. Real news. I went to jail for committing assault and battery and destruction of private property. I was committing domestic abuse and destroying hundreds of thousands of dollars of windows because I caught Bryant with his pants down. My heart was crushed and shattered into a million pieces. When Bryant answered the door to the cops, he was drunk, and sporting a motley of colors ranging from red welts to already forming blue bruises. I'm quite the artist. Anyhow, thank God for high-priced attorneys, right?

Coach's lip twitches, but he does a good job of hiding his smile. "I bailed you out of jail."

"Yes, you did! Do you think they'll drop the charges next time?"

"You're my witness if she knocks me off," Bryant tells him.

"Ha!" I laugh. "They'd never find your body!" Coach is looking at me with frustration knitted in his brows, so I raise my hand to see if it's still my turn to talk. He rubs the space between his eyes, and Bryant snorts. "Sir, may I borrow a pen and piece of paper?" He hands me the two items, and I write out a lovely little note and hand it back to him.

To whomever it may concern:

I quit.

Sincerely,

Zhanna Hale

"Alright, smart-ass," Coach says.

"You're not quitting," Bryant tells me.

I'm about to tell him what I do is none of his business anymore, but Coach interrupts before the feuding can well and truly begin. "Why don't you two take the rest of the day and talk this out? It would be good for you to establish boundaries for working with one another. I don't want any marital shit hindering this football team or my quarterback, and Zhanna, I need you on your toes to make sure my boys stay healthy. I need you both on top of your games. I believe in both of you, it's why you're here."

When the famous Otto Bullock tells you he believes in you, it's really something. "Yes, sir," we say in unison.

"Let's go before he fires us," Bryant says and grabs my hand, interlacing his fingers with mine.

"I already quit."

"See you tomorrow, Zhanna," Coach says as I'm pulled from his office.

Zina's standing outside, grinning when the two of us emerge hand-in-hand. "What's up, bro?"

My ex releases my hand, picks up my little sister, and spins her around. "Hey, sis!"

Those two should've gotten married. They get along so much better than we do.

Zina pulls on the arm of his shirt. "What's this shirt you're wearing?"

"My new team's shirt," he proudly answers.

"Holy shit! You're Voodoo now? Wait, how in the hell are the two of you going to work together and live in the same city?"

Bryant waves off the question. "We're going to be fine."

I'm glad someone has confidence we won't burn the city to the ground, because I sure don't. While Zina and Bryant catch up, I start to sneak off and make a break for it.

He reaches out and gently wraps a hand around my arm. "Not so fast, Z. You heard Coach."

I roll my eyes. "We can make up rules in my office with Zina as mediator."

"Nope. We're going to the lot, you're getting in my car, and we're going to grab a bite to eat in public where you can't commit another felony."

"We're not going anywhere. I can't take off work. I have stuff to do. You can't just waltz back in town and expect for me to drop everything. What are you even doing here?"

"I'm trying to win my wife back!" he shouts.

A few people look out of their offices.

"Shhh, keep your voice down!"

His face grows serious as he leans down in my personal space. "Zhanna, you have two choices. You can walk to my car of your own volition, or I'm picking you up, carrying you out there, and putting you in the damn thing."

"I'm wearing a skirt and heels." I point out.

"Five."

Huffing, I try to compromise with the ass. "Let's just stay out of each other's hair, okay?"

"Four."

"No more sleeping together."

"Three."

"Stop it, Bryant and listen to reason!"

"Two."

Assistant Coach Jed Jones heads in our direction again and frowns when he sees Bryant in my face. "You okay, Zhanna?"

My ex doesn't look away from me as he speaks through gritted teeth, "She's fine. Just stubborn as hell."

Jed chuckles. "That's why we call them 'the Hell Sisters'."

"One and a half," Bryant continues, stalling for time.

I start for my office.

"One," he says, turns me around, and scoops me up before throwing me over his shoulder.

I kick and yell like a banshee, attracting all sorts of attention. Not one person comes to help. Instead, they stare in awe at Bryant freaking Hudson being in their building. Since I just found out, I doubt many people know he's already traded to our team.

Meanwhile, I'm hanging upside down with all the blood rushing to my head. I pray he won't drop me on the hard ground.

Once we're outside, he stops at his black M5, and opens the passenger door. He slings me over his shoulder, sets my feet to rights, and keeps me from falling over from dizziness.

"You need to go back to California."

"I need you to listen to me, and listen to me good, Zhanna. I'm coming for you, and there's nothing you can do to stop me until you're wearing my ring, sleeping in my bed, and using my last name again. Wrap your mind around that because I fucked up the first time with you. There won't be a second."

"In other words, you're going to make my life a living hell until you finally realize I want nothing to do with you."

He grins at me. "Nothing?"

Gah. Okay. I want his body and his skills in the bedroom. "You know what I mean."

I slide into the car, with Bryant following moments later.

"Oh, I know what you mean. I'm taking it, you'd like to keep our little arrangement where we fuck each other senseless every time we're near one another."

He makes me sound like I use him, which I totally do, but there's an underlying sadness in his eyes he thinks he's hiding from me. I choose to ignore it. "Sure. We can keep that arrangement. It's working for me, and that's what's important—me and what I want for once. Don't you think so?"

"If that's what you want." He sounds resigned to the fact he's probably not getting much more out of this conversation.

"That's what I want. As a matter of fact, why don't we go to the nearest hotel and get a round in before lunch?"

He shakes his head at me. "No, I'm not running around in hotels with you anymore. You're my fucking wife! We both have residences that will suffice." He pauses, looking out the front window and releasing a sigh. "Your place or mine?"

I let the wife comment go. "Well, geez! Don't sound so freaking excited about it!"

Bryant turns the ignition over and revs the engine before he backs out of his parking space and drives away.

"We're going to lunch," he says five minutes later. "We're going somewhere nice and expensive and quietly making up rules to make you feel better about this situation. We're going to spend time together outside of the bedroom at my place."

My head whips around to him. "Did you already buy a place?"

"Bought it two months ago. Two blocks from your apartment, on Dauphine."

"You could've bought any place you wanted in New Orleans, but you bought a house two blocks from mine?"

He shrugs before he answers. "I wouldn't want traffic to be an issue for you when you decide I'm of use."

He's pouting, so I let him stew over there in his misery for a little while. A little while ends up being over thirty minutes away in the heart of the French Quarter at a fancy French restaurant named Bourdon's. At least, it's where I think we're headed, but instead, he pulls into a drive five houses down from the eatery until he comes to an iron gate. He presses a button on his visor and the gate opens. Fancy. The area beyond the gate is only wide enough for one vehicle. He parks in a two-car garage matching the blue, Victorian home, and exits.

"I bought a home with furniture, but some of it's hideous. The mattresses are lumpy. It would be a great help to me if you could get rid of the unwanted pieces and order furniture to replace them. You did a great job of decorating the home in L.A. Zina mentioned you know an interior designer?"

I have no idea when they could've had this conversation. "When did she say that?"

He shoots me an are you kidding me expression. "Outside of Bullock's office."

"Ah, I must've been ignoring you."

We walk through the gate to a private, overgrown courtyard complete with a koi pond and dilapidated furniture. This place could use some weed killer, paint, string lights, and nice furniture. I had to clean up the shared courtyard of my apartment building when I first moved in two years ago as well. It's nice to have a secluded place in the middle of the busy Quarter.

"So?"

"So?" I gaze up at him.

"Do you know an interior designer or not?"

"Yes, my neighbor, Leslie. I can put in a call to him and have him meet us here if you like."

He looks over his shoulder at me. "I think we have more important things to discuss first."

"I thought you were taking me to a public place?"

"We're going to Bourdon's, but first, we set the rules in place here. I want to change anyway. See if your friend can meet us here in a couple of hours." He walks through a kitchen that also needs work before heading into a den. "I'm not sure how comfortable the furniture in here is, but please have a seat and make yourself at home."

He takes off for what I assume is the master bedroom while I take a look around the narrow room with an original brick fireplace as the centerpiece. A large rectangular ornate mirror is hung above it. The couches are a hideous orange, but they can be recovered to be beautiful antique pieces.

I wander into the kitchen and look at its potential. It's hard not to picture myself here in these rooms, living with Bryant. When we attended LSU, he talked about playing for the Voodoo and us living in a mansion somewhere in the French Quarter or the Garden District. This house is three stories, but not a mansion by most standards. Still, this was the dream. Fast forward to today—we're living apart in the Quarter because we're divorced. It makes me realize just how precious and fragile love is.

"Are you ready?" he asks, pulling me out of my thoughts.

I turn to find him standing in the doorway to my right. "Food?"

"Before we go to a restaurant where there are steak knives, I'd like to try and calmly discuss your rules."

He looks behind me to the kitchen counter and back at me again. Then he holds a finger up to signal me to wait as he steps around me, grabs the knife block nestled against the tile backsplash, and puts it on top of the refrigerator where I can't reach it.

I put my hands on my hips. "You've got jokes?"

He shoots me a boyish grin complete with those damn dimples. "I don't want a pesky thing like my violent, untimely death to ruin my chances of getting back with you."

"Focus, Quarterback. Rules."

"Rule number one: you should always take your clothes off when we're alone,".

"In your dreams. Look, the only thing I care about is my job. Please don't jeopardize it."

He grows serious. "I would never do that."

Deep down, I know he wouldn't put my career at risk, but there's a great deal I didn't think he was capable of until two years ago. If someone told me the college kid who was after my heart from the moment, we met eight years ago would destroy it, I would've told them they didn't know Bryant, not the sweet Bryant I met at college all those years ago.

CHAPTER TWO

EIGHT YEARS AGO

HALE'S ROW IS A tract of land situated just outside the city limits of Baton Rouge. It's a haul from the stadium after a game on Saturday night, but every football team has partied here since my dad inherited the acreage his sophomore year at LSU. It's hard to tell how many students pass through our gates before and after a game, but it's hundreds on any given game day. Most come for a drink, the bonfire, and the game. And quite a few of our partygoers stay the night, opting to sleep inside tents or their cars rather than drive intoxicated.

Tonight, we're celebrating a victory after four long, brutal quarters against Western Mississippi State, bringing us one step closer to the conference title. It's a bit more crowded around the fire this evening, and the volume is about ten notches higher than usual.

Zina slides onto the back of the tailgate I'm perched on. "When was the last time you looked across the fire?"

I frown at her, confused as to what she's referring to. "What?"

"I heard a rumor that our quarterback decided to grace us with his presence tonight. I investigated and found him across the fire staring at you."

I immediately look across the huge fire, squinting and trying to see to the other side. It's no use with the smoke and flame in the middle. "Hudson is here?"

She giggles. "The one and only. And he's staring at you."

My dad was a famous college quarterback for LSU before he went to the pros as a coach for the Voodoo. He left his mark on college and professional football. I'm proud of his legacy, but I saw the toll the sport can take on a family. I'm not looking for a relationship that requires so much damn work. I want a relationship to be as effortless as possible. All of this is the reason I'm unconcerned with and unfazed by Bryant Hudson's supposed staring from across the fire.

"He's coming this way," she says and turns up her red solo cup to hide the tiny squeal of excitement that escapes her.

"No, thank you." I take the last swallow of my beer and slide off the tailgate to visit a nearby keg.

Zina is on my heels. "You're not seriously going to turn him down if he asks you out."

"I don't date football players." A sympathetic expression crosses her face. "Not everyone is dad, Zhanna. He played football at a different time when there were less security precautions on the field."

My father's brain was a ticking time bomb. He sustained several concussions when he played in college, and they left a lasting impact on his brain. He was diagnosed with post concussive syndrome when he began losing his balance. On the day he died, he was in the middle of the stadium he called home. Dad lost his balance on the concrete steps among the seats and tumbled down. A spinal cord injury instantly claimed his life. I'm not interested in sitting on the sidelines while holding my breath and praying nothing happens that will rip my partner from my life.

"He's with Ben Slate."

Ben Slate plays tight end for our team. Zina has the biggest crush on the guy, which probably means I'm going to be forced to spend my evening talking to his best friend, the quarterback.

As soon as I see Ben and Bryant, I fill my cup from the tap and turn on my heel before Zina can ask me to be her wing woman. I head for the hunting lodge my sister and I crash in on game nights. It's not far into woods from the vast open field that takes up a quarter of the property.

A masculine voice is much too close for my liking. "This is how all scary movies begin."

Turning on my heel to stop his progress, I find Bryant Hudson standing there with a red solo cup in his hand and a grin on his face. If dimples could kill, I'd be a goner. His dark brown hair almost touches his shoulders. His light green eyes sparkle with mischief. The tattoos on his arms do things to me I wish they didn't do.

"Are you following me into the dark woods?" I ask, giving him as much attitude as I can muster.

"I think it's more like you're leading me astray."

"I don't recall inviting you," I snark back, my hands on my hips.

He raises the cup to his lips and takes a drink. "I'm almost positive you did."

Zina and Ben trail after us with grins on their faces.

Bryant continues toward me, smirk firmly in place, until he stops directly in front of me.

"I know you're not accustomed to hearing this, QB, but I'm not interested."

His hand flies to his chest. "Ouch, woman. I haven't even introduced myself."

He's not going to like the fact that he's not getting in my pants tonight or ever. I'm sure guys like him aren't used to being turned down. "I know who you are."

He extends his hand to me. "Bryant Hudson."

I place my hand in his. He immediately brings it to his lips and places a kiss atop it. "Zhanna Hale."

"Beautiful name for a beautiful woman."

"Ugh." I roll my eyes. "Could you be any more of a douchebag right now?"

A choking sound comes from my sister.

Ben snorts.

"Zane Hale's daughter." One would think a sane man would take my rejection for the clear sign it is, turn his ass around, and leave me in peace, but not Bryant Hudson. No, he leans his head back and laughs at me. "I heard you were tough."

"My reputation precedes me."

"Not quite. I heard you were beautiful, but damn, they didn't do you justice."

I feel myself soften a hair toward him but hide it under a sarcastic laugh. "Does this work on other girls?"

His face grows serious. "I don't have time for women or dating, not with football. I don't usually bother to be honest. Plus, it's hard to find a meaningful relationship when over half the available women see me as a meal ticket."

It's probably best to set the record straight now. "I don't date football players."

Bryant holds up his large hand. "Whoa there, little lady. Nobody said anything about a date. How about a beer and a friendly conversation?"

His playful demeanor, the smirk on his handsome face, and his ability to take a not-so-subtle hint sets me at ease. "Yeah, QB, we can have a beer while I tell you how to step up your game on the field."

Ben spits out a mouthful of beer and nearly chokes through his laughter. "This chick is the best! I have to hear this."

"Is that right?" Amusement dances in Bryant's eyes.

"Uh oh. Can't take the heat from a girl?" I ask, winking at him.

He takes another few steps toward me. "I don't think there's anything hotter than a gorgeous chick talking football."

I suppress my stupid grin and lead the three of them to the hunting cabin without another word. There's a fire pit for warmth just outside the small two-bedroom cabin. It's surrounded by log seats we often use for smaller gatherings throughout the year.

Ben turns in a circle to check out the area. "Sweet spot."

Both guys take the lead on collecting firewood from our stack and starting the fire. It's November, so there's a chill in the air. It's nice to have heat and still be able to enjoy the outdoors this time of year.

I feel connected to my dad here. Our family spent a lot of time on this land when dad had down time from the team. Zina and I frequently use the pond and hiking trails on the land.

Bryant takes a seat next to me on the log. "Lay it on me. How do I step up my game?"

"Simple. Throw the damn ball."

Ben laughs. "I've been telling him the same thing for two seasons."

"We call you Chicken Shit Hudson." I blurt it out without meaning to.

Oops.

"Zhanna!" Zina chastises.

"What? It's the truth."

We love our boys, and we love our quarterback, but he's afraid to throw the ball.

Bryant's brows almost reach his hairline. "Chicken Shit Hudson?"

"I can't with this girl," Ben says, delighted beyond belief.

Lifting a shoulder, I shrug. "If the shoe fits."

Bryant quickly moves to one knee in front of me and takes my hand in his. "Will you marry me?"

I snatch my hand from his. "Who says I'm into guys?"

"Even more reason to take you off the market."

"Either way, I'm not into football players," I remind him.

He grins at me, almost toppling me over from the dimples. "You're discriminating against me?"

"No, I'm choosing not to end up with a man who is either going to be washed up by the end of college or by the time he's forty. I'm not marrying a man only to end up as his nurse."

Injuries are impossible to avoid in football. It's a full-contact sport where 200-pound and 300-pound men throw themselves at each other. Sometimes, players are lucky to never incur serious injuries, but they will indeed sustain them. Other players receive injuries that take them out of the game early. I don't want to live with a man who's pissed off at the world over his career ending early. It's hard to know which player will end up on the injured reserve list or which one will play until he's 40.

Understanding and compassion flash in Bryant's eyes. "Your dad."

"Yeah."

"I get it. It would scare me, too." Then he changes the subject, sitting back on the log next to me. "Are you a football fan?"

"The biggest."

"Favorite teams?"

Zina and Ben fall into conversation across the small fire as we do the same. I don't know what those two talk about, but they huddle in closer as time passes. I watch my younger sister out of the corner of my eye in case she decides to put the brakes on with Ben, but I give Bryant the rest of my attention.

I find he's more than just an attractive jock. He's also intelligent, driven, and disciplined. I'd even venture to say he's kind since he quickly moved on from trying to date me to treating me like I might actually have something to say about the sport he loves.

Zina and Ben wander into the cabin at around three in the morning. She gives me a thumbs up to let me know she feels safe with him, then they disappear inside. I'm not uncomfortable being left with Bryant. He's an easy-going type of guy, and he's easy to talk to. If I'm honest, he's one of the most attractive men I've ever seen, much less spoken to. If he weren't a football player, I'd give him a shot.

When there's a lull in silence, I peer over at him to discover him yawning. "I don't want to tucker out on you, but I have hours of film to watch in a few hours with Coach."

I admire an athlete's commitment to their craft. Training isn't only physical, it's psychological and analytical. A game is simply a battle fought in a long war.

"I should go to bed as well. The couch is very comfortable, but it does pull out into a bed if you would rather sleep on a mattress."

"I can sleep in my truck," he replies.

I offer him an easy smile. "I may not date football players, but I have a soft spot for them. You had a long game. Come inside where it's toasty and make yourself comfortable for the little bit of sleep you can get."

CHAPTER THREE

THEN

I SEE NEITHER HIDE nor hair of Bryant Hudson after we part at the hunting cabin on Hales Row the next morning, but Zina does. I've heard every single account of the man's performance at practice each day since from her.

Zina and Ben have been inseparable since the last game, and she's been his personal cheerleader on the sidelines each practice. I get all the details about Bryant and the team when she arrives back at our apartment at the end of each day.

I'm happy to hear he's throwing the ball more but thinking about the guy is starting to get out of hand.

I don't date, period, but I especially don't date football players. I don't have time with a double major. Thinking about Bryant is a waste of time… or a completely healthy fantasy. I haven't decided which. He's occupying more of my brain space than anyone before, and I've had one conversation with the guy. I'm ridiculous.

"Zhanna?" I turn around in the hunting cabin to find my godfather, Otto, standing in front of me with a smile on his face.

"Girl, what are you over there daydreaming about?"

I'm not much of a daydreamer. I prefer to keep my feet planted firmly on the ground, although, I do dare to dream sometimes. If I was honest with Otto about my current train of thought, he wouldn't believe me.

"I was wondering if our quarterback threw the ball tonight, or if he passed it off to his running backs."

"His pass percentage increased 25%."

My eyes almost bug out of my head at the drastic improvement. "Wow. Good on him."

Otto smirks. "I hear the great state of Louisiana has you to thank for our Win tonight."

I shrug. "He needed knocking down a few notches last Saturday."

"So, you called one of the best quarterbacks in college football a chicken shit?"

It's my turn to smirk. "It worked, didn't it?"

"The boy was a machine. You should've watched the game."

I didn't watch the game tonight because school always comes first, so I was studying for an upcoming test. I rarely miss football, but I heard the cheers outside the cabin while I hunkered down inside and buried my face in a textbook. When the shouts went up at the end of the game, I knew our boys had won.

"I'm glad he did well. What brings you to Hale's Row on a Saturday night?"

His belly bounces as he chuckles and looks around the old cabin. "I have fond memories of me and your dad's college days here."

Dad has been gone five years, but Otto still misses his best friend. "He did too. It's why he brought us here as much as he could."

He turns toward the door and hooks a thumb toward the party outside. "It's good you're keeping up the tradition. I'm going to head back to New Orleans early in the morning, but I wanted to stop by and see my eldest goddaughter."

"You mean your favorite goddaughter."

It draws a good laugh from him. "I have two favorite goddaughters, smart ass." He pauses and looks at me for a long moment before he smirks. "Something going on with you and Hudson?"

"He's a football player."

"He hasn't stopped talking about you. It seems you left a lasting impression on Bryant after insulting him."

"That doesn't say very much about him, does it?"

Before he can respond, Zina sticks her head in the door and smiles at us. "Bryant and Ben are here."

Coach snorts.

"Why would I care?" I ask a little too quickly.

Zina blinks at me. "Right."

"I'm going to let you kids be kids. Be safe," Otto says and motions us over for a bear hug.

After he leaves the cabin, Zina pulls me by the hand and leads me to the small fire outside. We don't allow many people to come back here, but I'm not surprised to find Bryant and Ben.

Even from across the fire, I can tell the QB is tired, but he casts the most beautiful smile in my direction.

Before I can analyze my use of an adjective or my penchant for his smile, Ben cups his hands around his mouth. "Hale-0, Chicken Shit Hudson-1."

"It was one game," I argue, but I find I'm genuinely happy about Bryant's improvements. And, it might be more than my fan status. I think I'm becoming a personal fan of his. Ugh. I don't even need to go there.

Bryant smirks from across the fire. "Coach Z, you should've seen your handy work."

"Coach Z?" I walk over to the log to have a seat beside him.

"I've been playing football since I was five. I've been primed to play quarterback since the sixth grade. I've never had another Coach get through to me like you did."

"It's because I have boobs."

Zina snorts, Bryant turns pink and looks away, and Ben laughs as he says, "She's got you there."

Without looking away from the fire, Bryant clears his throat. "Your theory is boobs are more effective than years of training, years of coaching experience, and an aging man swearing and insulting his players until they do something the coach likes?"

"Twenty-five percent, Chicken Shit."

If he's offended by my nickname, he doesn't show it. Instead, he seems amused by me. "They said your dad was a hard ass, too. He wasn't as beautiful though."

I wish I didn't like Bryant's smile so much. I can see how women could be easily charmed by him. He's talented, gorgeous, intelligent, and driven. He's also sincere and doesn't have his head stuck up his own ass like a lot of athletes. "Does that line usually work for you?"

He leans his head back as a bark of laughter escapes him. "I don't have a problem getting laid if I want it."

I roll my eyes.

"I'm sure. I bet the trophy wives are lining up for you."

The sobering expression on his face accompanies the shrug. "Unfortunately, the gold diggers are present at every practice and game. I can smell them a mile away though."

I feel bad for bringing it up. It's awful for anyone to have to deal with this. "My dad was lucky to find my mom, but I can't tell you how many players we saw down and out over the years because of that exact type of woman."

"It makes dating more difficult than it already is. It's why I don't date."

I arch a brow. "Are you making fun of me?"

He appears genuinely confused. "Um, no? I really don't date."

"At all?"

"At all."

"Ohhh," I say as it dawns on me what he's saying.

"Ohhh?"

I look across the fire to where Ben and Zina sit. They're sucking face and paying us no mind, but I still lean over to him and whisper, "You're a virgin?"

He laughs again, loudly, and abruptly. "No, sweetheart. I said I didn't date. Sex and dating aren't always exclusive."

"Are you a fuck boy?"

He's so tickled he can barely contain himself. "Me? Not hardly. Look, it's not difficult for a football player to get laid, but I have standards. I had a friend for a while until the season began, but I've been dry for months."

"Are you a unicorn? You act like going without isn't a big deal for a dude."

"I didn't say it isn't a big deal for a dude, but I don't make it my number one priority. What about you? Take the vow of celibacy until marriage?"

"I got duked in the back of a pickup at the end of a dirt road somewhere outside of New Orleans when I was seventeen. It left everything to be desired. I was drunk and ready to get it over."

He cringes. "Did he ruin you for good?"

I bat my eyes at him and then shoot him a grin. "Who me?"

"Ha. I can see your middle name is trouble."

I bump my shoulder into his, and his smile grows wider. "Too bad you're a football player. You're actually not a total bore to be around."

"Thank you? I think it's the nicest thing you've ever said to me."

"No, the nicest thing I ever said to you was, 'Throw the damn ball'."

His smile is full of dimples that should be criminal. "Touché." He bumps his shoulder into mine. "Too bad you don't date football players. You're a total babe, and you know football."

"But you don't date."

"I think I'd have to give it a shot with you."

"You don't want to date me."

He looks over at me with a sly grin. "Oh, I want to do a lot of things with you, Zhanna. But enlighten me as to why I don't want to date you."

"I drool when I sleep."

"That's it?"

"No. I also snore."

His voice lowers a few octaves into the sexiest sound I've ever heard. "I think I can handle you, Coach."

I'm aware that we're not talking about dating anymore, at least, not in the strictest sense. I'm also keenly mindful of the way my body reacts to the depth of his voice and the weight of his words. I swallow hard and turn away, embarrassed and surprised by the way my middle contracts and my nipples harden.

God, I've never been the girl that needed sex. I've had a few partners since I lost my virginity. One was a dead fish, and the other was a graduate student who knew exactly what he was doing. Being that I've had great sex, I can see what all the fuss is about, but I don't go a certain time period and think, God, how will I go on if I don't get laid? Feeling like I want to jump his leg is out of character for me, and completely inappropriate considering I'm not going to let him in my pants as a reward.

Bryant licks his lips and looks down at mine.

Why, oh, why do I mimic him?

He takes it as a sign to lean in, coming super close to kissing me. He gives me time to back out, his gaze back on my hazel eyes as he reads me like a book. Just before he touches me, I sharply inhale air, shocked that I've let him get so close.

He draws back an inch. "Shit. I'm sorry. Fuck, I swear I'm not that guy."

I smile, uncomfortable in my own skin, and stand from the log to put some space between us. "It's okay. No worries."

He stands as well and runs his hands through his silky brown hair. "It's late. I should go."

We're both twenty and adults as far as the world is concerned, so we don't have to do the awkward thing. "You don't have to go. Please, stay on the couch again. If I let you leave as tired as you are, my dad will haunt me. I'd love to see the old man, but not when he's angry about his alma mater."

I'm on the receiving end of his brilliant, white smile, and I'm once again a bit stunned at its effect on me. "Thank you, for being cool."

I shrug it off like it's no big deal. "There's no need to be awkward."

"I'm glad to hear it. Does it mean we can be friends?"

"Yeah, QB." I can't stop the flirty smile from spreading across my face.

"We're friends."

I don't know why it makes me gleefully happy.

CHAPTER FOUR

THEN

I'M DREAMING ABOUT BEING Khal Drogo's willing concubine when my buzzing phone pulls me from sleep. I reach for my phone and pluck it from my nightstand. "Hello?"

No one says anything, so I look at the screen and see it's buzzing with text messages from an unknown number. Wiping the drool off my cheek, I open the message.

Unknown: Zina said you're a Pearl Jam fan. I heard Jeremy on the radio and thought of you. She said you might be pissed she gave me your number, but friends should have each other's phone numbers. Right?

Unknown: FYI: This is your friend, Chicken Shit.

Unknown: Please don't put me in your phone as 'Chicken Shit'.

I laugh at him and save his number.

QB: It might bruise my already fragile ego.

Zhanna: I think your ego is just fine.

QB: Did I wake you?

Zhanna: Yes. What are you doing up at 3 am?

QB: Writing a paper. I'm sorry I woke you.

Zhanna: It's okay. Are you alright?

QB: Tired. Go back to sleep, woman. We'll talk tomorrow.

Zhanna: Night, QB.

QB: Night, Coach.

    I sleep in the next morning since my class doesn't start until noon on Thursday. Zina texts me from Ben and Bryant's house while I'm in a public relations class and asks me to meet her at football practice. She makes it sound urgent, so I meet her at the practice field after my two-hour class. She's standing right next to the head coach like she owns the place.

    Coach Paul Tombs was my father's favorite rival when they played together in the pros, but Dad respected the man and his talent. Dad always gave people their due. Zina was the son my father always wanted. She loves football more than I do, and she aims to follow the coaching path like our dad. She'd be one of the first female coaches if she ever makes it, and she's tenacious enough to do so.

I take my eyes off my sister and search out Ben and Bryant on the field. Bryant and I lock eyes seconds before he's tackled to the ground.

"What the hell was that Hudson?" Coach Tombs yells.

I have a feeling my presence at practice is a surprise to Bryant, and his sack might be my fault. I hope he isn't hurt.

"Her?" Coach asks and points down the sidelines to me. "You dream big, Hudson." Then the head man waves me over. "Are you dating my quarterback, sweetheart?"

"No, sir. We're just friends."

The Coach smirks like it's the funniest thing he's heard all day. "I'm going to let you in on a secret, Zhanna. Football players don't take their eyes off the ball and risk getting sacked over a friend, no matter how pretty she is. Linebackers are big ol' boys."

Zina snorts her agreement. "Tell it, Coach."

"At least, the boy aims high. Going after a football princess and all."

"I'm not here for Hudson. I'm here for Zina. She asked me to meet her here." I don't know why I'm defending myself to a man I barely know.

Coach turns his attention back to the field. "What in the hell are you maggots looking at?"

I almost fall over from embarrassment when I also shift my attention to the players and find them staring back at me with their helmets off.

"That's her?"

Bryant smiles at me, happier than a pig in mud. "Coach Z meet the team. Fellas meet Zhanna Hale." Then the idiot jogs over to me, both of us smiling with an entire football team watching.

Why am I smiling at him like this?

"Friends, my ass," Tombs mumbles before shouting at Bryant. "What are you doing, Hudson? I didn't blow the damn whistle. Get your ass back out on the field!"

The man is going to have a premature heart attack and blow out my eardrum in the process.

Bryant runs back to his team, but he's still grinning when he glances back at me. Then he winks which elicits an entire chorus of catcalls from his teammates. For the rest of practice, I stand beside Zina, soak in the atmosphere I grew up in, inhale the scent of fresh turf and sweat, and listen to the sounds of football. It takes me to a bittersweet place in my mind and heart where I have the fondest memories of my dad, but it also reminds me just how much I miss him.

After practice, I find myself waiting outside the facility with Zina as she waits for Ben to shower and reappear.

"He's got it bad for you."

"Bryant?"

"Duh."

"I don't date…"

She sighs in frustration. "Yeah, yeah, I know. The entire world knows. You don't date football players. I think you're making a big mistake with him though. He's a great guy."

I don't doubt Bryant's awesomeness. I've grown to like the guy after three conversations. I like him more than I should and definitely more than I want to. "Maybe. Maybe not. I don't want to raise two kids by myself when they still need a dad. I don't want to navigate all of my children's big life moments alone because of a game. And I don't want a game to dictate my entire life, because it does right down to where you live and the life you can create outside of football. Everything revolves around the game."

Professional sports are a huge commitment on both the athlete's and the family's parts. I can talk about it all until I'm blue in the face, and most people won't understand. It's where my grief has taken me though.

"I heard a rumor," Bryant says from behind us, "that two beautiful women were waiting outside the locker room. I didn't believe it until I saw it with my own eyes."

"You're an idiot," Zina mutters and nudges me in the ribs. "Hey, Quarterback, where's that hot tight end I've seen around here?"

Bryant turns around and slaps his ass. "This tight end?"

Why does he have to have such a great personality? He could make it a lot more difficult to like him. And, God. You can pop a quarter off his juicy ass. So many erotic images of my hands on his bare ass flitter across my mind.

"Close your mouth." Zina whispers.

I immediately do as I'm told before Bryant sees the physical effect he has on me. Ben exits the locker room before we head to the lot outside with those two holding hands along the way.

"I'm heading to Ben's," my sister announces when we reach our cars. "You should come."

"Nah, I think I'll head home."

"Suit yourself." She kisses Ben before she gets into her car to follow him home. I get a little wave through the window as they pull off.

Bryant opens the latch on his tailgate and eases it down. "I don't know why they take two separate cars everywhere. They're always together." He pats the tailgate. "I'm not going to complain though. It means I get to see you."

I ignore his comment because I honestly don't know what to say. I don't want to lead him on, but I'd be lying if I said I didn't like the way he makes me feel every time I'm around him. "I should go."

The two dimples on either side of his brilliant smile are my undoing. "Come on, Coach. You don't date, and there's no one in dire need of your presence like me."

"You make it hard to say no."

His smile fades into something less genial and more smoldering. "Good. Now, hop your pretty ass up here and tell me what's happening with yourself."

I wish he weren't so easy to be around. I slide onto the gate as he does the same. His arm touches mine as his masculine-scented soap wraps around me. Of course, he smells good. So good. Too good, but that's beside the point. I need more self-control around this dude. My nipples are hard enough to spear a fish.

"I'm winding down for Thanksgiving break next week. How about you?"

"I'm practicing until Wednesday. I'm ready to eat and have a day off from football." After a pregnant pause, he asks, "Have you eaten dinner?"

"No, not yet."

"Eat dinner with me? I don't want to go home and listen to the sounds your sister and my tight end make, and I sure as hell don't want to dine alone when I could be dining with you."

"Gross, I didn't need to hear that about my sister."

He laughs. "You should hear Ben."

"Even grosser."

His laughter grows louder. "Not a Ben Slate fan?"

"He's an excellent athlete, but I don't have the same affinity for players that my sister does."

"So I've heard. It's a pity, too."

"How is that?"

He shakes his head and slides off the gate. "Nothing." But he turns around to face me, his eyes holding things I'd rather ignore. "That's not true. There's something. I can't stop wondering what it would be like to kiss you. I know you don't date football players, but kissing and dating aren't the same thing."

Giggling, I elbow him in the ribs. "Is that your argument for kissing me?"

He grins. "Yes. I mean, no. There are many reasons why I want to kiss you, but mainly in the name of curiosity."

"Curiosity killed the cat."

"Or at least gets you sacked."

"Is that what that was?"

"God, you're beautiful, Zhanna."

"Are you saying that so I'll let you kiss me?"

He takes a few steps with his long legs and covers the ground between us. He wets his lips and looks down at mine. "No, but I hope you'll let me kiss you anyway."

"Because you think I'm a football princess?"

"No, woman. I want to kiss you because you're tough, intelligent, beautiful, and you're not begging me to marry you. Hell, you won't even go out on a date with me."

"You don't date either," I remind him.

"I'd give it a real shot with you."

"Why?"

"Because you're not like other girls."

I consider him for a moment. "You don't know me. We've had like five conversations."

His knees touch my shins, and his breath is hot on my face. "Then I'm alone in this insane attraction?"

I look up at him as he towers over me and try to figure out exactly what it is about him that makes me a little weak in my resolve. I think about lying to him, but it's not my style. "No, you're not alone."

"But you don't date football players, so a kiss would mean nothing."

I have a feeling if he kisses me, I'll feel a whole lot of something. "Now he's getting it."

"Then you won't stop me if I do this?" He leans forward, presses his lips to mine, touching his palm to my cheek.

I don't stop him. In fact, I'm overwhelmed by his scent, touch, and the feel of his facial stubble against my skin. I lean into it, kissing him back as I close my eyes and pretend like hell there isn't a chance he'll penetrate my walls. My mouth parts for him as he touches his tongue to mine, my entire being coming alive as I tug him closer.

He groans against my mouth and captures both sides of my face in his hands. "Fuck, Zhanna. We have to slow down. Anybody could be watching."

The concern in his voice when I feel so wildly abandoned is like a punch to the gut. It feels a lot like rejection.

God. I'm so stupid.

"No, Z. Not that look. It's not what I meant."

"It's fine," I say and wave it off. It's not fine. I kissed a player, and it's on a train headed nowhere fast. "You're right. With you being the quarterback, anyone could be watching. I'm going to go. It's getting late."

He reaches for me as I turn to go. "Don't leave it like this. Have dinner with me."

I offer the biggest smile I can muster. "It's okay, QB. I need to get home."

I slide off the tailgate, around his large body, and walk a few spaces over to my car. He doesn't say another word until I unlock my car and climb inside.

"Zhanna!" He calls after me, but I pretend not to hear him as I put my car in drive and pull away.

CHAPTER FIVE

THEN

I pull my Jeep into Hale's Row. It's not entirely uncommon for me to sleep out here by myself on a night that isn't game night. I enjoy a good hike on our private land first thing in the morning. Sometimes I'll practice yoga on the dock at the pond, and sometimes Zina is so damn loud, I need to get away from her to think. This place is my church, my refuge from the world, so when headlights flash behind me, I'm taken off guard for a moment. I quickly realize who it must be at the same moment my phone rings. I stop the Jeep without answering the phone to close the property gate at the drive. Bryant gets out of his truck and is hot on my heels.

"Let me do that," he says and closes the gate before turning to face me again. He jams his hands into his front denim pockets and looks at the ground for a moment. "So, I fucked that up, and I'm sorry."

I've had time to cool down as the heat of our time together passed, and now, I can see he did us both a favor by stopping it. "It's okay. You were right to stop it."

"No, you don't understand. I watched you walk to your car, and it felt like I was making the biggest mistake of my life if I let you go without exploring this thing between us. We've only had five conversations?" He takes a few steps toward me, but I retreat toward his truck until my back touches it. "But I felt more alive when I kissed you than I did the day my dream college team asked me to throw the ball for them for four years."

He comes to stand in front of me, and God, the way he gazes at me does strange things to my insides. He reaches up and tucks my hair behind my ear, an electrical current traveling through me at his touch. My heart beats faster, my breath comes quicker, and my insides turn to lava.

"If you don't feel this, I'll fuck off. I won't ever push my luck again. But I don't think you'd still be standing here if I was totally off base."

I open my mouth to tell him to fuck off, but my voice fails me.

More than that, it's not what I want. I'm not sure exactly what I crave, but I know it's him. I just need to get him out of my system and allow it to run its course. My plan is much better than continuing to deny that I want to sleep with him. "Just one night."

"Baby, there's no way I'm getting over this in one night."

I can't do more than one night, because I actually like the guy. He's not an entitled athlete. He's shown compassion. He's hot as hell, and I want to know what he looks like with all his clothes on the floor of my hunting cabin. "Just one night… and no one can know."

"Just one night? What happens after tonight?"

"Tonight?" I squeak.

I look down at my yoga pants and hoodie. I'd really like to feel at least a little sexy.

He smirks. "You're thinking too much."

Then he leans down from his gigantic height and kisses me. I think about objecting to his methods, but the man can kiss.

All my thoughts and objections fall to the wayside when he lifts me into the air. I wrap my legs around him, and then we're on the move. His truck door clicks open before he sets me on his seat. He never breaks the kiss. His hands start to explore, shift, and move as he easily navigates my body. An unintended moan slips from me before I can stop it.

I grab a handful of his shirt, and pull him back to me, but he stops just short of my mouth. "The first time I sleep with you won't be in my truck. Your place or mine?"

"The only time. And the hunting cabin will do just fine."

I slide out of his truck and head for my Jeep.

"What?" he asks with the biggest smirk on his face. "I don't get a goodbye kiss?"

I roll my eyes but there's a grin playing on my lips. "One night, QB."

When we reach the hunting cabin, we're all over each other before we can get to the door. I blindly unlock it. We burst through, yanking at each other's clothes. With one foot and the keys still in the front door, he slams it shut and takes his shirt off. He picks me up again as he walks to my room.

His hands run up my sides as he pushes my shirt up and over my head. Without bothering with the lights, he lays me down on the bed, hovering over me. The sheer white curtains allow the moonlight to illuminate the room enough for me to see the planes of his body. I don't know a straight woman alive who wouldn't drool over his 6'5 hard bod. My God, he's fabulous in every way. I hope the thing poking me in the leg is equally as wonderful.

I reach down, unbuckling his belt and pushing his pants down. I've never wanted anyone this bad, not like this. I can feel him under my skin, breathing my oxygen and driving me wild. Bryant tugs my yoga pants down until they're off.

He reaches for his pants and plucks a foil from his pocket. I don't know or care why it's so readily available but thank heavens he thought of it before now. After he rolls it on, he crawls back onto the bed until he's seated between my legs.

Bringing his lips back to mine, he slows the pace of his kiss. I grow impatient and reach between us to grab him, pulling him to me until he's lined up where I want him. Wrapping my legs around his waist, I wait for him to do the rest.

And I wait.

I break the kiss. "Are you okay?"

He sighs, rolls off me to the other side of the bed, and throws an arm to cover his eyes. "I keep wondering about what happens after tonight?"

"That's what you're thinking about right now?"

"Zhanna, listen, I don't want to do something that means when this is over you'll pretend we're strangers. I don't know why I feel that way, but I do."

"What do you want from me?"

"I…"

"A relationship? We're not going down that road."

"No, but maybe…"

"You want to be my fuck buddy? You know that would never work. You'll catch feelings." I scoff, knowing I'm right.

"For fuck's sake, I want you! I don't know exactly what that means yet, but it means I want the shot any other guy would get. I want to take you out on a date and not be afraid that sex means the end of whatever this is between us. And don't bullshit me, Coach, you're feeling this pull too."

He's right. I'm drawn to him. I like our conversations and how down to earth he seems. He's gorgeous, chiseled, intelligent, and kind, but he's a freaking football player. I can't bring myself to attach myself to that kind of loss and pain. I didn't have a choice the first time. So, I lie. I lie to protect myself and my heart. "You're wrong. This is just…"

He interrupts me by placing a finger over my lips. "False start, baby. Let's try this again." He rolls to his side to face me and touches his hand to my belly. "Let's play a game I like to call 'Lie Detector'. When you tell the truth, you'll be rewarded… dearly. First question… will you go on a date with me?"

"No."

"My fault. I led with the wrong question. Is your name Zhanna Hale?"

"Yes."

His middle finger slips down my center. "Jesus, fuck, you're wet."

Boy, he isn't lying. He's more than capable of turning me on.

"Next question. Do you want me inside of you?"

"Yes."

His finger inches inside, moving over my clit. The moan that leaves me isn't of my own volition. He curses under his breath.

"Would you date me if I wasn't a football player?"

"I don't have time to date."

"If you did?"

"No."

He pauses the amazing thing he's doing between my legs. "Why?"

"Because…"

He moves his hand and nearly has me convulsing within ten seconds. Oh, he's good. Too good. It's exactly why I can't date him. He's the type of guy a girl falls in love with. I don't have time to fall in love, and I sure as shit don't want to hitch myself to an athlete.

Just when I think I'm going over the edge, he stops. "I bet you'd like to come. Now, tell me, why won't you date me?"

"You're a football player."

"I'll quit."

"No, you won't."

"You're right, I won't. But I think you'd be happy if you gave me a damn chance."

I'm desperate for relief. "Fine. One date."

"Two weeks of dates."

"One date," I counter.

He flicks my center.

My traitorous eyes roll back in my head. "Okay. Two weeks."

"There are fourteen days in two weeks. I want fourteen dates."

I pull at his arm to remove it from the promised land. It's time I take care of business myself but pulling at him is like trying to move a brick wall.

"Tsk, tsk, tsk. I'm in control of when you come."

I hate that his words turn me on even more. "Fucking fine! Fourteen dates. You got it, buddy."

His deft fingers move up and down the center of me until I'm writhing beneath him. I forget he's naked beside me and could be doing this in an entirely different, more fulfilling way. I also forget my own name and basic identifying details as he pushes me closer and closer to the precipice of bliss. Unable to control the moans or the pleas that roll out of my mouth, I arch my back and surrender.

Bryant swallows my cries in a kiss as I reach for him to anchor me here to earth as my world shatters into a gazillion pieces. His name crosses my lips as I fall apart around him, and there's not a thing I can do to stop it. He's perfect in every way, except one.

CHAPTER SIX

NOW

AFTER WE HAVE A quiet dinner at Bourdon's, I stare out of Bryant's window onto Dauphine Street and watch the tourists and locals pass by on their merry ways. From the frame of this window, their lives seem so much easier than mine. They have a destination and a purpose in mind. It feels as though I've been floating around waiting for my purpose since our divorce. I'm both aimless and restless. As thirty looms closer each year, I feel the pressure to start a family, but I can't start a family until I can find a way to rid my life of my ex-husband.

When the doorbell rings, I turn from my place in the empty dining room to answer it and find Bryant standing in the arched door frame staring at me with the most beautiful green eyes I've ever seen. The look in them reminds me of the first night I almost slept with him. I now know the look is one of love. For all his faults, I can't deny the man loves me. Looking back, I see maybe he already loved me that night.

"What were you thinking about just now?" he asks, his eyes softening even more.

"The hunting cabin."

"It's where I realized I first loved you."

The doorbell rings again, but the expression on his face and the tenderness in his eyes holds me in place.

"When did you know?"

"When you called me 'Chicken Shit Hudson'. But, Z, the moment I saw you across the fire at Hale's Row, I knew you were something special."

The front door opens.

"Knock, knock." Leslie's deep voice booms from the foyer.

"Who doesn't lock their front door in New Orleans?" Zina asks, likely behind the big fella.

The click-clack of Leslie's shoes sound across the old hardwood floor until they bring him to the open dining room with Zina on his five-inch heels. With his favorite black leather Jimmy Choos on, Leslie towers over Bryant. He's a formidable man with a wide chest who prefers to wear the burnt orange and royal blue, Aztec-modified muu-muu in his down time. He's a performer at a local nightclub five nights a week and has the voice of an angel. Not only is Leslie my neighbor, he's also my friend. As soon as we met, Zina and I adopted him because we fell in love with his outrageous personality and kind heart. It was Leslie who pulled me out of my depression when I moved to New Orleans from California after Bryant and I split. Some days, he wasn't so nice about it. It took a while to see he was giving me the tough love I needed to get out of the bed and move on with my life.

"Bryant, please meet Leslie. Leslie, my ex."

Leslie outreaches his humongous, French-manicured hand to Bryant. "Pleasure, Suga."

Bryant shakes his hand. "Thanks for coming over so quickly. I appreciate the favor."

"Anything for my girls." Leslie passive-aggressively starts the dick-swinging contest.

Bryant's jaw tenses at the possessive nature of my friend, but he smiles tightly. "You're free to look around. I'm not attached to anything here." He moves his attention to me. "I'm not attached to anything of the previous owners."

Leslie dramatically snaps his fingers back and forth. "Ooooo, you two are going to burn down the entire block if you keep on with those smoldering gazes. Never seen two people who just need to fuck and get it over with."

"Leslie!" I scold and hopefully, it's enough to remind him we are not Team Bryant.

"Girl, that man is fine. F-I-N-E. Fine."

Bryant smirks from across the room. "You know, I'd really like to be the one to show you around." Then he offers my friend his arm like a gentleman.

My soon-to-be-ex-friend doesn't even attempt to hide the swoon or the drool as he lets the football player lead him off like he's Scarlett freaking O'Hara—if Scarlett was a large man with beautiful mocha skin in a muumuu. I let them go ahead of me as I take a moment to gather myself.

"I give you two months before you're living together again," Zina says and reminds me she's still in the room.

It angers me that she finds humor in the situation after what he did to me. "I know you think it's cute and romantic that he showed up here to win me back, but it wasn't long ago you were calling for his balls because I couldn't stop crying over my broken heart. He's still the same guy who let another woman blow him in our house."

"Believe me, I still aim to collect his penance, but you have to find a way to forgive him for your own peace of mind."

She's right. I need to forgive Bryant. It's been long enough, but today isn't a day for forgiveness when he's infiltrated both my personal and professional life. Today isn't the day I give him absolution when he has my sister, my best friend, and an entire football organization eating out of his big hands.

Sighing, I give up fighting for her to have my back. "I'm going. It's been a long day."

"Okay. I'll wait for Leslie and come over after he's done with Bryant."

For the first time in my life, I decline her support and company. It doesn't feel much like she's on my side today. "I think I'm going to lie down. I'll see you at work tomorrow."

Hurt flashes across her face, but I'm too crushed by today to have the energy to make it better. "Okay."

Opening my car service app, I order the next available ride. I can't stand to be in the house any longer, so I stand outside near the street and wait. I'm happy when the driver pulls up to the curb just a few minutes later because Bryant steps onto the porch with determination in his eyes. I shake my head to indicate I don't want him to follow and then climb inside for the short journey home.

***

FRIDAYS IN FOOTBALL AREN'T like most people start their weekend. Since it's July, we're in the off season, and it means Friday is a workout day for the players. Zina, an athletic trainer, and me, a physical therapist for the team, stand by for injuries and observation. Being Bryant is a new player to the team, he's working out with rookies and a few team veterans at the practice facility. I do my best to ignore him, but it's nearly impossible when I can feel the heat of his stupid, gorgeous stare. I hate that I'm uber aware of his presence, so I welcome the distraction of Leslie texting me.

> **Leslie: Can you talk?**

> **Zhanna: No.**

> **Leslie: What do you think of recovering this chair with an expensive ivory chenille and placing it on his side of the bed? I was thinking it would look perfect with anything the man takes off his body and carelessly drapes over it.**

I blink at my screen.

Forget the picture of the hideous chair attached to the message, I can't believe Bryant has Leslie still swooning over him. I lift my gaze from my phone and find the quarterback across the room. I'm already in his sights when we make eye contact. As I glare at him, pure guilt crosses his face.

> **Zhanna: I think you should have free rein of the house.**

There, that will serve Bryant right. Let the man have run of the house and fill it with his animal prints. He'll have to pay Leslie twice to fix it.

> **Leslie: Ooooo, no girl. Mr. Football Star said to defer all decisions to you as the woman of the house. So, I'm deferring to the woman of the house.**

Zina snorts from over my shoulder. "Bryant is so going to break Leslie's heart."

I move my phone from her view to keep her out of my business.

Zhanna: Bryant needs to find a new woman of the house because it ain't me.

Leslie: Be careful what you wish for, Suga.

He sends a picture of an ivory fabric I'm sure he could write a thesis on.

Leslie: I'm thinking this is the one.

I roll my eyes, choose to ignore it, and get back to focusing on all the players, except one. My phone must buzz a thousand times in my back pocket during the morning. Leslie is persistent when he's got a bone to chew on, but I'm not going to play into Bryant's hand.

When we break for lunch, my ex follows me down the hall to my office. I can't wait to throw every swear word in the book at him for telling my own friend to refer to me as the lady of the house. I turn the corner to my office and come to face Leslie seated in my chair with his smoothly shaved legs crossed and his feet on the desk.

Before I can ask him what the hell he's doing here, he twirls a perfect dreadlock around his finger and bats his eyes at the man behind me. "Ooooo, look at all those mus-cles." Then he mumbles unintelligible words under his breath that are very likely X-rated.

"Hey, Leslie," Bryant greets, and then he averts his attention to me. "Tell me what's wrong, baby."

Zina skids to a halt behind my ex and looks around him. "Par-tay!"

"Why in the hell are you ignoring my beautiful ass?" Leslie demands.

"Zhanna, we need to talk." Bryant says.

Coach Jed Jones sticks his head in the office. "I had no idea you were married to Hudson. Huh. Go figure." Then he pops back out and goes on his way.

My office phone rings, and for some reason it sounds shriller than usual. I walk past my neighbor to answer, but Leslie beats me to it. "Zhanna Hale's office."

We wrestle over the phone, although it's really more like he's holding one of his large tree trunks of an arm out with his hand on my forehead to prevent me from gaining ground. No matter how hard I push I can't reach him, so I switch tactics and swing my arms to grasp at anything that will give me purchase against the giant.

"Give me the phone."

"No, I'm sorry, Fletcher, Mrs. Hale-Hudson is no longer interested in your services."

"I'm going to kill you in your sleep," I threaten.

Fletcher is my real estate agent. I've been waiting for his phone call all morning, and now, I'm going to look like a crazy person if I call back and make up an elaborate story to explain Leslie's mistake.

"Is that Fletcher Carson from school?" Bryant asks, jealousy laced in his voice.

Zina volunteers entirely too much information. "Yep. Fletcher has been trying to get in your wife's panties since he found out she was available and back in New Orleans."

Bryant hands rest on his hips. "Isn't he a real estate agent now? Why do you need a real estate agent?"

"Well, I guess my plan to sell my house under the shade of night and sneak out of the country is blown to shit now," I quip.

Otto walks into my office and stops in his tracks when he sees Leslie.

"Does he work here now?"

Leslie returns the receiver to the cradle without a goodbye. "You wish I'd bring my fairy godmother ass in here and bring this place to life. I'd decorate the shit out of this place. Can I get an amen?"

"Amen," Zina sing-songs.

I feel pressure in my chest, my head begins to pound, and pure hot anger wraps around the base of my spine. I don't know who to yell at first.

"Enough!" I yell. "Out!"

"Baby," Bryant protests.

I hold my hand up to stop him from saying another damn word, closing my eyes and taking a deep breath. The room goes silent enough to hear a pin drop. I do my best to hold back the tears. I'm not one to cry easily, but it's been a rough two days. And I'm ovulating, meaning my eggs are jumping to their deaths as we speak.

Otto is the first to realize I'm barely holding it together. "Uh oh."

"I," I begin but have to pause to hold it together. "I am not your wife. I'm not his wife," I repeat to the others in the room before focusing on Leslie. "I don't give two fucks about ivory chenille or being the lady of his house, not after he was with another woman. I am done being nice about it. You've all forgotten how hard it was for me after he cheated, so the next person to call me his wife or treat me like his wife will receive a swift kick in the balls or ovaries."

I march out of my office dashing tears away and head home until Monday when I'll look for another real estate agent.

CHAPTER SEVEN

THEN

I WAIT FOR BRYANT at Hale's Row after the game two nights later, but he doesn't show. I expected to see or at least hear from him after he begged for not one, but fourteen dates. It's been two days, and I'm acting like he didn't call after we slept together. We didn't have sex, so I don't know what I'm freaking out about. He gave me a great orgasm. What's the big deal? Lots of guys can do that. Okay, maybe not a lot. Bryant Hudson is sort of a unicorn, but it's not a biggie.

"What are you thinking so hard about, Coach?"

I spin around in my bedroom. Bryant leans his tall body against the door frame with his arms crossed over his wide chest.

"What are you doing here?"

He smirks and peruses me from head to toe before he crosses the room in four long strides. His toes touch mine as he looks down at me. "Ben offered Zina a ride to New Orleans, and I figured I'd take the chance to catch up on rest while he drives. You might as well ride with us. There's no sense in driving separately."

"Are you keeping your hands to yourself?" I ask, trying my best not to grin at him.

His smirk grows wider. "Do you want me to keep my hands to myself?"

I open my mouth and promptly shut it. The man knows how to do a hell of a lot more with his large hands than throw a football, but I'm a wee bit upset with him for not showing at Hale's Row last night. It's stupid and irrational, but it's how I feel.

"You look tired. Late night?"

A dimple appears on the right side. "Is this your way of asking if I was with someone else last night?"

"For there to be a someone else, there must be a someone. I'm not your someone, QB."

The frown on his face does nothing to mar his beauty. "I was with Coach Tombs until two. I went home and climbed straight in the bed. I was aching from the two sacks I took."

"Where was your left tackle?"

I can feel his frustration as he launches into the reason behind his late-night visit with his coach. "It's why I didn't come see you after the game. Lawrence and I had words after the game about me taking unnecessary hits. We were shouting in the locker room, and Coach wasn't happy about it." Bryant leans into my space as he lifts his hand and tucks my hair behind my ear. "I didn't want you to have to be around me when I was in such a surly mood. But I wished I was at the cabin with you."

Butterflies take flight in my tummy, and I feel like an overexcited, boy-crazy prepubescent.

"God, you're beautiful, Z."

How does he do it – make me feel and ache for him? And how long can I fight him when he's so charming and perfect?

"You have to stop talking to me like that." It's the only way I'll survive a road trip and fourteen dates with him.

"We'll have to agree to disagree on the matter then." He tips my chin up with his hand. "Zina called shotgun, so you're in the back with me. Want to snuggle like we did the other night?"

Zina walks in and interrupts us. "Whoa. You two are absolutely gorgeous together. But why are you standing so close to one another?"

"I was just telling your sister not to drool on me in the backseat."

Zina smirks like she's done something she shouldn't have. "Oh yeah! Shotgun!"

The little heifer set me up. I slice my finger across my throat to let her know what I think about it. "I know where you sleep, and Ben won't be too far from your baby pictures."

My little sister gasps. "You wouldn't."

"I would."

"I could return the favor with Bryant."

"I was cute as shit when I was a kid. I didn't have weird tendencies like you did."

Bryant points his finger to her and then me. "Y'all look just alike."

It's my turn to smile at my sister. Ben walks up to share the doorway with her, and she goes mute. I pick up my suitcase and send a wink in Zina's direction. One day, she'll find the perfect man to love her even though she was obsessed with having a penis when she was young. Weird kid. "See y'all in the car."

The trip from Baton Rouge to New Orleans is just over an hour, but as usual, the ride puts me straight to sleep. I'm thankful for the reprieve from having to pretend there's not something bubbling between me and the quarterback. However, I pay for it by waking up in his arms. I know Ben nor my sister missed it while I was unconscious. I play off my immediate escape from his hold by sitting up and stretching, but Bryant has none of it. He pulls me directly back to his chest and wraps his arms around me.

"We're fifteen minutes out," Ben announces.

I squirm against my captor. "Let me go."

"Mmm."

Whatever that means

I struggle again and this time he releases me to pop up into an upright position and scoot away from him. "Fifteen minutes to Mom's?"

"Yeah," my sister says, a little too happy for my liking.

The trip comes to an end as Ben pulls into the drive of the large, brick home I grew up in. My mom and both of my grandmothers stand on the front porch waiting for us with huge, warm smiles. My heart soars when I see them.

"I can't believe Grandma Rose is here!" Zina says about our grandmother who lives in a nearby home for patients with dementia.

We haven't seen her since the summer, and steady communication is difficult when she's not always lucid. Seeing her here to greet us brings a smile to both of our faces.

Zina and I both leap from the car and charge Mom, Grandma Rose, and our Granny Hazel. We wrap the women in hugs and although Grandma seems confused, she's still happy to see us and to be in the middle of so much excitement.

"Phillip!" she yells my deceased grandfather's name and takes off down the porch stairs in a hurry. We rush after her to prevent her from falling, but she's too quick. She walks past Ben and heads straight for Bryant.

Bryant is more than a little bewildered as my strange grandmother wraps her short arms around him.

My mother reaches her first and gently reminds her, "Rose, this gentleman isn't Phillip."

"I'm sorry." I apologize quietly to Bryant and attempt to extract him from the situation.

Then he does something wonderful and unexpected. He wraps his arms around my grandmother and hugs her back. "There, there, love."

"I've been looking everywhere for you," she tells him, the confusion evident in her voice.

"Mrs. Rose, why don't we scrounge up something to drink for Mr. Phillip?" Mom asks, hoping to assist.

Grandma leans back and smiles at Bryant like he's her savior. "Be right back, sweetheart."

God, I haven't seen her smile like that since before my grandfather died ten years ago. My heart further melts into a big pile of goo when my sweet Grandma Rose looks back at Bryant as she walks away and waves the sweetest little wave. The big, tough quarterback smiles at her like she's the love of his life and waves back. It feels like I'm watching intimacy not meant for my eyes, but I'm glad I saw it. I'm glad I saw her happy again.

"Would you like to come inside?" I ask, all of a sudden endeared to him on a level I didn't wish was possible.

"Yeah, I really would. I'd like to see the place where you grew up."

I don't know why I'm inviting him further into my life. I don't know why I can't shake him. I should be running for the hills and far away from him. He's going to hurt me, and it may be completely unintentional, but it'll hurt just the same.

Zina and I lead the guys inside to the large family room filled with large, comfy taupe couches and a brick fireplace. Ben and Bryant both busy themselves looking at the pictures on the walls of our family while we step into the kitchen and help Mom and our grandmothers with cookies and drinks, because honestly, I don't think Zina or I know what to do with these two dudes in our house.

"Can I help with anything?" Bryant steps in behind us and asks.

I swear to the good Lord above, my mother blushes as she steps forward and shakes Bryant's hand. "Robin Hale."

"Bryant Hudson. Your home is as lovely as your daughters, Mrs. Hale."

"Oh." My mother giggles. "Please call me Robin."

Oh my God.

Kill me now.

I glance across the room at Zina who's working through her breaths to keep from laughing. Bryant shoots me a wink as Ben steps into the room.

Granny Hazel loses her fucking mind when he does. "Well, damn, I didn't think my lady parts worked anymore." Then she pops her teeth out and winks at Ben. "My teeth come out, Tiger."

If that isn't bad enough, she then sticks her tongue in her cheek and does a blow job motion.

Ben doesn't know whether to run, laugh, or cry.

Bryant and Zina have chosen laughter.

My mom is mortified, and Grandma Rose is oblivious as she stares at Bryant.

"I'm moving in," Ben finally says, and it's the last straw for Zina who bursts into unbridled laughter.

"Phillip let's go sit, sweetheart," Grandma Rose says, pulling Bryant by the hand.

He very sweetly goes with her into the family room without a second thought.

"You girls brought home Bryant Hudson and Ben Slate. A woman couldn't ask for better son-in-laws." Mom fans herself.

Zina snorts. "Or hotter."

"Well," my mother says as she rubs the back of her neck, "they are quite handsome."

I laugh. "Cougar much?"

I help her load a plate with cookies before going after Bryant to rescue him from my poor, confused grandmother.

In the family room, Bryant helps my grandma sit on the couch before taking a seat beside her.

Grandma Rose leans over and whispers to him as she primps her hair and bats her lashes. "Phillip, do you think we'd be in trouble if we held hands?"

Bryant leans over and whispers back, "I think it would be okay if we held hands. But don't you go and try to take advantage by putting the moves on me, Rose."

Her hand flies to her chest and a gasp leaves her. "I wouldn't dare. I'm not that kind of girl."

My heart does a weird flip flop thing in my chest. Tears prick my eyes as my sister sidles up beside me. "You're fucked."

"Yeah," I agree.

I don't know many men in their young twenties that would sit with a strange woman and pretend to be her dead husband. I also don't know many dudes who would drop whatever he had planned for the day to spend it with an aging woman who found love again, albeit faux love. And I sure as shit don't know guys who would understand the situation within a few moments.

So, yeah, I'm fucked. He slithered underneath my skin, and I don't know if it's possible to work him out of my system.

CHAPTER EIGHT

THEN

BRYANT AND BEN LEAVE around five to make it to Bryant's parent's home outside the city for dinner. And when Grandma Rose wakes shortly after, she has no recollection of Bryant being here. But I'll never forget that he was here and what he did for her and us.

The hardest part of loving a patient with dementia is the pain that comes from watching them deteriorate. They're in and out of lucidity. The confusion it causes the patient is the most heartbreaking thing about it. There's nothing the people around them can do but play along and hope they'll remember soon.

As I lie down at midnight, my thoughts center on Bryant. I send him a text to see if he's awake.

> Zhanna: Hey you.

God. Why is this so hard?

> Zhanna: I just wanted to thank you for everything you did for my family today. You were amazing.

Three little dots dance at the bottom of my screen indicating he's typing. I really hope I didn't wake him.

> Bryant: Hey, gorgeous! You're welcome. I'm glad I could help. The women in your family are all beautiful and kind.

Zhanna: Did I wake you?

Bryant: No, I was actually thinking about you.

His words make me want to leap from my bed, jump up and down, and shout in glee. But I manage to contain myself.

Bryant: What are you doing right now?

Zhanna: I was headed to bed.

Bryant: Want to go on a date?

Zhanna: When?

Bryant: Now, before you change your mind.

Zhanna: Now?!!

> **Bryant:** I'd like to show you something. Are you up for a field trip?

> **Zhanna:** Now?!!

> **Bryant:** LOL

> **Zhanna:** Does the field trip involve a shovel, duct tape, and rope?

> **Bryant:** She's got jokes. I'll pick you up in thirty.

> **Zhanna:** I'll meet you in the drive. I don't want to wake anyone.

> **Bryant:** I'll be the lucky guy waiting on you with a big smile on his face.

Yeah, he's a unicorn.

The man who has slowly gotten under my skin is waiting for me in the drive when I emerge from the house half an hour later. I have a moment of deja vu as I walk toward him. He rolls the window down in a big, black diesel truck and smiles at me. My heart does that weird thing again, taking my breath away. It feels like I've been here before

56

with him and felt the emotions swirling around inside me.

He opens the door, steps down from the tall truck, and meets me at the front of the vehicle. Without a word, he escorts me to the other side and opens my door. As I pass him to climb inside, I catch his masculine scent and grow weak in the knees. It smells like he rolled around in pheromones before he arrived. My poor ovaries can hardly stand it, but I manage to climb into the truck without breaking my neck. Just before he closes the door, he winks at me. Even though it's a small flirty gesture, I feel it all the way down to my toes.

Once inside the cab, he looks over at me and says, "My parents want to meet you."

I choke on my spit.

As I struggle to recover, Bryant claps me on the back to help me out. "Too soon to tell you we're getting married? They'd like to meet their future daughter-in-law."

I choke harder and then squeak. "Tonight?!"

He looks at the radio clock. "If you're really gunning to tie me down, I suppose we could fly to Vegas and be married in the next five hours or so. Soon enough for you?"

"Now, he's got jokes."

He chuckles. "I noticed you didn't object to the marriage bit. Duly noted. It means I have a real shot. I'm going to count this as a point in the win column."

"You're awfully full of yourself tonight."

"Just positive thinking. The law of attraction and all that jazz."

After he pulls from our neighborhood, he turns the radio on, and we quietly listen to classic rock as he drives out of town. The passing scenery changes from upper class to a peaceful upper middle-class neighborhood with rocking chair front porches, large, wooded lots, and manicured lawns.

"Is this where you live?" I ask as he turns into the drive of a red brick home with large white columns.

"It's where I grew up." He pulls past the house to a fenced backyard and kills the engine. "I don't have a lot of time to visit home with football on my plate. I stay in Baton Rouge most of the time."

We climb from the vehicle and head to a gate located on the side of the lot. Inside the fence, he leads me to a massive oak tree. On the top of it is the biggest tree house I've ever seen.

"Whoa," I say, craning my neck.

"I was six feet tall by middle school, so my dad had to engineer a house for a bigger-than-average kid."

"How long did it take to build?"

"My dad and I did this together. It took us a year because I was playing football all the time."

"It's great you have memories of this. It's important to cherish them."

"Up you go," he says and waves his hand in front of an attached wooden ladder. "You don't seem twenty. You act older. It's one of the many reasons I'm drawn to you."

"I had to grow up," I tell him as I begin to climb ahead of him. "My mom fell apart when my dad died. I took care of Zina so mom could hold everything else together."

"She seems like she's in a good place now."

"Yeah, she is. The first year was hard though."

"What was he like? Your dad?"

I smile at the mention of Dad. "The famous Zane Hale?" I laugh. "He was super intense about football, but he was laid back about everything else. He was a good dad and an awesome husband. I can understand why my mom fell apart a little bit when he died. She lost her best friend, the person she was supposed to grow old with, and the father of her children at the same time. I can't imagine raising two kids on my own."

"It's why you don't date football players."

"Yes. I don't ever want to have to tell my children their father is gone. Not until I'm old and it's time."

"There aren't any guarantees in life, Coach. Anything could take us out at any moment. I could play a game and take hit after hit all night and walk off the field only to be hit by a bus outside the stadium. You can't let fear make you afraid to connect with someone. What if I'm meant to be the father of your children? You're fucking with fate by turning me down."

I come to the landing and wait for him but look into a small window to see glowing lights. "Oh, this is about fate now?"

"It's been about fate since the moment we met, Z."

When he's up the ladder, he takes my hand, guiding me around the outside of the house until we reach a door. We step inside to a scene out of a movie. Warm Christmas lights are hung from the ceiling, and soft music plays from a record player beside a double bed.

"There's a refrigerator and sink? This is a house, not a treehouse."

"It's my man cave," he replies, jamming his hands into his pockets as he nervously looks at the floor for a moment. "I just realized what this looks like. I didn't bring you here with expectations."

I smile to put him at ease and have a look around the room. There's a television centered in an entertainment center, and bookcases are built on either side. The cases are full of board games, books, and gaming equipment.

"Would you like a drink?"

I pick through the books. "No, I'm okay. I love this place. It's very you."

"It's not a hunting cabin on a bunch of acres, but it's my little spot away from everyone."

"It's cozy."

"You're beautiful."

I've ignored all of his attempts at complimenting me prior to now, but he's irresistible. I can no longer deny the attraction or the growing emotions I have for Bryant. Seeing him with my grandmother forced me to look past the football player in him.

God. Do I really want to go down this route with him?

"You're not so bad yourself."

His hand flies to his chest in shock. "Did Zhanna Hale just compliment me?"

"You know."

His long legs bring him to me in three strides. "I know what?"

"You know you're attractive."

"I'm more concerned with what you think about the situation." He lifts his hand and touches my cheek before he swipes his thumb over the apple of my cheek. "I'd give a prized organ to know what goes through your beautiful mind."

"In regards to you? Oh, that's easy! You never cross my mind."

"Baby, you texted me at midnight. That tells me I crossed your mind."

I'm sure a legitimate and plausible explanation exists as to how I was texting him and absolutely not thinking about him at the same time, but I can't think while he's touching me. Also, the cologne he wears must be made of Aphrodite's tears. He has an unfair advantage over me.

"Don't overthink this thing between us. It's existed since the moment I laid eyes on you. I feel you down to my bones, and I know you feel it, too."

I do feel it, but I wish I didn't. There has to be a way to fuck him out of my system. If he would cooperate, I could get it over with, and I intend to do just that as I stand on my toes and press my lips to his. He pulls me into him and kisses me harder as my arms circle his neck.

He pulls back slightly after breaking the kiss. "You agreed to fourteen dates. This is not a date."

"Whatever." I tug him back to me by the front of his shirt.

He stops short of my puckered lips. "I mean it, Zhanna. I have fourteen dates to plan."

"I swear to Jesus, if you don't stop talking, there won't be any dates."

He must realize I mean business because he stops running his mouth and kisses me like it's his job. He bends down slightly, grabbing me by the hips and lifting me until I wrap my legs around him. Walking backward to the bed, he perches on the edge.

His rough hands slide underneath my shirt against the sensitive skin on my back and travel down to my hips. Thrusting up, Bryant presses his hard length against me. The friction is enough to make me break the kiss, moan shamelessly, and throw my head back in ecstasy. I've needed another release since the moment he made me come Thursday night.

"Fuck, baby," he murmurs against my throat as he cups my center and groans. "You are so sexy. And soaked through your pants."

Before I can reply, he flips us and presses my back to the mattress. His fingers hook inside the waistband of my black yoga pants, pulling until they're on the floor. My panties follow soon after.

Spreading my leg, he runs a finger up and down my seam. I reach for his belt, but he backs away. "You make it fucking impossible to resist you, but I need you to tell me I still get my fourteen dates."

"Yes! Oh my God! You'll have your fourteen dates. Now, will you please take your clothes off?"

"You don't have to ask me twice." Bryant is naked in less than half a minute, and he's rolling on a condom two seconds after. He lines himself up and pushes inside. There's resistance due to his size, but it isn't painful. "Fuck, Zhanna. You feel good."

I reach for him to come closer. He starts to move inside me as he kisses my mouth. He takes his time exploring every inch of my body with his hands and mouth. I've never been so turned on and lost in the rapture of the moment. Bryant adjusts himself several times, pushes my legs back, and changes his angle until I almost sit straight up. He touches a sensitive spot I didn't know existed. A jolt shoots through me. I arch my back in an attempt to find it again, desperate for the release I've sought for three days.

"I've got you, baby. Let go," he says so quietly, I almost don't hear him.

Moments later, I dive over a cliff of bliss, completely unraveling around him as his name spills from my lips. I could let the sea of ecstasy sweep me away for the night, but then I'd miss him losing himself in me.

Once I've ridden my high, he slows down the pace. As he catches his breath, he lowers his forehead to mine and deeply gazes into me. "So fucking beautiful."

I wrap my legs around him, not quite able to speak just yet, and move my hands down to the perfect globes of his ass. He pushes his hand under my cheek, bringing me closer. "Jesus, fuck. You're the best damn thing I've ever felt." I expect him to begin to rush toward the finish line at any moment until he says, "I need to make you come again."

I've never had multiple orgasms, not that I've had the experience under my belt to be disappointed by it, but I'm not sure it's possible. "Is it possible?"

"God, I hope so."

And seconds later, I shatter as he rubs against my newly discovered favorite spot. I call out his name a second time and wait for him to follow. When he pulses inside me, a strange disappointment overcomes me at his having a barrier between us.

CHAPTER NINE

THEN

THANKSGIVING COMES AND GOES quickly. I don't see Bryant again until Friday morning when we head back to school, but we text a lot, probably too much. The more we talk, the more I like him. Also, I can't stop thinking about the sex. I've never been sex crazed, but damn, all I think about are the two orgasms he gave me.

He reaches across the back seat of Ben's car and squeezes my thigh. "A penny for your thoughts?"

"What are you two whispering about back there?" Zina asks from the front passenger seat. "It's not like we don't know you two have been talking nonstop."

I would've been embarrassed by Zina's knowledge prior to Bryant wrapping Grandma Rose in his arms and giving her peace instead of more confusion. At this point, I don't care if my sister and Ben know Bryant and I are talking.

"I was thinking about how amazing Bryant is in bed," I confess just to throw Zina off.

She spits out her drink and sprays it across the windshield. "You slept together?"

"Everything is going to be sticky," Ben complains before he catches up. "Wait, what? Did you tap that ass, my man?"

Bryant stares at me as though I've lost my mind. "I can't believe you told them."

I shrug. "I figured if we keep sleeping together then they'd find out eventually anyway."

His dimples make a grand appearance, and my lady parts grow hot and bothered. "We're sleeping together again?"

"Yeah, QB. I like your moves."

"What has gotten into you?" Zina asks.

False Start

Bryant Hudson is under my skin, and I'm on the fence between continuing to fight the good fight and giving into the insane attraction I feel for him. It's not just his looks or him being great in the sack. He is a really good person.

Ben snorts. "Bryant did."

Bryant pops him on the back of the head. "Watch how you talk about my future wife."

My sister is so confused. "I feel like I'm in the twilight zone."

The quarterback tugs at my shirt until I cross the backseat and snuggle into his waiting arms. It feels right to be there. For once, I just take a deep breath and let it be. I stop fighting. Maybe he'll surprise me and keep giving me reasons to want more of him.

The ride home is quick, too quick considering Bryant's deep, beautiful voice is quietly singing along to the song playing over the speakers of Ben's car. I enjoy hearing him croon and also love the fact that he doesn't care if I hear him. Once we arrive back at our apartment, the guys help us unload our bags before they head home to grab their gear for practice. As Zina and Ben suck face in a long goodbye, Bryant pulls at the hem of my shirt until our toes are touching. Then he leans down and kisses me. I've never been one to care for public displays of affection, but when he kisses me, I can think of little else.

"I want my first date tonight," he says after he breaks the kiss.

"You have a game tomorrow. You'll be in bed early."

"Nothing fancy, beautiful. Just you, me, and a little grub."

An idea pops into my mind. "Can you meet me at the cabin after practice?"

He touches my hair and presses the sweetest kiss to my forehead. "Whatever you want. I hate having to go to practice."

"I'll see you soon enough, QB. Go before you're late and piss the coach off."

He briefly kisses me again. "I'll see you. Don't promise dates for anyone else while I'm gone."

I salute him. "You got it, Captain."

"Smartass." He has to drag Ben away from my sister's mouth, but they eventually make it out of the apartment intact and likely with a pair of blue balls.

I spend the day preparing a nice meal for Bryant and wait for him at the cabin. I find it difficult to concentrate on anything other than him. I often think back to what he said at the treehouse about nothing being promised to us. I know I was scarred by losing my dad at a young age, and I've let it dictate parts of my life. I've fought falling for an amazing guy because of what happened to my father. Maybe it's time to stop battling my feelings.

I lie on the couch after I light a fire, and then I curl up and wait. Sometime later, a gentle shake wakes me.

Light green eyes fill my vision. "Has anyone told you how beautiful you are today?"

God. This guy makes it impossible to stay away. "No, not a soul has impressed upon me the effect of my beauty today."

He leans forward and softly presses his lips to mine. "I'm not worthy of your beauty, affection, or desire."

"Did you turn into a poet while I wasn't looking?"

"Yes. As a matter of fact, I've been quite creative today."

I sit up and lean my head against my bent arm and hand. "Do tell."

"I did something. I hope you're not mad."

"Uh oh."

He tightly shuts his eyes. "Fuck. I hope you're not mad. I sort of talked to the head physical therapist on the team and asked him if you could shadow at tomorrow's game."

I nearly knock him over as I sit all the way up. "Shut up. You did not."

"I can't tell if you're happy right now."

I throw my arms around his neck and squeeze tight. "I'm floored and overwhelmed that you did this for me. Why?"

"Look at me." I lean back a hair to look him in the eye. "I will always want you to be happy, Zhanna, even if it means you're truly happy with someone else."

False Start

Emotion sticks in my throat. "I wish you didn't make me happy."

He tucks my hair behind my ear. "I know, baby, but we're written in the stars. Can't fuck with fate."

"We've known each other for three weeks."

He grabs my hand and places my palm over his heart. "Feel how fast it's beating? You do this to me. And this." He lowers my hand to his crotch. "And you've got me all fucked up here." He moves my hand to the side of his head. "I may have only known you for three weeks, but when you know, you know."

I hug him again and avoid saying anything else. I'm too scared to dive in the deep end with him just yet. I'm not convinced I'm ready to live with the constant fear of being attached to a football player. "I was waiting for you to start dinner. What time is it?"

"Five. I have about 4 ½ hours before I have to make curfew in my hotel room."

Football players at the college and professional levels have a curfew at ten the night before a game, and they're required to stay in a hotel room the night before as well in order to limit distractions.

"I hope you know how to grill."

"I learned from the best."

"Your dad?"

"Yeah."

"Good, I bought steaks and potatoes."

"Could you be any more perfect?"

I ready the potatoes for the oven, humming to myself while Bryant goes outside and lights the grill for the steaks. I join him on the tailgate of his black truck out by the grill and snuggle in close when he wraps his arm around me. We listen to an acoustic country playlist and talk about tomorrow's game. It's easy to be with him. I enjoy every laid back second we spend together.

After dinner inside the cabin, we cuddle on the couch.

"Dinner was amazing. Thank you," he says, pressing a kiss to my forehead.

I move to straddle him as our hands intertwine with one another. "You're welcome."

"Will you wait for me after the game tomorrow? There are some people I'd like you to meet."

"I can't believe you were able to get me in the door to the physical therapy department. I can't thank you enough."

He releases my right hand and touches his hand to my face. "I'm a little nervous to have you on the sidelines, but I'm glad you're going to be there. The experience will be good for you."

"How did you know I wanted to go into sports medicine?"

"Zina." The saddest expression crosses his face. "I hate to go, babe, but I don't want to piss Coach off by missing curfew."

"It's okay. I knew you couldn't stay."

"Would you let me stay? Now that people know?"

I shrug and smirk. "I guess it depends on how you play tomorrow."

He leans his head back and laughs. "She's got jokes."

I know he's nervous to play tomorrow. Our team is undefeated in our conference this year, and the mounting pressure to hold onto the title grows with each game as the end of the season nears. He likely won't sleep well the night before a big game, so he needs to scoot and arrive at his hotel to at least attempt a decent night's sleep.

A strange feeling erupts in my chest when I realize I don't want him to go tonight. I'd rather him stay and us sleep by the fire. "You only have half an hour until curfew."

"Are you kicking me out?"

"Yes. Otherwise, the great state of Louisiana will blame me for their quarterback riding the bench because he pissed off his coach."

"They would indeed be angry. Alright, I'll go." He stands, stretches his long body, and then reaches out for me. I also stand, go to him, and lay my head against his chest. "Tonight was perfect. Thank you."

"You're very welcome."

"Are you staying out here tonight?"

"Yes, but I'll lock up tight until the morning."

He nods, seemingly happy with my response. "I'll text the instructions on who to meet tomorrow at the stadium. In the meantime, get some rest and stay hydrated. You'll be on the field tomorrow. I can't tell you how happy it makes me."

He kisses me goodnight right before I lock up behind him. Once the door is closed behind me, I touch my lips and smile to myself. When I lie down, my mind is full of him.

***

THE NEXT MORNING, I wake up early to Bryant's texts.

> Bryant: Good morning, beautiful.

> Bryant: I'm sending over Ben's cousin, Charity, with a pass that will enable you to access virtually any area of the stadium.

> Bryant: Can you meet her at the gate at 10?

> Zhanna: Wow! I'm going to watch from the sidelines tonight! It's been such a long time. Thank you! Thank you! Thank you!

> Bryant: Baby, Charity is waiting at the gate for you. Let me know when you have the pass in your hands.

I look at the time and see it's five past ten. I jump from the bed, rush out of the cabin, and practically jump in my Jeep to head for the gate. It takes me a few minutes to reach it at the front of the property where a girl waits inside a blue Honda.

I unlock the gate as Charity exits her vehicle on five-inch wedges. She walks smoothly across the gravel. It's a miracle she doesn't tip over or suffocate in her tight pants and shirt. I'm not sure how she's breathing considering they're painted on. Her long, platinum blond hair is perfectly curled in loose waves down her back. She's a knock-out.

With long, beautiful nails, she hands me an envelope. Before I can thank her for making the trip, she turns on her heel and marches back to her car.

"Thank you!" I say after her.

She might be rude, but I don't have to be.

Strange.

I turn and head back to the gate to close and lock it when Charity finally says something. "What do you have?"

I pivot. "Sorry?"

"What do you have that I don't? I've been chasing after Bryant since freshman year. He told me he didn't date, but he's giving you a pass and hooking you up with an opportunity with the team. A man doesn't do that unless he's got serious feelings for a chick. He's been screwing me for two years, and he's never done anything more than give me an orgasm."

Pure envy and a ridiculous possession fill me. The urge to close the distance between us and knock her off her rocker almost overtakes me.

Oh my God. What's wrong with me?

She grins when she sees she's gotten to me. "You didn't know about me?"

I recall my conversation with Bryant from a few weeks ago. "You're the woman he was seeing before football."

She laughs non humorously. "No, sweetheart, I sucked him off this morning in his truck outside the stadium."

She drops the bombshell and sways her ass back to her little car.

I'm so angry and blindsided. My fists are clenched as my blood pressure skyrockets. I jog across the country road to her before she can open her door. "You forgot something." I hand her the pass. "Please tell Hudson he can go fuck himself. And for future reference, chicks before dicks. Learn how to fix a woman's crown instead of trying to tear her down."

On the way to my Jeep, I pull my phone from my jacket pocket and look at the texts Bryant has sent since I left to open the gate.

Bryant: I keep thinking about how amazing it was to spend time with you last night. I feel deep shit for you, Coach.

I don't read anymore of his bullshit. I delete the feed and block his number. Just when I decide he's a great guy worth giving a shot to, he turns out to be an asshole. Granted, we aren't together, though he's said he wants to be. He shouldn't lead a woman on if he still wants to sleep around. It's common fucking courtesy.

"Ugh!" I shout in frustration.

CHAPTER TEN

THEN

I PACK UP THE cabin and make sure the fire is out before I lock it. My chest aches as I think about Bryant and who I thought he was. It hurts so much worse than it should after just weeks of knowing him. After I climb into my Jeep, I crank up a sad country song and instead of crying, I sing my heart out. Fuck Bryant Hudson and the horse he rode in on. I don't need a man in my already busy life, and he doesn't have time to have a relationship with football on his plate, even if he wanted one.

My phone rings and Zina's name flashes on the screen. "Hello?"

I can tell she's been crying as soon as she speaks. "Where are you?"

"I'm headed back to the apartment. I'll be there in ten minutes. What's wrong?"

"Grandma Rose is sick, like bad sick. She has pneumonia in both lungs. She didn't start feeling ill until two days ago. Mom said we might want to come home, so that means she's bad sick. Right?"

Shit. She's right. If Mom called us home, then Grandma Rose is really sick. "I'll be home in five."

I step on the gas and almost run into Bryant on the way into our complex. He brakes for me as I zip in front of him through the entrance. I park and take the building stairs two at a time to our second-floor apartment. I don't have time to wait on Bryant or to hear him out. We need to get on the road to New Orleans.

"Zhanna!" he yells after me, but I keep trucking toward my front door.

Zina has it open before I can push my key into the lock. Her face is stained with tears. My heart breaks as I pull her into a hug. It's time to put on my big girl panties again and take care of my baby sister.

"I packed you a bag."

Grabbing her by the hand, I pull her out of our apartment. "Let's go."

She closes the door and as we turn for the stairs, I run into Bryant's large chest.

"Baby, we need to talk."

With one index finger in the air, I start counting. "One, I'm not your baby. Two, I don't have time to talk to anyone." I walk around him and take the stairs quickly.

"Zina? What's wrong?" he asks, frowning at seeing her upset.

"Grandma Rose is sick. Mom said we should come home."

"Shit." He runs his hands through his hair. "I'll be there after the game. Ben, too."

I roll my eyes. "Don't bother."

Bryant puffs his chest out. "Woman, I don't know what that crazy bitch told you, but I'm most certainly not fucking off. One, in hindsight, sending Charity with the pass wasn't the smartest decision I've ever made. Two, you are my baby. I don't care if you're mad, that shit isn't changing. Get it through your thick skull. Three, I haven't touched anyone else since before the season began. I've told you this, but you didn't know me well enough at that point. So let me tell you, when I say something, it's the truth. Even when I fuck up, I'll tell you the truth."

We reach my car and throw our bags in the backseat. "I don't have time for this. I have to go."

"I'll be there after the game. Please unblock my number."

"Move, Bryant."

"Tell me you heard me, Z."

"It's hard not to! You're practically yelling. Now fucking move, or I'm kicking you in the dick."

He moves after another long look. "Please unblock me."

After I climb inside my vehicle, I turn over the ignition and drive away with Bryant staring after us.

"What happened with Charity?" Zina asks, crossing her arms over her chest.

I give her the rundown. "I thought he was a good guy."

"That bitch is lying. Bryant talks about you nonstop. I swear the boy is in love with you."

"We've known each other for three weeks."

"And it doesn't change the fact that he's practically obsessed with you."

I try like hell not to think about him as we drive seventy-five minutes away. I'm grateful Zina drops any more conversation about Bryant. I don't want to argue with her about him right now.

When we pull into the large hospital parking garage and park, Zina looks at me and touches my hand. "Ben said Charity has been looking for a rich husband since she was eighteen. She wants to land Bryant, but he's never wanted a relationship with her. He wants one with you. I know it's difficult to hear the things she said, but it doesn't mean they're true. He should have the opportunity to defend himself."

"She just seemed so confident and…"

"Gorgeous? Doesn't change the fact that she never made it past bed warmer status. He chose you. It also doesn't change her bitchy personality. Bryant had an arrangement with her for a short time, before you."

"I'm out of my depth with him," I admit, sighing.

"I get it. You guys light up when you're in the same space. There's so much sexual tension between you two. When the passion burns hot like that, it's a lot to take in. It would be easier to believe Charity than to put yourself out there to be hurt by a man who has the power to do it."

I know she's right. I'm scared of Bryant for many reasons. If he hasn't been with Charity, then I need to decide if I want to see something through with him. Shit or get off the toilet as they say. "Let's go check on Grandma Rose."

***

THE SMELL OF ANTISEPTIC fills my nose as we walk through the hospital lobby. I put Bryant out of my mind, focusing on being present for my family. My grandma needs our prayers and support.

We find our mom inside Grandma Rose's hospital room with a magazine in her hand. Our grandmother has an oxygen mask over her face as she sleeps soundly.

"Hey, girls," Mom greets and stands to hug us before she gives us an update. "She's having a hard time breathing. They may have to put a tube in her chest to help her."

Tears prick my eyes. "Will it hurt her?"

"No, they'll sedate her so she's not uncomfortable."

"How did she become sick this fast?"

Mom takes my hand and rubs her thumb over the top. "When her memory comes and goes, she doesn't always have the ability to communicate how she's feeling. She's lost in another time."

We sit for hours as we wait by my grandma's bed. She wakes herself up coughing but doesn't stay awake for long before she dozes again. After a late lunch, I pass time by holding my grandmother's hand and watching her favorite shows. She may be asleep, but a familiar sound in the background might be comforting. The nurses come in, checking on their patient and updating us with her worsening condition. She's not responding to the antibiotics fast enough.

As day turns into night, Grandma Rose continues to struggle breathing. Mom offers to turn the game on for us at seven, but I ask her to leave it on the Golden Girls. Plus, I don't want to see Bryant on television and think about the Charity situation. It's hard, but I need to tuck the situation away until later and focus on what's in front of me.

Zina announces we won the game when she returns from the vending machine around 10:30. "Twenty-four to ten."

"Good game."

"Hudson threw the damn ball."

My smile is instant. The familiarity of an inside joke about how I met him warms me.

"What's going on?" Mom looks between the two of us.

"Zhanna's tapping dat ass."

Glaring at her, I show my appreciation. "Thanks."

"I hoped you'd warm up to him. He seems like a nice young man," Mom says, but she isn't fooling me.

"You think he's hot."

"He's a very handsome young man."

Zina gives mom the business about Charity, and Mom's mouth drops open. "He left on game day to chase you?"

"Sho 'nuff did," Zina answers for me. "Ben said Tombs almost had a massive coronary and threatened to bench Hudson. Bryant left anyway. He gives a shit what you think."

I was so angry and upset about Charity and Grandma Rose when I saw him. It didn't register that he'd left when he had somewhere important to be. If it gets out he left against the coach's orders, pro teams could push him back in the draft next year. Before I can reply, Grandma has a coughing fit. The three of us leave our seats to check on her.

Her nurse comes in and gives her a breathing treatment, so we step outside to stretch our legs. Trekking down to my car to grab my bag for a change of clothes, I run into Bryant and Ben a few yards from my Jeep. Bryant's hair is down instead of pulled back in his usual man bun.

"I'll go inside and check on my girl," Ben says, saluting us as he leaves.

Bryant jams his hands inside the front pockets of his athletic pants and chews on his lip. "You didn't unblock me."

"Shit." I reach for my phone. "I forgot all about it once I hit the road. I'm sorry. I'll do it now."

I quickly unblock him.

"How's Rose?"

"She's not good. They're giving her a breathing treatment to hopefully open up her airway."

"We got here as fast as we could."

"You made record time. You shouldn't have risked speeding, though, not at the risk of hurting yourself."

He sighs and looks away for a moment before his eyes are back on me. "Can we talk about Charity?"

"She said she…"

"I know what she said. She told me. She's been taken care of. She's not allowed back at our place. I don't associate with people like her, and I really don't want to hang out with someone who's coming between me and you. She's gone. I hope I never lay eyes on her again because for most of the day I didn't know if you'd ever talk to me again. And I don't like the way that feels."

"I'm so…"

"I know you need to take things slow in the relationship department. You spent the last five years telling yourself you'd never be with a player, but you were letting me in. You were letting me close until Charity. So, if you're going to take you away from me, go ahead and do it now. If it hurts this bad after three weeks, I don't want to know how fucked I'm going to be after six months or a year. I have deep feelings for you, Zhanna. I'm not ashamed of it, but I'm also not naive enough to think you're there yet. If you gave us a real chance, you'd see how good we'd be together. I'll never hurt you. If we're going to do this, you can't have a foot half out of the door waiting for me to fuck up so you can leave. I can't live waiting for it to happen."

I need to make this right. "I'm sorry I believed her without speaking with you first."

I pause before pushing my next words out. "You scare me."

"I know, babe. I think it's best if I take a step back and let you figure it out. You've got school and Rose on your plate. I don't want to crowd you."

My phone buzzes in my pocket. I wouldn't normally answer it in the middle of such an important conversation, but Grandma Rose is in the hospital. I apologize before answering it. "Hello?"

My mom's voice comes over the line. "Sweetheart, they've decided to ventilate Grandma Rose. You may want to come back up and see her before they sedate her."

"Yes, ma'am."

Hanging up, I relay the news. "I'm sorry to end this conversation, but they're sedating Grandma Rose soon. I need to go back up."

"Can I walk you inside? You can tell me about Rose on the way up."

"I'd like that."

I fill him in on her worsening condition as we walk inside the hospital before taking the elevator to the third floor.

"I'm sure Mom would love to see you and say hello."

"Sure."

He follows me inside and Grandma lights up. I can hear her call for my grandfather, even through her oxygen mask and ragged breathing. "Phillip."

Bryant doesn't miss a beat with her as he walks past me to the side of her bed and sits down. He takes her hand in his and places his free hand on top. "Hello, love. Are you tired?"

She nods her head.

"If you need to rest, I'll still be here when you wake," he assures her, his voice gentle for her.

I can't believe he's here with my grandmother, once again bringing her comfort by pretending to be her husband. He's promising to stay beside her while she sleeps, and I pushed him away.

Fuck.

Bryant sits on one side of my grandmother while we gather on the other side. She fades in and out over the next hour as we wait for them to process the physician's order to sedate and ventilate her. Each time she wakes, she looks for Bryant, squeezes his hand, and smiles through her oxygen mask. Even in extreme discomfort and confusion, his presence seems to bring her the same comfort it brings me.

When the medical staff crowds in the room to start the process, my sweet Grandma Rose becomes terrified. I've done a good job of holding it together until I see her scared.

She constantly looks to Bryant for comfort.

He takes it all in stride. "You're doing a great job, Rose. Focus on me, sweetheart."

God.

I'm going to be a blubbering mess soon. My grandmother is so sick, and I scared away the perfect guy.

She pulls her mask off and struggles to breathe as she tells him, "I love you."

77

"I love you, too, Rose."

I turn around and fight to breathe through my tears. I need to pull myself together.

CHAPTER ELEVEN

THEN

AFTER A SHORT TIME, I've grown somewhat accustomed to being touched by Bryant any time we've been around each other. It's a slap in the face when I can't hug him anymore. He doesn't crowd me like he used to. I miss his nearness as we camp in the ICU waiting room.

"Why don't we go home and grab some shut-eye? We aren't doing Grandma any favors if we don't take care of ourselves."

"I rode with Ben. I can drive you home in the Jeep," Bryant offers.

"Aren't you tired?" I ask.

"I'm still wired from the game. It'll catch up with me soon enough, but I'm wide awake for now."

I throw him my keys. "Okay. I'll take you up on your offer. I'm dead on my feet."

"How mad was Coach Tombs that you left this morning?" I ask once we're inside.

"Stroke level."

"Yeesh."

"He'll get over it."

There's a lull in conversation before I apologize again. "I'm sorry… for believing Charity."

"I'm sure she was convincing."

"Although there's no excuse for believing her, she completely blindsided me."

"If I put myself in your shoes and some dude says you blew him while we've been talking, I'm blowing a gasket. I don't know if I'm keeping my cool by the time I get to you. So I don't blame you. I just think I need to give you space to figure out if you really want to pursue this with me. And to be honest, I can't invest anymore emotions in this until I know you're on board. I'm just as afraid of getting hurt as you are."

He's right. Of course, he's right. I completely understand where he's coming from, but the distance I forced him to put between us hurts more than I thought it would. I lose myself in my thoughts for the remainder of the trip. Bryant turns the radio on to drown out the silence. I'm grateful for it. I don't want him to hear my hushed cries.

As soon as we pull down the long driveway, I leave the vehicle without a word and head inside. I head straight for my room, lock the door behind me, dive under the covers, and take deep breaths. This is my process for dealing with stress when I'm overwhelmed. I just need a few minutes to catch my breath after a hard day.

"Zhanna?" Mom calls and knocks at my bedroom door. "Sweetheart, are you okay?"

I sniffle one time, and then I get my shit together. "Yes, ma'am."

"I've told Ben and Bryant they could stay in the pool house as long as they need it." She's such a hospitable, southern woman.

I throw the covers back and leave the bed to open the door. "Thank you for setting them up."

"Are those tears for Grandma or Bryant?"

I dash them away. "Ugh. Is my face red and splotchy?"

"Yes, dear. Are you going to be okay?"

"Aren't I always?"

Disapproval flashes across her face. "It's okay not to be okay sometimes. It's part of being human. You don't have to be so tough all the time, sweetheart. Now, talk to me about Bryant."

"He's giving me space and I hate it. I mean, I thought it's what I wanted."

She smirks. "Reverse psychology. Well played, Bryant."

"What?"

"He gave you what you thought you wanted in hopes you'd see you actually want what is right in front of you. It looks like it worked out for him."

"He's a football player."

"And against all odds, he captured your heart anyway."

"I can't go through what you did with Dad and two kids."

"The moment you decide to love someone, you take the risk of losing them one day. That's the price of love. For all the pain I've felt over your father's death, I wouldn't change one second of the time we spent together." Mom smirks and pats me on the arm. "If you can't sleep, come wake me."

She leaves my door and heads for her own bed.

A text sounds from my phone somewhere under the covers. I have to tear the bed apart to find it.

> Mom: Watch this video and make sure you read the lyrics.

The video is a song I know well, *The Dance*.

I click the link and the video loads, and it's the last thing I remember.

***

"ZHANNA, WAKE UP, SWEETHEART."

I turn over, cover my head, and snuggle deeper into my bed.

"Zhanna."

My eyes pop open, and my vision fills with my mom's worried face.

"There's been some news on Grandma."

"Is she okay?" I ask.

Her eyes gleam with unshed tears as she shakes her head. "No, Grandma passed away about thirty minutes ago."

"I thought the ventilator was supposed to help her."

"I don't know what happened, but she was older and very sick. We can find solace in the fact that she's no longer suffering." Mom pulls me into a comforting hug before we wake Zina together and share the same news.

False Start

After a great big group cry, we slide into my mom's bed and sleep close together until nine. I rise to find Bryant and Ben in the kitchen cooking breakfast.

"Morning. We didn't want to wake you a little earlier, but Rose passed away at about four this morning."

Bryant vacates a bar stool, takes two long strides, wraps his arms around me. "What do you need, Coach?"

God. Why does he have to smell so good?

"I don't know. I guess Mom will know about arrangements."

I sit with them as they cook breakfast, but I'm in a daze. It's weird how someone can die and the world just keeps moving. It doesn't pause for anyone. After Zina and Mom wake up, we eat in silence after we thank the guys for their hard work. No one quite knows what to say. What topics are appropriate for the recently bereaved?

We clear the table and clean the kitchen for the next little while, also in silence. I'm relieved when Ben and Bryant are forced to leave for football practice. The pressure to entertain is too much, too soon. I spend the day with Zina and Mom taking care of arrangements (Grandma was thankfully prepared), sifting through old photographs of Grandma Rose, and trying to imagine what Grandpa Phillip and our father said when Grandma made it to the other side.

I also think of Bryant. I find myself wondering what he's doing. Is he thinking of me as well? Or have I completely ruined any real chance with him?

I click on my main social media app and look through my sister's and mom's feeds to read the sympathetic messages others have left for Rose. And then I curiously look up Bryant, who I've not added as a friend yet.

He last posted a picture of a rose and captioned it, "Rose, thank you for letting me be your Phillip. I'm so happy you're with your true love now. Rest in peace, sweet lady."

He took the time to search for a picture and tell the world about my grandmother. Lending her comfort, he held her hand while she was dying. He drove all the way to New Orleans after a game to be at the hospital…after I told him to fuck off. He left the stadium under orders not to do so from his coach and went out of his way to set up a shadowing experience with the team's physical therapist. The man has shown me time and again he's not only a good guy, but he's also shown me how much he cares for me.

I'm a grade A idiot.

I send him a text to see how his day is going.

> Zhanna: Hey you. I hope you guys were able to get some sleep this morning. I know it wasn't much. I didn't thank you for driving here, so thank you.

Tucking my phone away, I return to his social media account. His account is full of video highlights, pictures, and news articles about him as a player. I notice there's nothing personal on his page except the sweet comments his parents leave. They couldn't be prouder of him, and it shows even through the internet. But it's sad that no one in the media really takes the time to get to know athletes beyond their talent as a player.

I don't hear from Bryant for the rest of the day. And as time goes by, I begin to worry about him and us. I don't know which way is up or down anymore. I'm probably just more emotional than usual because of Grandma Rose, but he did say he was giving me space, something that would've made me happy a few weeks ago. Now, I dare to say I miss him. I miss his presence, smile, eyes, and kind heart, and we've only been apart for mere hours.

God. What is happening to me?

"What's wrong?" Mom asks as we clean up takeout leftovers a neighbor brought over. "You're sighing a lot."

"Am I?"

Zina snorts. "Yes, like a million times."

"It's been two hours since practice let out, but I haven't heard from Bryant. I think I messed up."

"Is this about what we talked about last night?" Mom asks.

"Yeah."

"He told you he was giving you space, and yet he still woke and cooked breakfast for you this morning. I think it says how he really feels. He's been very giving in the short time you've been, erm, dating. I think it's time you give back some, even things up a bit."

I cock my head to the side and take her in. "What do you mean?"

"I mean, if you haven't heard from him, be the one to reach out with a call, or even better, a surprise visit."

"He's in Baton Rouge."

"You have a car and it's barely over an hour's drive."

I don't have an argument for that, but I try anyway. "And what if he's not talking to me, and I show up at his place out of the blue? I will have driven all the way for nothing. Worse? What if he's with a girl, and it's why he's not communicating. If I show up, things will get awkward fast."

"Pussy." Zina says.

I bite my lip and look to my mother for help.

"You're letting your fear control you. The real question, sweetheart, is do you want to be with him? If so, get in your car and go. Text us when you land."

"But..."

Zina pushes me toward the door. "You heard Mom. If you want him, you have to be willing to go more than halfway sometimes. Bryant is in Baton Rouge. He's not with another girl, because the guy is insanely obsessed with you. All you have to do is show or tell him how you feel, and he's yours. He wants you. You want him. He chose you. Are you going to choose him?"

I don't waste a second picking up my purse and keys and kissing my mom and sister goodbye. They wish me luck and ask for a report as soon as I've arrived. I drive faster than I should, making the drive in an hour.

Pulling into the drive of the home he shares with Ben, I park beside Bryant's truck. Ben's car isn't here, so I hope Bryant isn't with him. I could be waiting all night. I take a few deep breaths and leave my Jeep.

Here goes nothing.

At his front door, I ring the doorbell and wait. And I wait some more before pressing the button again. This is stupid. I shouldn't have come here. It's probably best he doesn't know I came desperately pining after him.

Pathetic.

I turn and go to my car after I finish berating myself for thinking this was a good idea. After turning the ignition over, I back out of his drive.

"Zhanna!" he yells, and I slam on the brake.

He walks up to my vehicle and taps on the window. I roll it down, and then my tongue almost falls out of my mouth. There's no denying he just woke up. His hair is rumpled, he's shirtless, and his shorts ride low on his hips.

"I'm sorry. I didn't realize you were sleeping. I'll just go."

"What? No. Park and come in, babe."

I hesitate.

"You okay, Coach?"

"I…" I start and stop several times. "Do you like to dance?"

His brows knit in confusion. "Yeah, with the right girl."

Stop being a chicken shit, park your damn car, and go inside al-fucking-ready.

I hesitate for a few more beats before I listen to myself and park my car. Bryant walks back down the drive alongside me as he runs his hands through his hair.

When I've come to a stop, he opens my door and offers me his hand as I step down. He crowds my space as I crane my head back to look up at him. "Are you okay? I mean, I know you aren't okay, but…"

I place my hand on his arm to ease his worry. "I'm okay. Let's get you out of the cold."

I don't miss the fact that he doesn't throw his arm around my shoulders like usual. I don't know why it took him pulling away for me to realize how much his touch means to me.

Once we're inside the home, he leads me through a foyer, living area, and then into a large open kitchen with an island in the middle.

"Let me throw a shirt and shoes on," he says, and I almost object to it but end up saying nothing.

When he returns, his hair is brushed. I mourn the loss of his sexy bed head.

He holds his phone up. "I just saw your call. I crashed after practice."

"I know you must've been exhausted."

"Yeah, but I should've waited until I talked to you and made sure you were doing okay before I passed out. I didn't mean to go to sleep. I called it resting my eyes." He laughs.

"Oh, you don't have to call and check on me."

He casts a frown in my direction. "What do you mean?"

I shrug. "I don't know. I guess you wanted to take a step back, so things changed and…"

"Whoa. I don't want to take a step back. Fuck, Zhanna. It took everything I had not to text you all day. Fighting it wore me out more than watching film did. I don't like not talking to you. I thought I was doing the right thing by giving you what you wanted."

"And what do you think I want? I didn't have time to respond to you giving me distance. My grandmother was dying, and we had to go upstairs in the middle of our conversation. I've had a lot to process since Charity showed up yesterday morning. And then today…today you didn't talk to me during film or after practice, and…" I bite my lip unsure of my next words. I'm winging this by the heart I'm wearing on my sleeve.

Bryant takes a few small steps toward me and closes the gap between us. "And you thought I'd moved on?"

I look down at my shoes, afraid to say it out loud. "No. Yes. I don't know. I thought maybe I'd pushed you away for good."

"Z, look at me, baby." His green eyes are full of compassion as he stares deeply into me. "You didn't push me away. I'm afraid of being the one to push you away by crowding you and pushing you faster than you're ready to go."

"I want the dance," I say, and I'm met with confusion. I forget the lyrics and fumble. "Something about wanting the pain and the dance. Or is it not wanting the pain, but wanting the dance? Shit, I forget which."

He presses his lips into a thin line as he tries not to laugh. "Babe, what are you talking about?"

"The Garth Brooks song. My mom sent it to me." I wave it off. "The song is called The Dance."

Two dimples make an appearance. "Yeah, babe, I know the song."

"So that's what I want."

A bark of laughter leaves him. "Forgive me for being obtuse, but you'll have to be a little more explicit about what you want."

I bite my lip, hoping putting myself out there will suddenly become easier. "You. I just want you."

The side of his mouth curves into half a smile. "Christ, you're so fucking beautiful it hurts to look at you."

"Yeah?"

"Baby, as soon as I saw you standing across the fire, I knew I had to talk to you."

I cringe. "I called you 'a chicken shit'."

"You didn't kiss my ass. You didn't throw yourself at me, and as hard as it was to hear, you told me the truth about my game. You immediately had my respect because you treated me like I'm a person instead of a stat. And what can I say? I'm strangely turned on by your insults."

I get tickled with him. "There's plenty more where that came from."

Bryant tucks my hair behind my ear and touches his palm to my cheek. "I'd like to look forward to hearing them each and every day."

"Every day?"

He leans in closer, so close that his breath whispers across my lips. "Every fucking one."

"Will you hurry up and kiss me? The anticipation is killing me."

His smirk turns into a grin. "What am I going to do with you?"

"I have a few suggestions, but the first thing I'd recommend is…"

He presses his lips to mine and cuts my words off. I was going to say, "kiss me," but I guess he got the hint. He cradles my face in his hands like I'm the most precious thing in the world to him and kisses me slowly with a sense of urgency. My hormones surge as my hands begin to wander all over his perfect body. We get lost in each other and abandon the world for a little while.

CHAPTER TWELVE

NOW

AFTER I WALK OUT of my office and leave Otto, Leslie, Zina, and Bryant behind, they leave me in peace. To ensure they leave me that way, I don't go directly home. I park close to Jackson Square in the Quarter, leave my cell in the car, and walk the streets of the city I love more than any other place on earth. I don't know if past lives exist, but if they do, I'm pretty sure I lived here before. There's something both brazen but easy going about New Orleans.

I find a bench on Bourbon Street and watch the street performers–the silver men, the artist formerly known as Prince, and Michael Jackson, and other part-time acts I haven't seen before. For about an hour, I sit quietly and watch the city pass by, desperate to be alone with my thoughts. When I've had my fill, I stroll down the streets through the tourists and pop into shops here and there. I mostly wander to pass the time, so I don't have to face the emotions swirling around inside me. It's all too raw, too painful to remember.

By the time the sun sets, I'm tired of walking. I want to go home, have a drink, and forget that I ever fell in love with Bryant Hudson. But the city is alive this evening and the news of his contract with the Voodoo broke. The people of our hometown couldn't be more excited to have a local boy as their new quarterback, and there's already talks of his franchise hopes. His name floats around the city like he's the second coming of Jesus. When I've had enough of hearing his name, I walk back to my car and drive the few crowded blocks home.

At home, I finally check my phone and see quite a few messages.

Zina: Are you okay?

Bryant: I'm sorry.

Leslie: Biiiiitttcccchhhh, get your cute ass over here when you come home. M'kay? M'kay. Need help picking out countertops, cabinets, and general kitchen fuckery for homeboy.

Bryant: I'm at your house. Where did you go, baby? Please come talk to me.

Leslie: Mr. Football Star is on your front step if you're avoiding him.

Leslie: Also, he looks like a sad puppy dog right now.

Zina: Let me know you're okay.

Zhanna: I'm fine, but it would be nice to have yours and Leslie's support. It feels like you've all so easily forgiven him for tearing my heart out. You're supposed to

> be on my side, but it doesn't feel like you are right now.

> Zina: I am on your side, dummy. You're miserable without him, and don't you dare deny it. If I didn't know being with him is exactly what you want, then I wouldn't give him the time of day. You still love him. If you didn't, I'd back off.

> Zhanna: If Bryant and I get back together it won't be because we were pushed together.

I put my phone down and grab the biggest bottle of wine in my fridge I can find and head next door to Leslie's house. He opens the door before I can knock.

"Oooooooo, girl, is that a chilled red?"

"I'm a rebel. Who says you can't chill a red?"

"Let's air her out while you tell me where you've been."

"I walked around the Quarter. I just wanted to be by myself and alone with my thoughts for a while."

"And?"

"And what?"

He hmphs. "I know you. And I may have only known him for a day, but I also know you when it comes to him. You went to that place."

"What place?" I ask.

"The place where you overanalyze the man and the situation. It's not complicated. Do you love him?"

I don't hesitate because there's no use in lying to myself or Leslie. "I'd sacrifice a lot not to."

"Can you forgive him?"

"I've tried."

"Forgiveness isn't the hard part, it's the forgetting how much it fucking hurts. But it's possible to move on. It's possible to trust again, boo."

"Pour me a glass?" I need alcohol if we're going to continue talking about my ex.

Leslie sets a large glass of wine in front of me. "Do you know he loves you?"

"Yes, he loves me, but I don't know if it's enough." I shrug. "It's complicated."

"You want me to kick his ass?"

"No."

"Good. I'd hate to mess up his gorgeousness or injure him where he can't play."

I'm grateful when my friend shifts the conversation slightly away from my relationship to Bryant's kitchen. I do my best to detach from the fact it's his kitchen, not ours. If it was ours, it would have an entirely different feel to it. It would be for a future family and not a millionaire bachelor. "This," I say and hold up a dark mahogany swatch of wood stain. "This is beautiful."

After another few glasses of wine, I really get into it. I sort through swatches like a demented, drunk, interior-decorating queen. Within a few hours we've finished the entire bottle of wine and have his entire kitchen laid out from the walls to the flooring.

"I'm really good at this." I glance up at Leslie to find him dazed and confused. I snap my fingers in front of his face. "Yo. Are you alive?"

"Bitch, you are drunk, so I need you to hold it together when I tell you that your ex-husband is about to step onto my porch and knock on the door."

"Shit," I slur. "Quick, hide me."

He arches his right brow. "Why?"

"I don't want to see him."

"Tough shit. We're showing him this fabulous new kitchen you put together for him."

As Leslie heads around the kitchen bar for the front door, I sneak off for the back door to slip out before anyone can detect my absence. As soon as I open the back door, a possum's shiny eyes glow back at me as it starts hissing. I let out a scream and slam the door. Two heavy sets of footsteps run toward me.

"What's wrong?" They both ask in unison.

"Possum."

"Jesus. I thought someone had broken into the house to take your behind," Leslie also slurs.

Bryant grins. "Been drinking, baby?"

I hold up my finger and thumb to indicate a teensy amount. "Just a little bit." Then I burst into tears because seeing him reminds me how much it hurts to love him.

Leslie's hands go to his hips. "Ah, hell."

"She drunk-cries when she's emotional," Bryant says.

Leslie turns to him like he might knock him out. "Motherfucker, I know. I've been drinking with the bitch ever since she moved in. And the damndest thing happens every time she drinks wine and talks about you – she cries." He points at Bryant then at me. "You broke it, you need to fix it. You aren't supposed to make her cry. Get your shit together, Mr. Football Star." My friend pivots on his heel like a diva, tosses his long dreads over his shoulder, and sashays off into the sunset in an aqua blue muumuu and black yoga sandals.

I try to walk around Bryant but don't make it far. He hooks me in crook of the arm and spins me around. "Not so fast, Hudson."

"Hale," I correct.

His jaw tenses at the reminder. "Baby, listen…"

I yank my arm from his clutch. "Come see what we did for your kitchen."

He follows without another word. I pull out a bar stool at the kitchen island for him to sit and begin to lay samples in front of him as I explain each choice. It all comes together like a puzzle in front of us. I'm happy with the end result. I can't wait to see how Leslie makes it happen.

Bryant frowns at my presentation.

Shit.

"You don't like it."

"No, it's beautiful, Zhanna." I can tell he wants to say more, but he refrains as an overwhelming sadness clings to him like a rain cloud. Leslie pours us another glass of wine and tries to pour the quarterback a lowball of scotch. "No, thank you," he says.

Leslie lifts a brow. "You might need it. I'm putting on Grease, and then we're going to sing and dance our drunk, beautiful asses off."

Bryant changes his mind. "Leave the bottle."

My friend turns to me and holds his hand for me to take. "Come on, Sandy."

"Okay, Danny."

We do exactly as he said and dance our asses off. Bryant moves into the living room to watch and laugh at us. Before I can reach the end of the movie, I cuddle into my friend's armchair and fall asleep.

"Up you go," Bryant says and jostles me awake as he picks me up

I manage to open one eye. "What's happening?"

"We're getting you home and in bed."

"Night, boo boo!" Leslie yells as we walk through his front door.

"I love you!"

"Bitch, you better."

I try to wave at him, but my arm is like a wet spaghetti noodle.

Bryant chuckles at my attempt. "You're the cutest drunk in the world."

"You don't have to carry me. I can walk."

He pulls me a little tighter to his chest. "I know, babe, but I've got you."

He carries me to the house as I lay my head against his broad chest and shoulder. I doze off again before we reach my door. I'm vaguely aware of him reaching for my keys and then laying me on the bed.

"You can't sleep in jeans."

I pull the covers over me and snuggle into the sheets.

He pulls it off. "You're still wearing your shoes, Coach."

Pulling my shoes off causes a shiver to form over my skin. The discomfort of cold air hitting my feet nudges me awake. "Cold," I say as I sit up and pull at the covers again. I'm out like a light as soon as my head hits the pillow.

Bryant shakes me from sleep again. "Take some aspirin and drink a glass of water for me."

I sleepily comply and swallow the pain reliever before I lie back down. Bryant climbs into bed behind me moments later and pulls me to the middle of the bed. "In case you're sick," he says.

"Okay." I pull his arm from his side and slide it around me.

"Z?"

"Yeah?"

"Will you remember this tomorrow for me? Remember that you wanted me close?"

"Yeah."

"I love you more than life itself."

CHAPTER THIRTEEN

NOW

A LIGHT SNORE AT my back wakes me. I snuggle into Bryant as the morning sunlight streams through the window. The birds happily chirp outside until my mind fully wakes up and realizes Bryant is snoring at my back with his heavily-tattooed arm thrown across my middle. I throw an elbow into his ribs making him grunt in pain.

"Huh? What?" he asks half unconscious.

"Why are you in my bed?"

He looks around the room. "Ah. You were drunk. I stayed in case you were sick."

"Remind me why you were at Leslie's again?"

He moves his arm, rolls over to his back, and sighs. "I'll just go. I don't want to fight with you, Z." He leaves the bed.

Who is he and what has he done with my ex-husband? Since when has Bryant ever given up so easily?

"What's your deal?"

He sits on the side of the bed and rubs his face. "I don't have a deal."

"You totally have a deal. You're pouting."

"I'm a grown man. I don't fucking pout." He stands and stretches his tall, muscular body.

I almost orgasm on the spot.

"Did you come over for a booty call?"

"No, Zhanna. I came over to check on you because I haven't heard a word since you left work at lunch. I was worried. I also wanted to apologize for putting my house's redesign in your lap."

He throws on his shirt as he sits to put on his shoes. Then the man walks out of my room and front door, slamming it shut behind him.

The front door opens again almost immediately. Bryant is standing in the door frame a few seconds later. "I hate the kitchen you designed, not because it's unappealing, but because it's not the French Country kitchen you've always wanted. As soon as I looked at the house, I knew the kitchen was perfect for what you wanted. A big place for the family to gather over food, wine, and hot cocoa. You designed a beautiful kitchen last night, but it's not what I had in mind."

"It's not my house nor is it my kitchen," I reply, and the sudden urge to vomit hits me like a train. "Oh, God."

I run into the master bath and heave. Bryant comes in behind me and turns on the water in the sink. When I'm done, I sit back on my heels as he presses a cold rag to my face.

"You drank too much last night, babe."

"I was trying to forget."

"Forget what?"

I push his hand away and pick myself off the floor. "Falling in love with you."

I leave him in the bathroom and head for the kitchen. I need food on my stomach if I'm going to stave off nausea.

"You don't mean it," he says as he comes to stand behind me at the refrigerator. "I fucked up. I own it. I'll never regret anything more than cheating on you. No matter how it shakes out between us, I'll never regret being someone you used to love."

I'm not immune to him. That's the problem. He's always held the power to hurt me like no other. I'm not unaffected by his words. They pull at my heartstrings and make me want to lean back into his chest, so he'll wrap his arms around me. They make me want French country kitchens, food, cocoa, wine, and the family it comes with.

He isn't someone I used to love. I still love him very much. And that's the thing about love, it doesn't give a damn how much it hurts when you're betrayed, the love just doesn't fade with the presence of pain. Love hurts, but it shouldn't, and it didn't always. His love used to be the most comforting warmth I've felt since my dad died. Bryant has never just been my lover, he's always been my best friend, too. So, in one fell swoop, I lost both. I'm angry and bitter about it. How does my husband, my best friend, and my lover commit the ultimate sin when he's supposed to love me?

"I ask myself everyday what I did to deserve it. For the life of me, I can't figure it out."

He wraps his arms around my waist as he leans down and tucks his face into the side of my neck. "Zhanna, baby, it had nothing to do with you. You didn't do anything wrong. You're the best wife a man can ask for."

It's hard to reconcile his past actions with his current words. How can I be such a great wife if he dropped his guard enough with another woman to be intimate with her? I know his words are meant to ease my pain, but they sting.

"Let me make you breakfast and my hangover cure," he says, and my ears perk up.

Bryant's hangover cure actually works, so I'm not turning it down. I slip from his grasp and have a seat at the bar while I watch him work. To be such a big guy, he moves like a gazelle.

He throws bacon in a frying pan before he whips up a batch of eggs for us. "Mind throwing toast in?"

"Not at all."

I busy myself with the toaster and listen to his deep hum. His voice is one of my favorite sounds in the world. An overwhelming sadness settles over me as I realize how much I miss this small thing about him. Really, I miss much more if I'm honest. I sniffle and excuse myself to the bathroom before I become a blubbering fool in front of him. Inside the master bath, I count to twenty several times as I attempt to rein in my emotions.

A knock comes at the door. "Zhanna? Are you okay?"

"Yes," I lie. "Just felt queasy again. I'll be out in a minute."

"I'll wait for you to see if you feel like eating."

Why does he have to be a great guy? He's thoughtful, compassionate, and worships the ground I walk on, except for the one night he didn't.

"Please go ahead and eat without me." I wipe my eyes, wash my face, and stall for time. I have to return eventually though, so I put on a brave face and handle business.

When I emerge, Bryant is standing on the other side of the door with a worried expression on his face.

"I'm okay."

"Feel like eating or do you want to lie on the couch?"

"I think I can handle food."

We sit beside each other at the bar with orange juice and food, enduring an awkward silence. I don't know why he's being quiet, but I don't speak for fear I'll let my emotions rule me.

"What finally won you over? You know, back in the day when we were in school? What made you take a chance on me?" He picks up my empty plate and stacks it on his before he takes them to the sink.

"Grandma Rose."

"You would've done the same."

"I would hope so. It was one of the kindest acts I've ever witnessed."

He turns around and leans against the sink. "Will you give me fourteen dates to change your mind?"

The reminder of the first time we were intimate brings the saddest smile to my face. The memory is bittersweet. My memories of falling in love are some of the most beautiful ones a person can have, but the problem has never been his ability to make me fall for him. It's being faithful. I'm not one to believe that people don't cheat, because they do, and people cheat for many reasons.

"Just give me fourteen dates. Let me show you I'm still the man you loved."

He's still the man I love, present tense, but telling him so will only fuel his tenacity to reunite with me.

I sigh. "We can't keep doing this. I left you. I divorced you. I need to move on with my life. We can't continue sleeping together."

"I agree. Fourteen dates and absolutely no sex."

I hesitate, because I don't want to hurt him, but he steps toward me with sheer determination on his face.

"What do you have to lose, Z? A few hours each date? After fourteen dates, you either want me back or you don't. I'll walk away and stay away if it's what you want."

"I don't think you'll stay away."

He takes another step with his long legs. "I don't think you want me to."

"What do you think this will accomplish?"

"I think it'll show you we're meant to be together. We've always been fated to one another. I fucked up, Z, but I didn't stop loving you."

"Not even when you let her touch you?"

"Not even then. I know that's hard to understand because I betrayed you, but it's the truth."

A knock comes at the back door of my kitchen. "It's most likely Leslie, who has a key."

I hear the knob turn, and then my friend. "Yoo hoo, lovers! Cover up! My beautiful ass is in the house!" He peeks into the kitchen. "Ohhhhh, looks like some serious shit is going on in here. What are y'all talking about?"

I roll my eyes. "You have no boundaries."

He waves it off as he walks in wearing an emerald, green and yellow, African-motif muumuu. "Girl, I know. Seriously, what's the topic of conversation?"

"I asked her out on fourteen dates."

"Why fourteen?"

"Because eight years ago, I asked her out on fourteen dates and never really got them. If she doesn't want me after fourteen dates, then I'll stay away."

"It's a fair deal," Leslie adds his opinion on the matter.

"What?! You're supposed to be on my side!"

He draws an imaginary heart with his index fingers complete with long, pointy yellow nails. "Suga, I'm on the side of love. Did you give the man fourteen dates?"

"Yes, we've gone on tons of dates over the last eight years."

He shakes his finger at me. "Nuh-uh. Did you agree to fourteen dates before you were a couple?"

I glare at my friend. "Yes, but…"

"But nothing, honey child, if you promised Mr. Football Star fourteen dates and didn't deliver, you still owe the man his dates."

"We're divorced for Christ's sake!"

Leslie purses his lips in displeasure at my volume. "And a deal is a deal. I've never known you to go back on your word."

My blood pressure is steadily rising. My dad always taught me that a person's word should mean something. You should never go back on your word if it's in your control. "You know what? Fine! I'll go on eleven dates, fourteen minus the three I went on when we were dating, but it won't change anything."

Bryant smirks at me and rubs his hands together. "Be ready, baby. I'm coming for you. I'll make you fall head over heels for me again."

This will show him he needs to move on once and for all.

CHAPTER FOURTEEN

NOW

I DON'T SEE OR hear from Bryant for a few days, but he's waiting for me in my office Monday morning. "Good morning, Coach."

"Shouldn't you be working out?"

"I wanted to tell you good morning, you know, start my day off right. I also wanted to ask you out on a date."

He's already at this again. I decide to play his game. I'll play it right until the end when he's sorely disappointed I'm still not taking his ass back. "Sure. Where are we going?"

"You could sound happier."

Crossing my arms over my chest, I shoot him an eat shit look.

He glares back. "I'll pick you up Friday at seven."

"Where are we going?" I ask not sounding any more delighted with the idea of a date.

Bryant places his hands on his hips, puffing his chest out and giving me all sorts of attitude. "It's a surprise."

Rolling my eyes, I sigh. "Fine. Whatever."

"Fucking perfect," he bites out.

Coach Jed Jones walks in and rambles about another player's hamstring injury when he suddenly realizes Bryant's in my office. "Oh, hey, man! How's it going so far?"

"Good, man. Thanks."

It takes Jed a minute to read the room. "I'll see you in the weight room, Zhanna. We'll talk there."

Bryant watches him leave. "He has a thing for you."

"He's happily married."

He grunts.

"I guess guilty minds think that way about their peers."

I could've slapped him and had less of a response. Hurt flashes across his face.

He holds a hand up and swallows hard. "I deserved that." Then he hooks a thumb over his shoulder. "I'm going to work out."

"Bryant…"

"It's okay, baby. I gutted you. I don't know what it feels like, but I deserve every ounce of pain you dish out. And I'll take it because I love you. Have a good day."

Then he's gone. I hate the person I am when I lash out at him. I know it's because he hurt me and somewhere deep down, I want him to hurt too. I'm not proud of it.

Something has to change.

***

ALL WEEK I'VE TOLD myself I'm not putting effort into Friday, and I've avoided any talk on the matter from anyone. But, as it inches closer to Friday, I panic about my outfit, hair, and makeup. I don't want to look like I don't take care of myself, but I also don't want to look like I went through any extra care. It sends the wrong message.

By Thursday night, I'm borderline hyperventilating about toeing the line between pretty and friendly. I try on several outfits, then play with my makeup. I'm lost in the art of the perfect smoky eye when my bell rings.

I'm a total dork for answering the door at nine at night in yoga pants and full warpaint.

"I brought beignets and coffee," Bryant says and holds up a Cafe du Monde box.

I frown at him. He looks me up and down. He's a real fan of yoga pants. "Our date isn't until tomorrow."

His smile falters. "It's cool. I can leave them with you."

"No, please come in and share them." I open the door wide for him to pass through. "Let's put them on the coffee table in the living room. I'll grab us plates from the kitchen."

On my way to the kitchen, I debate whether to take my makeup

False Start

off so I don't give him the wrong impression, but he knows me well enough to know why I'd take it off.

When I return to the living room, Bryant is on the couch with his arm draped across the back, white paper coffee cup in his hand. He looks at home even being as large as he is on the loveseat. I've been here before – being at home with him, tucked into his side on the couch as we relax and unwind together. It was my favorite part of the day.

I clear my throat as I shake off the memories. "What took you to the cafe?"

"I was walking around remembering the time we got so drunk and rowdy in that old bar down on Bourbon that they threw us out. Do you remember that night? If you told me that night Ben and Zina wouldn't be together forever, I would've thought you were crazy."

"Yeah." I smile. "It was a good night. I thought they'd be together forever, too."

He sits forward on the couch and opens the bakery box. "The beignets are still warm-ish, but we can pop them in the microwave and nuke them if you want."

I sit beside him, and hand over a plate and napkin. "They're okay the way they are. Thank you for bringing them."

He gazes up at the television show paused on the screen. "What are you watching?"

"Vikings."

"Gruesome."

I laugh. "Yes, but I'm obsessed with it. I have the biggest girl crush on Lagertha. She's a badass."

He snorts. "Am I at risk of losing you to a woman?"

"No. I like being with a man, but I find women to be beautiful."

He turns to face me. "Can I ask you a question?"

"I guess so."

"Please don't get mad."

"I'll try.

"Have you been with anyone else?"

Putting my beignet down, I look away. "That's none of your business. You forfeited the right to know."

"I get your anger, because just the thought of you with someone else hurts and pisses me off. I wish there was some way for me to ease it all for you. Seeing you in pain has always been hard for me. Being the one to cause it keeps me up at night."

My gaze lands back on him. "You don't sleep?"

"I can manage three hours at a time before I'm up. I still find it difficult to sleep by myself after sleeping beside you for so many years."

I don't tell him I also miss sleeping with him, snuggled up against his broad, massive, tattooed chest. I've always felt safe and precious in his arms. I also miss waking up a hot, sweaty mess because we've become so tangled in each other during the night that we don't know where I start or he ends. I also remember the nights when I woke to his hands wandering over my body. It was wild and reckless. We never could get enough of each other, even in our sleep.

"Have you tried taking a supplement?"

"Yeah. It makes me groggy the next day. I can't be groggy. I could get hit and injured."

"Problematic." An idea that drives me mad with jealousy pops into my mind, but I ask before I can stop myself. "Have you tried sex?"

"We haven't had sex in two months." He ensures I pick up the fact that he hasn't slept with anyone else. "I haven't slept with anyone else in eight years."

I close my eyes and swallow past the painful reminder of his infidelity. He didn't sleep with the woman, but she put him in her mouth, and he finished. I don't know why him finishing makes it worse, but it does.

He reads me like a book. "I didn't mean to upset you. I'll go."

He stands to go with slumped shoulders and an expression of pure agony on his face. He hurt me, and I keep hurting him back, even when I don't mean to.

I reach up and grab his hand and tug him toward the couch. "Stay. Please."

"Are you sure?"

I gently tug at his hand, and I'm relieved when he sits. Except, I don't let go of his big, rough hand.

He squeezes. "We don't have to do this."

"Chicken shit."

He smirks and two beautiful dimples make an appearance. God, I realize how long it's been since I've seen him smile. It's been longer even since I've been the one to make him smile. How has the world been deprived of such a wonderful thing? "You've always scared me, Zhanna. You have a lot of power over me."

If he knew he had the same power over me, I'd already be in Vegas again, getting married at another chapel by an Elvis impersonator.

I lay my head against the back of the couch, allowing my gaze to settle on him. He gets better with age. He's sexier now than when we first met. Instead of verbally responding to him, I leave my seat and crawl over to straddle his lap.

"I don't want to be angry with you. It's exhausting."

"What are you saying?"

I lean forward, pressing my lips to his. He freezes against me for a moment before kissing me back. His hands come to cradle the back of my head as his tongue slips into my mouth and dances with mine.

He breaks the kiss enough to whisper against my lips, "We can't."

"We can." I'm so turned on by his touch, smell, and prowess.

The man can kiss. I'm so turned out by the hardness between my legs, I clench and rub myself against him.

"Fuuuuuuck," he groans.

Unzipping and unbuttoning his jeans, I work to pull him out. As soon as I wrap my hand around his length, he bucks. I nearly combust on the spot. I've always been aroused by his pleasure. The mere thought of him losing control makes me want to do the same. So I maneuver around as I pull my pants off like I'm doing a weird interpretive dance. When I'm straddling him again, he reaches underneath my shirt and pulls it up and over my head.

"You're fucking perfect."

I ease down on him as he hisses. I start to ride him and buck uncontrollably as I'm filled with the need to release around him.

"Slow down, beautiful."

I don't, not when I feel whole again, like I can breathe for the first time in months. I'm desperate for it.

"No," he argues, grabbing my hips to stop my movement. "This isn't going to be a quick fuck this time." Bryant brings his forehead down to mine. His pale green eyes have a hint of moisture in them as he pleads with a whisper, "Just be with me tonight."

He searches my face for understanding. He's asking me to lay myself open raw for him. He wants more than a quick romp. I know me—I'll open myself and give him everything. What will be left of me and us when we're done? It's why I prefer the less intimate fucks. I don't have to connect with him and stare the facts in the face–I still love him, and I think I always will. And yet, what can be done about it when he's torn my heart out once already? How can I possibly make the leap again after what he's done? How do I trust that it won't happen again?

I close my eyes and disconnect as I begin to move again, but this time at a much slower pace. A moan escapes me when he pulls my bottom lip between his teeth.

"Open your eyes."

I ignore his request and continue moving, leaving my eyes closed and my soul shut to him. Except, he creeps underneath my skin anyway and sinks into the very fiber of me with his mere presence inside and around me.

"Goddamnit," his deep voice cracks over the words. "Open your eyes and look at me, Zhanna." When I hear his desperation, my lids fly open and a single tear escapes. Upon seeing it, he swipes it away with his thumb. "There she is."

I look away, feeling too exposed, and try to also pull away. I want to escape the urge to drown myself in him. I want to dive into the deep end of Bryant Hudson and drink him in one mouthful at a time. But I don't ever want to feel the heartache he gave me again. The fear keeps me from letting him get too close.

"Please," he whispers against the skin of my neck. "Just be with me."

"Hold onto me, baby," he says, warning me I'm close before I feel the first quake of an orgasm.

I wrap my arms around his neck and press my lips to his. I'm on the precipice of falling apart. My mind goes blank, my eyes close, and my back arches as I come undone around him.

"Bryant," I murmur like a quiet prayer.

"I've got you."

I'm gone. Lost to ecstasy. No longer in this world. When I descend from the higher plane, Bryant is close to finding his own release. I can feel it in the slight tremor of his muscles, the quickening of his breath, and the stiffness of his legs.

"Zhanna," he says, then he pulses inside of me. He wraps himself around my body and lets go, whispering things I can't decipher but anxiously want to know.

When we've both come back together, he searches my face once more. I'm not sure what he's looking for or what he finds.

He leans back against the couch and takes me with him, where I lay on his chest. I listen to his heartbeat and breath sounds beneath my ear. It's calming and eventually, it lulls me to sleep with him still connected to me.

When I wake, I'm floating in the air, weightless and free, in Bryant's arms. I wince from the soreness between my legs and hips.

"What's wrong?" he asks.

"My hips hurt."

"Shit. I should've moved you from that position, but you were sleeping so well."

"You can put me down."

"I know, but I'm not going to."

I'm far too exhausted to argue with him.

He carries me to the master bath and sets me on the white marble counter. "Where are your towels?"

"Beneath me."

Stooping below, he quickly grabs a small cloth before he wets it with warm water and cleans me up like a gentleman. He cleans himself up as I slide off the counter and head for my bed. When I get there, I do something I haven't done in a long time—I pull the sheet and comforter down on the other side of the bed.

CHAPTER FIFTEEN

THEN

JUNIOR YEAR FLIES BY. Before I know it, we're in our last year of undergraduate. So many things will change for us in the spring when Bryant and I graduate. He'll be drafted into the league, and I'll attend grad school wherever he ends up playing. He told me from the beginning of our relationship that nothing will change between us when he's playing in the league. He wants me with him, no matter what.

We're attached at the hip most days, even though we're both busy with school and his football schedule. He always makes time for me. We often steal moments alone at the cabin—camping, hiking, fishing, and just hanging around a fire. We rarely spend a night apart, except for the night before a game when he has to stay in a hotel.

I'm still terrified I'll receive a phone call one day about him being injured on the field, but I try not to focus on it and worry myself to death over something that may never happen. When he arrives home black and blue from practice, I aim my attention at making him comfortable and sated, because even after a hard day at football, we very rarely go without making love. I'd rather focus on feeling great than being a nervous Nancy.

As I walk the sideline, practice unfolds on the football field in front of me. "Hudson! What the fuck was that?" Coach Tombs shouts at him, then he spots me on his field. "Shouldn't you be over the honeymoon phase by now?"

"What?" Bryant shouts across the field. "She's hot!"

He jogs over to meet me near the goalpost. "Hey, baby. I'm so fucking glad to see you. Coach is killing us."

"I heard that!" Tombs says, quick as can be.

The quarterback pats the top of his thighs for me to jump up and lock my legs around him. There are cameras all over a college football practice, especially with a Heisman contender QB slated to be a first-round pick in the spring, so I'm hesitant to put our relationship on national television.

Plus, he's filthy.

"Come on, baby."

"Stop."

He smirks at me, holds his arms out wide, leans his head back, and shouts at the top of his lungs. "I'm in love with Zhanna Hale!"

The team hoots and hollers to support their leading man as I laugh at them. He picks me up and spins me around as I giggle harder. Then he lowers and kisses me for the entire world to see.

Continuing to laugh, I kiss him again. "You're insane."

"You love me anyway."

"To the moon and back, Quarterback."

"I have to go before Coach makes me run laps like a rookie."

"I'll be the girl watching from the bench and having the dirtiest thoughts about what I want to do to you tonight."

"Fuck. I'm wearing a cup, babe. And lots of people are watching."

I peck him on the lips and unwrap myself from his sweaty body. He awkwardly jogs back to the huddle while I find a place to sit on an empty bench. He only has a few minutes left. We rode to school together this morning, so I wait for him to finish with practice.

I waste the last part of practice texting Zina. I haven't heard from her all day and begin to worry maybe she and Ben had a fight. The closer it gets to Ben graduating and going into the league, the unhappier Zina seems to be. Ben graduates a year earlier than her, and he could end up virtually anywhere in the country. He'll have the wherewithal to fly her back and forth, but long-distance relationships are hard on strong, solid couples. Ben and Zina are in their early twenties with their entire lives ahead of them. I don't know if they'll last the year apart. Furthermore, I suspect my sister knows this and is pushing Ben away before he can be the one to hurt her first.

After practice, Bryant throws his arm around me, and we follow the team to the locker rooms. I remain outside and wait while I check my messages.

Zina: I'm fine. Busy with school. See you at the apartment later?

Zhanna: See you there.

"Why's the love of my life frowning?" Bryant asks when he emerges from the locker room freshly showered.

"Zina."

"Is she okay?"

Bryant and Zina have become like brother and sister over the last year we've dated. He worries as much about her as he does me.

"I'm not sure."

"Ben?"

"Maybe."

"He's been off, too," he says, frowning as it dawns on him.

We walk to his truck with his arm around my waist and me tucked into his side. He opens the door for me, kissing me before climbing up. Then he rolls the windows down and allows the hot, humid August air flow inside the vehicle. It's not so bad once he gets going.

When he heads for the interstate, I ask, "Where are we going?"

"You'll see, Miss Impatient. Just sit back and enjoy the ride, baby."

Enjoying the ride puts me to sleep. When the car stops and wakes me, it takes a moment to recognize my surroundings. "We're in New Orleans." I have another look around. "My dad is buried here."

Bryant wears his heart on his sleeve when it comes to me, but he's still confident, strong, and dominant when he needs to be. I'm accustomed to him being a rock of strength both physically and emotionally. When he intakes a harsh, shaky breath and speaks with tremor in his voice, I realize something is amiss.

"What's wrong, QB?"

It takes him a minute to find his words. "We've been together a year now."

"Yeah?"

"Wait. Hold on. I'm fucking this up." He rubs a hand over his face and then through his shiny hair. "I came here because… no, not that part yet. We're here because I didn't think it was right to… no, not that part yet either."

I touch a gentle hand to his. "What's wrong? You know you can tell me anything."

He opens his mouth to talk and promptly shuts it when nothing comes out. Then he opens his door, leaves the truck, walks around the front of it, and opens my door. He reaches across me, unbuckling my seatbelt, before he guides me to the sidewalk beside the cemetery entrance. We walk into the cemetery with our hands intertwined and weave through the rows of crypts until we stop at Dad's.

Bryant's sweaty hand releases mine as he turns to me with terrified eyes. He drops to one knee and pulls my hand into his. "Baby, I know we've only been together a year…."

"*Oh my God*," I say and slap my free hand over my mouth.

"But I think I loved you from the moment you called me 'Chicken Shit Hudson' and told me to 'throw the damn ball'. We're so good together. You're perfect for me in every way. I can't imagine my days not being full of your smile and love. I came here to ask your dad's permission for your hand in marriage. I wanted him to be a part of this. So will you do me the honor of being my wife?"

"Oh my God," I repeat.

"Ring!" Ben whisper-yells from somewhere nearby.

I look up and find my mom, Zina, and Ben doing a terrible job at hiding five rows down.

"Shit," Bryant swears while reaching into his pocket, pulling out a black ring box, and opening it. "Marry me, baby?"

Tears prick my eyes as I gaze down at him. His eyes are full of so much hope and love. The slight nervous shake in his hand is uncharacteristic but also very cute. I can't imagine not having him in my life every single day. Maybe we're too young to marry by most people's standards, but no one can deny how amazing we are together.

"Yes."

His eyes grow large. "Yes?"

I nod my head as a smile spreads across my face. "Yes!"

He jumps up and places the ring on my finger. Then he cradles my face in his hands and kisses me. When he breaks the kiss, he turns over his shoulder and shouts, "She said 'Yes'!"

Picking me up and spinning us around, he places me back on my feet.

I'm not ready to let go of him yet, so I wrap my arms around his neck, tuck my face into the side of his neck, and breathe him in. "I love you to the moon and back, Quarterback."

He holds me tightly as he kisses the top of my head. "I love you more than life itself."

***

AS WE LIE IN bed and stare into each other's eyes, I think about how lucky I am to have Bryant. I fought the attraction and the feelings as hard as I could, and yet, I'm beyond grateful he persisted in chasing me. The love we share is beautiful, passionate, and rare.

"What are you thinking about?" His voice is deep but gentle.

"That I'm a lucky girl."

"Even though I'm a chicken shit?"

"Especially because you're a chicken shit. It's my weakness."

"Then I'm the lucky one. What other woman would have me?"

I reach across the bed and pinch his nipple. "Don't talk about other women in our bed."

"Ouch!" He hollers. "You called it 'our' bed, so I'll forgive you."

"Good thing. I have more where that came from." I reach across the bed once more and attempt to pinch him again, but he covers my hand with both of his and stops me.

"Marry me."

"I already said yes."

"I mean marry me now."

"Do you want a quick engagement?"

"Seriously," he continues, releasing my hand and reaching out to touch my cheek. "I want to marry you tomorrow."

"You have practice tomorrow, and a game the next day."

"Sunday then."

I snort. "Do you know how long it takes to plan a wedding? It takes months and sometimes years."

"Not in Vegas."

"I don't have a dress for Vegas or anywhere for that matter. A pretty dress is literally my only requirement for getting married."

He leans in and kisses me. "Yeah? Go buy a dress then. Take my credit card. When you get back, I'll book the red eye flight for Sunday."

"I can't tell if you're being serious right now."

He presses the palm of my hand against his chest. "As a heart attack."

"My mom and sister will kill me if I elope."

"They're invited along with my parents and Ben. The thing is we don't have large families or friend networks. I'd rather have an intimate ceremony in Vegas while we're surrounded by a few close friends and family than an extravagant event that will stress us out and financially break us."

"You're serious about Vegas?" I study him closely to see if he's pulling my leg.

"I'm serious about marrying you as quickly as possible. Until you're using Hudson as your last name, I won't be satisfied."

Searching his eyes, I think about his proposal. A big wedding doesn't make any sense for either of us. Plus, I've never been the type wanting a huge wedding and large, frilly dress. We don't have a large family, and Zina is my best friend, so Vegas makes sense. "This is really happening. We're getting married."

"Yes, baby. God, yes. We're getting married. So what do you say to Vegas?"

"I can buy a dress?"

"I can't wait to see you in a wedding dress." He pushes my hair behind my ear and tugs on the lobe. "I never want to forget how you look in it."

"Should we call our parents?"

"I suppose we should probably give them as much notice as possible. "

Bryant calls his mom first. I'm elated she's excited about our engagement. She nearly breaks the speaker on his phone when he tells her we're getting married in another state in three days. "Bryant Aiken Hudson, I don't have a dress!"

"What is it with dresses and weddings?" he asks, scratching his head.

"It's a wedding" his mother and I both shout at the same time.

"And you're wearing a tuxedo for the pictures," Mrs. Hudson adds.

Next, I call my mom in New Orleans to share the good news. She's equally happy and offers to fly everyone out on her dime.

My sister immediately answers her phone when I dial her. "I can't believe you're engaged."

"Me either, and I have more news."

"I knew it! You're pregnant!"

"No, doofus. I'm not pregnant. We're getting married Sunday in Vegas, and I'd like you to be my maid of honor."

"Oh my God. Are you moving out? Do I get my own apartment?"

"Is that a 'yes' to be the maid of honor?"

"Hell yeah!"

CHAPTER SIXTEEN

THEN

WHEN A PARENT DIES, it can leave one feeling like an orphan. I miss my father more than ever as I stand on the side of the double doors to the Two Hearts Chapel in the heart of Las Vegas. When they open, I'll walk down the aisle to my soon-to-be-husband, but Dad isn't here to do the thing fathers do when their daughter gets married – walk me down the aisle and give me away to the man I'll spend the rest of my life with. Mom offered to do it, but I didn't want anyone taking his place. In my heart, I know he's beside me every step of the way.

Glancing down at the ivory lace dress, I smile. It was my only requirement for marrying. I found it at a thrift store and didn't care that it had been worn before. It was THE dress with a sweetheart neckline and a mermaid skirt.

"Are you ready, dear?" the owner asks.

Beatrice is an elderly lady with short, gray, curly hair who believes in love.

Am I ready? I'm twenty-one and taking one of the biggest steps of my life. Marriage happened so fast from the moment he proposed until now. We've only been together a year. What if we don't know each other well enough to commit the rest of our lives to each other?

Beatrice saves me from my thoughts. "Don't do that. Second guessing won't do you any good. I've been in this business a long time and developed a sixth sense about couples. I know when two people are in love for the right reasons. The first sign is the wedding party and guests are happy about the union. Girlie, the people in the next room are happy for you both."

She's right. This is right. Our love will get us through the hard times and cold nights as long as we have each other, and I truly believe it.

"I'm ready." I straighten my back and focus on the rest of my life.

Beatrice opens the doors, and I immediately focus on Bryant's pale green eyes. As he gazes at my dress, his eyes becoming glassy with tears. I barely hold it together as I walk down the aisle.

I stop in front of Elvis and peer over at Bryant, taking one hand off the bouquet and pulling his hand into mine.

"You may be, uh-huh, seated. Thank you very much," Elvis says, starting the ceremony.

On the other side of Bryant is Ben, his best man. Zina stands as my number one on my right.

"Dearly Beloved, we are gathered here today in Viva Las Vegas in the name of burning, burning love. The King knows a thing or two about love, uh-huh." Elvis does his famous dance move and freezes with his fingers out like pistols. Zina snorts behind me. "If there's anyone that opposes this marriage let them speak now or forever hold their peace, but don't be cruel." The impersonator pivots his hips again. "Who gives this woman away?"

My mom stands from the front bench in the small chapel. "Her sister and I."

"Thanks, Mama," Elvis replies. "And little Sister, I'll be your teddy bear. Uh-huh."

I hand Zina my bouquet and turn to face Bryant. He takes both of my hands into his and inhales a shaky breath. "I love you."

I mouth it back as Elvis continues. "Bryant and Zhanna are here because they can't help falling in love. Bryant Aiken Hudson, do you promise to honor, love, and cherish Zhanna as your wife for all of eternity?"

"I do." He squeezes my hand and smiles.

"Zhanna Hale, do you promise to honor, love, and cherish Bryant as your husband for all of eternity?"

"I do."

"Do we have the rings? Uh-huh."

Ben and Zina hand over the rings.

"The ring is a token of your love and commitment to each other. Do you promise to forsake all others and support one another?"

"I do." Bryant answers quickly.

"I do."

"You may exchange rings."

Neither of us have seen the wedding bands yet, so I'm pleasantly surprised when he slides a beautiful diamond encrusted band on my ring finger. I'm nervous to slide the rosewood ring on his finger. I hope I picked the right one. We look at our bands once they're on and grin at each other. Maybe it means I chose well.

"By the power vested in me by the state of Nevada, I pronounce you husband and wife. You may kiss the bride."

Bryant doesn't waste a second pulling me into his arms, dipping me, and leaning down to kiss me. I can't believe I'm kissing my husband. I can't believe I'm married.

"That's my boy!" Ben says.

"Get her, bro," Zina adds.

Someone claps, two women (most likely our mothers) giggle uncomfortably, and his father clears his throat. Bryant doesn't stop kissing me.

When he finally does, I'm out of breath and horny as hell. He sets me to rights, pressing a kiss to my forehead.

"I present to you, Mr. and Mrs. Bryant Aiken Hudson."

Turning to the small group behind us, we hook our arms, and walk down the aisle together as husband and wife. All the fears I had in the moments leading up to the ceremony are gone. I feel whole, like I'm right where I'm supposed to be.

"What are you thinking about?" my husband asks me.

"I can't imagine being anywhere but here."

"I love you, Coach."

"I love you, too, QB."

When we leave the chapel, we leave in a limo. I'm not a gambler, so I'm not into the whole casino scene, but it's one of the biggest reasons people come to Vegas. So, we do the tourist thing and visit a few casinos, sit at a few blackjack tables, and lose about a hundred bucks before we both decide we don't like losing our money.

False Start

We eat a late dinner with Ben and our family, and by the time it's over, we're both anxious to get away from everyone. But my mom insists on finding somewhere for us to dance as husband and wife.

We give in and find a piano bar not far from the restaurant. Bryant and I instantly fall in love with the vibe of the place, and then we get lost in each other as they play *Can't Help Falling in Love* and *Love Me Tender* while we slowly dance in each other's arms.

***

THE NEXT MORNING, I wake completely sated and hungry. The smell of bacon has my tummy rumbling. Or it could be the sheer amount of energy my new husband and I expended together last night in the honeymoon suite.

"Bacon," I grumble.

"She's alive." Bryant chuckles.

I open one eye, then the other, and turn over to find him at the small table in the room with a breakfast feast in front of him.

"It took 5.6 seconds for you to wake after I took the cover off the bacon. Impressive."

"You ordered me bacon?"

"And much, much more. Come eat, babe. I wore you out last night. You must be starving."

I wrap the sheet around me and leave the bed to sit in his lap. After giving him a good morning kiss, I grab a piece of bacon and chow down.

"Mrs. Hudson, did you use me for my bacon?"

I pick up another strip and inhale it. "Yes, yes, I did."

I can't stop my girlish giggle at hearing my name as Mrs. Hudson.

"Best sound in the world," he says as he nuzzles his face into my neck. "I could listen to you laugh all day."

"I love you, hubby."

"Mmm, I like the way that sounds. Say it again."

"Which part?"

"Both."

"I love you, hubby. What time is it?"

He presses a kiss to my neck. "Seven. Our flight leaves at noon. Are you ready to head home?"

We decided to finish out our leases until the end of the school year since we already committed to providing half the rent for Zina and Ben. It would be wonderful if Zina and Ben did a swap, but things are strained between them. I thought it best not to push the envelope, so we'll crash between both places. We don't want either one of them to feel abandoned because we're now married. They're our best friends. I just hate it's not working out between them.

"What are you thinking about?" he asks as he often does.

"Why do you ask?"

"I can see the wheels to your brain turning just by looking at your eyes."

"I was thinking of Ben and Zina and where we're going to call home when we land. I don't want one to think we chose the other over them."

"Being in the middle of their drama sucks."

I hold up my glass of orange juice. "Here, here."

Being between two people we love sucks. Zina isn't just my best friend, she's my sister, and Ben is the best friend and brother Bryant never had as an only child.

After we devour breakfast, we take a long bath together in the hotel's claw foot tub. It's nice to relax. When we return, Bryant will go straight back into football and school. I'll log clinical hours, a course load, and being a wife to a football player. At the pro level, wives have their own clubs. Thankfully, it's not the case at the college level.

I don't know why I'm nervous about returning home. The only thing that should change is my last name and the fact we both wear a ring. We're already cohabitating and spending every moment together.

"What's wrong?" he asks, always perceptive of my moods as we walk through the concourse of the airport. "You're frowning."

"Why did you want to marry me?"

He chuckles and slides his arm around my shoulders as he leans in and kisses me above the temple. "Babe, we've been married less than 24 hours and you're already busting my balls about it? What's wrong?"

"I was wondering what would change now that we're married. I don't want us to change."

"Oh, baby, change is inevitable. Next year, we'll likely be living somewhere else. You'll be at a new school, and as long as all goes according to plan, I'll be playing in the league. We'll grow older and wiser together. Change is good. Change is progress. But it's okay to be a little unsure of the future. We're young, and there's a lot to look forward to and be unsure about."

He always says the right thing to calm me when I worry. "You're right. Change is inevitable. I just need a moment to adjust."

When we've climbed into Bryant's truck, he turns to me again. "I sprung marriage on you. I expect you'll need a minute to catch your breath. I'm okay with that. Just promise me something?"

"Yeah?"

"We'll always work our issues out between us. We'll do whatever it takes to make it work. I love you, and I never want to live without you."

I lean forward to kiss him with a smile playing at my lips. "I think I can grant your request."

Turning on a country station, Bryant drives us to school. We both missed our first class of the day and don't want to grow further behind in assignments. When he turns into the lot for the science building, there's media vans parked all over the place.

"Did someone win the Nobel Peace Prize?" Bryant asks.

"You don't think…"

"Nah, they couldn't care less if a football player gets hitched."

Bryant stops his truck a few yards from a media van for a major sports network and leans over to kiss me. "Have a good day, wifey. I love you. See you on the field at four."

"There they are!" Someone shouts and I look past him to see all the reporters looking our way.

"Bryant Hudson!"

"Is she with him?"

"She's with him!"

"Go!" I shout before they stampede the truck and block us.

Bryant squeals tires out of the lot and heads for the practice field.

"I thought you said no one cares if you get married."

"I was very wrong. Why would they care?" His reply is gruff and a sign of his unhappiness.

"You're Bryant Hudson, and it's a big story in the sports world. You married Zane Hale's daughter. They want the scoop," I tell him.

When we reach the coach's office beyond the lot, he's waiting on us with his hands on his hips. "Most men evade the ball and chain as long as humanly possible, and you went out and married it at twenty-one."

"I had to take her off the market, Coach."

Coach Toombs smirks. "Are you joining us for practice today, Zhanna?"

"Do I get a whistle?"

"Are you blowing it at your husband?"

I can't help but smile at the title. "If he needs his ass whipped into shape, then yes, sir, I'll make him dream about whistles tonight."

"You're definitely your father's daughter." Coach says.

My smile widens. "Thank you."

"When's the honeymoon?" Tombs asks.

"March," his quarterback replies.

"Where to?"

"She loves the mountains and the outdoors. Football will be over, so maybe somewhere quiet with snow on the ground late in the season."

"Congratulations to you both," Tombs says.

Then practice begins with the blow of his whistle.

CHAPTER SEVENTEEN

NOW

I T'S BEEN A LONG time since I've reached for someone on the other side of the bed. It's been even longer since I reached and found nothing but an empty pillow. I look up to see if I somehow missed Bryant on the edge, but there's nobody there. I sniff the air, hoping for coffee or bacon, but find nothing. I throw the covers back, climb from the bed, and grab my robe as I search for him in my home.

I come up empty.

Maybe he went for beignets and coffee.

I call him, but he sends me to voicemail. I frown at the screen and send a text.

Zhanna: Where did you go?

I stare at my phone for twenty minutes, willing it to ding with a message from him.

For the next hour, I reserve a tiny piece of hope he'll return with pastries. But with each minute that ticks by, I know he left in the middle of the night. He's never left our bed in the middle of the night without waking me first and telling me what's going on. I guess it isn't our bed, and I shouldn't expect things from him I don't intend on returning.

I have a cry session in the shower. I need to get it out of my system before I'm forced to face him at work. I can't believe I softened toward him last night and let him in. I laid myself bare for him, and he snuck out in the middle of the night. I can't win for losing.

On the drive to work to the other side of New Orleans, Bryant messages me back.

Bryant: Can we talk after practice?

I ignore his message.

> Zina: Why is Bryant moping?

I wait until I'm inside my office to text her back.

> Zhanna: How the fuck would I know? He snuck out of my house this morning.

> Zina: Ouch. You okay?

> Zhanna: I'm already ready for the day to be over with. I don't know why he left, but he should've left a note or woke me to let me know he was leaving.

> Zina: I'm giving him the evil eye.

> Zhanna: I'll be on the field in a minute.

I steel myself to remain strong when I'm on the field and pull on my big girl panties. Once I'm outside, I take in a deep humid breath of Louisiana air and release some of my tension. Throughout the day, I ignore the many attempts Bryant makes to engage me in small talk.

"Did you need something?" I tersely ask him before lunch.

"Baby, we need to talk after practice. I'll leave you alone until then."

I don't reply and instead, take an early lunch to get away from him. He doesn't try to talk to me in the last half of practice, and I leave the facility while he's showering in the locker room. I don't know if my heart can stand hearing why he left me in bed this morning.

He shows up at the front door with a bouquet of flowers and a sympathetic smile. Standing aside, I open the door wider for him to come inside.

"I'm sorry it's late. It took me a minute to find a florist who would open and also had lilies and orchids in stock."

"You've been looking for lilies and orchids all afternoon?"

"You hate roses."

"I don't hate roses."

"They're not your favorite flower. You had lilies and orchids the day we married. I remember you smelled like them all day."

Why does he make it so hard to dislike him? Why can't I just stop loving him and gain immunity to his kindness and dimples? He spent hours looking for the perfect flowers because he's thoughtful and kind.

A sob escapes me.

"Z?"

"Why did you do it?" I cry.

"Baby… She…"

I cut him off. "You sacrificed this… us, for an orgasm with a woman who meant nothing to you. I could see if you fell in love with another woman, but you didn't. I mean that would be awful, and I'd still be devastated, but you hate her."

"Yeah, babe, I hate her."

"Then what did you gain by killing us?"

"I lost everything I give a fuck about."

"You still have football."

He scoffs. "The dream was football and you. For a while, I had my cake, and I was eating it too, but I took you being there for granted.

Football isn't the same without my favorite coach."

"Why did you leave this morning?"

"Because I was overwhelmed. You let me sleep next to you for the first time in almost two years. I couldn't sleep all night because you were so close. I was inhaling your scent and touching your skin. I was afraid you'd be pissed we slept together again. I didn't want a perfect night to end that way, so I left."

I don't know what to say, so I buy myself time by taking the flowers into the kitchen for a vase.

Bryant follows. "I didn't want to leave. It's just you're pissed at me most of the time, and I didn't think I could handle it if you woke up angry. Not after you connected with me last night. Thing is, I want this to work between us. I want to earn your trust back, but we can't do it alone. We need help from someone."

"Like who?"

"A therapist we both agree on. Someone you feel will be fair to us both. It isn't about winning in therapy. It's about working past our problems and finding a way to be together. Because you can't tell me you weren't there with me last night. I felt all of you, baby. You gave that to me, and the only reason I can think you would do that is you still love me. I've wondered for a while now, but after last night, there's not a doubt in my mind."

He's asked me to therapy before, but I was too angry to consider it. Something changed, and I'm not sure when it happened. Bryant crawled underneath my skin again when I wasn't looking. He made me remember all the great times we've spent together and how amazing of a man he is. He made me remember falling in love with him, and he spent all afternoon looking for the stupid flowers I carried when we were married.

I was scared this morning when he wasn't there. It was the first time in eight years of knowing each other that he wasn't there in the way that I knew he wasn't going anywhere. I didn't know if I'd pushed him too far in my anger.

"Okay, I'll try one visit."

His eyes light up like I haven't seen them in ages. He clasps his hands together and brings them up to his lips. "You won't regret this."

"Can you be at my place after work? We can ride together."

I stick the flowers in the vase and place them on the counter beside me before I turn around to face him. "I think I'd rather take my own car, you know, in case I don't feel like talking after. Do you already have an appointment?"

"Yes, I found someone who can fit us in and keep our details private."

I can tell he wants to object to me meeting him there. He wants to escort me home and make sure I'm okay, that *we're* okay, or as okay as we can be right now. "I get it. I'll back off."

"It's not what I meant. I just don't know how I'll feel after. I may be upset and want to be alone."

"Okay," he says.

"Don't make me feel bad for it."

"Of course, not. I get it. I really do."

"Thank you for the flowers. They're beautiful."

"You're welcome. I'm going to head home. I need to sleep after last night."

"I'm sure. Rest well. And this doesn't count as a date."

He hesitates to leave, smirking at me.

"What?" I ask, knowing he has something up his sleeve.

"Did you hear about Ben?"

Outside of professional football, I haven't heard Ben Slate's name in months. Zina doesn't talk about him, and we didn't keep in touch after the divorce since he's Bryant's best friend. "No."

Within a few strides he's standing in front of me, two dimples on each side of his full lips. He leans down and presses a kiss to my cheek. "Check the sports channel."

"Just tell me."

"And ruin the surprise?" He leans his head back and laughs.

I inch to the side and take off running as soon as I clear him. Down the hall I go with a massive football player running after me. I skid on the floor in front of my bedroom door but manage to turn the corner just in time to get inside the room. Bryant and I make it around my bed and to my nightstand where my phone is located.

"What are you doing you big ass ogre?" I ask.

"Giving you a hard time."

"Does Zina know?"

"Nope. It's why I'm giving you a head's up."

I wrench my phone from his big, meaty paws and dive onto the bed. He dives after me and tickles me until I hand the phone over.

"Enough. Okay! Just tell me already." I shout through laughter.

"He's trading to Voodoo. Announcement will come next week. He's laying low at my place with his son until the press release."

"Why was this deal such a secret? Nobody has even predicted a trade for Ben."

"Personal issues. Ben needed to be back home in New Orleans."

"I'll come by and check on him soon," I offer, having missed Ben over the years.

"Thank you. I know he'd really appreciate it."

"You're lying on top of me, and I can't breathe. Can you get off me?"

"You always know just what to say to make a guy feel special," he jokes, and then he scoots to the side but doesn't stop peering down at me. "Hey, Coach?"

"Yeah, QB?"

"Please don't give up on us yet. It's not even half-time."

"Are you calling an audible?"

"I'm saying false start, baby. We've been backed up five yards, but we're still halfway down the field. It's only second down, and we have plenty of time to move the ball." Then he leans down and briefly kisses my lips. "I'm going to let you rest. I'll see you tomorrow at work."

I walk him to the door and lock up before he'll leave my front porch. As I'm nestling into my pillow, my phone buzzes on the nightstand.

Bryant: Sweet dreams.

Zhanna: Sleep tight, don't let the bed bugs bite.

CHAPTER EIGHTEEN

THEN

I'M A SOUTHERN GIRL through and through, so when Bryant is drafted to the Los Angeles Spartans as the number one pick, we celebrate the fact we're not going somewhere cold.

When we land in the City of Angels, it doesn't take long before I feel completely out of place.

"Aren't you the cutest little thing?" the realtor says to me like I'm five, and then she flirts with my husband. "I heard you were tall."

I glare at her dumb ass. "Six feet is *short* in the league."

Read: Football players are tall, you dumb bitch.

I mean if you're going to flirt with another woman's husband in front of her, then be smart about it.

Bryant squeezes my hand and suppresses a laugh. "What do you think of the house, baby?"

I haven't had time to look at the stupid mansion this heifer dragged us to because I've been too busy keeping a close eye on her before she drags Bryant into a closet and assaults him. "I've seen better."

The realtor, Adrienne, rolls her eyes at me when Bryant isn't looking. The woman is trying my patience. I'm not a violent person, nor am I rude, but I won't tolerate her behavior. "Next time you roll your eyes at me, we'll be finding another agent." I take a few steps toward her. "And next time you touch my husband, I'm going to break your ass in half. Capeesh?"

I start for the door and Bryant follows after muttering to the woman.

Outside in his brand-new SUV, he laughs. "Rawr! Tiger! That was so hot. I'm not even going to lie, watching you go alpha made me hard."

I huff. "I think we need a new agent."

"I think you're right. She's now terrified of you."

"I think we should work with a male agent."

He opens the door for me and pats me on the ass. "I think we'll do whatever makes you happy, boss lady."

As he walks around the car, I wonder if I'm being irrational. Should I be comfortable enough in my relationship to be unconcerned with who lays their little hands on him? I trust him, so why does it matter?

"What are you thinking about over there?" he asks as we head down the highway to our hotel room.

"I'm sorry if I overreacted. She was being a bitch."

"What do you think I'm going to do if a dude does the same shit? You think I'm going to take it for half a day before I say something? No. The first motherfucker to put his hands on you is answering to my fists. I'll ask questions later."

He makes me feel better about the situation. As we leave the subdivision of mansions, I notice a beautiful Spanish mission style home near the front of the neighborhood.

"Wow." Bryant ducks down to peer out my window.

"It's for sale, but I bet I couldn't sell enough organs to afford the down payment." When he pulls into the drive of the house, I turn to him. "What are we doing?"

"Let's have a look."

The house has to be the most beautiful I've ever seen.

"You can't be serious."

He points to a sign in the yard. "They're having an open house. It doesn't hurt to window shop. We can pretend to be far wealthier than we are."

My parents were well off, but I've never had any type of money of my own. When Bryant signed to the Spartans, they were kind with their salary offer. It's probably more money than a young couple should have, and we won't ever really want for anything.

There's only one other car in the drive, which I assume is the realtor's. We park and head to the double mahogany front doors with a large iron lion head knocker.

"That's cool as shit. If we don't buy this house, we're at least getting one of those."

I laugh at his excitement. He's so much like a boy at times.

The door opens and a very attractive man with cropped black hair steps out. "Bryant Hudson?"

"Yes, sir?"

"You're our new quarterback. Jim Newton," he replies, sticking his hand out. "It's a pleasure to meet you."

"Nice to meet you, too, Jim. Are you a Spartan fan?" Bryant asks.

"Born and raised. I love them even when they suck."

Bryant chuckles. "The testament of a true fan. Are you showing the house?"

"Yes, please come inside," Jim says, stepping to the side. "I'd love to show you around."

We follow Jim through the house as he does his best to focus on the details of the light stucco walls and Spanish tile throughout the home. Each room seems bigger than the last as we walk through arched doorways. The house is so large and so empty it echoes when we speak. There's a gym, complete with a sauna, a movie theater, a pool with a hot tub and grotto, but our favorite is the huge open eat-in kitchen. The home boasts 8 large bedrooms with ensuite baths, and four additional full baths. There's a full basement that was used as a bar and pool room by the previous owners. A barber shop sits outside the master suite.

The bedroom has its own covered balcony, and I can imagine us having breakfast in the warm California morning together before we start our days. As we walk through the kitchen again, I can imagine two laughing kids playing with Bryant while I cook a meal for the family. Or maybe we'd decorate cookies for each holiday and spend time swiping each other's noses with sugary icing.

I gaze out of the back of the home to the pool and what appears to be a pool house as Bryant comes up behind me, wrapping his arms around my middle. "What do you think?"

"I think this is entirely too much home for us."

"It is, but we can afford it."

"No, we can't."

He whispers against my ear. "I want to fuck you in this house and knock you up with my babies inside this house."

My nipples tighten and my uterus contracts at his words. "Yeah?"

"Let's make and raise babies here, Coach."

It's how he talks me into buying a house we'll never be able to fill. "Do you realize how much furniture it will take to make it not look so empty?"

"I don't care, baby. I can tell you love the house. It's the first one you've seemed to like all day, and the agent is a dude, which is a total plus after the last nightmare."

I sigh. He doesn't ask to get his way often, but he's going to win this one. "Okay. It's your money."

"Babe, no it's not. We're married. It's our money. Even if we weren't, you're my partner. We share our lives, and it includes financials."

"Are we going furniture shopping?"

He kisses the side of my neck. "Yes. We need a bed first and foremost. I want something big and comfy. Decorate the house as you like."

"What if we decorate it together? It could be fun."

If my husband thinks the idea is ludicrous, he doesn't show it. "Okay, baby. Whatever you want."

"I want it to look like we both live here."

The agent sneaks up behind us and almost scares the bejesus out of me. "Did you have any questions about the property?"

"Yeah. Where do we sign?" Bryant asks before placing a kiss at my temple.

***

BRYANT SPEEDS UP THE process of us moving into the house by playing the state's new "it" man in sports. People love him and eat up his southern charm. His dimples don't hurt either. Within two weeks, we've moved in with virtually nothing but a few personal

Tonight, the moonlight casts across our bed, illuminating his green eyes. I wrap his long hair around my finger and play with it. It's become a source of comfort for me in the last eighteen months we've been together. I enjoy the way his silky brown hair feels against my fingers.

"You're going to put me to sleep." His deep voice rumbles in the quiet night.

I snort. "I thought that was the point of us lying here in the dark."

He reaches across the bed and hooks his arm around me before he effortlessly moves me across the bed to him. "Come here, smart-ass. God, I love you."

"I love you, too."

"The house is quiet, but one day, we'll remember this and wish we had a little piece of it again."

"Yeah?"

"Yeah, babe. Before we know it, we'll hear the pitter-patter of little feet all around us. And we'll be pulling our hair out, wishing our names were something other than mommy and daddy, at least, for a little while."

I press a kiss to his chest and then snuggle into his massive arms. "I just hope we aren't the couple who hates each other after they have kids."

He kisses the top of my head and gives a gentle squeeze. "We could never hate each other. We're a team, and nobody can ever come between you and I. We've always been on the same page, and it's important for us to stay that way when we have babies. If we do that, we'll survive anything."

I trace the tattoo of my name in script on his chest and smile as I briefly remember him coming home to surprise me with it. I thought he was out with the guys for a beer, but he'd booked an appointment for the tattoo instead. I was dumbfounded when he first took his shirt off before I began crying tears of joy.

"I always want to be this happy with you."

He chuckles. "I'm going to do stupid shit like leave the seat up in the middle of the night. You won't always be this happy with me."

"If that's the worst you ever do, I think we'll make it as a couple."

CHAPTER NINETEEN

THEN

BRYANT'S FOOTBALL SEASON BEGINS in mid-July as a rookie. He starts training before the veterans come back at the end of the month. He's tired when he comes home each day, but he's still attentive in all the ways he's always been. He's beginning to feel the difference between college football and professional football.

When graduate school starts in August, I'm relieved. Sitting at the house all day without Bryant grows boring quickly. My mind needs stimulation. Trashy television doesn't do it for me. I haven't ventured out enough to meet anyone, so I'm looking forward to meeting a friend or two at school. Bryant talks about his new teammates all the time, and it makes me miss Ben and Zina even more than I already do.

Zina is attending her senior year back in Louisiana, and Ben was drafted to Detroit. The two of them broke up, so we haven't seen either of them since we moved to California. If they were still together, we'd likely be flying back and forth between Michigan and Los Angeles at least once a month. I miss them both, and I miss them being together. They were a great couple. Too bad Zina doesn't want to do long distance. I think she made a really big mistake letting Ben go, but dating a professional football player isn't easy without the distance.

"Coach!" Bryant yells as soon as he walks in through the garage.

"In here!" I call out from our master bathroom.

Tonight, we're going to a party thrown by one of his teammates. I'm excited to meet the other women who have experience with the fame and fortune that goes along with having a husband or boyfriend in the league.

"Wow," he says as he comes to a stop just inside the bathroom. "You look…"

I smirk. "Yes?"

"I better stay on this side of the room before I ruin your hair and makeup. You look good enough to eat."

"Don't say things you don't mean," I tease.

He licks his lips, takes two strides across the room to me, and goes down on his knees. And then he pulls my long red, sleeveless dress up and sticks his head underneath. I can't help but giggle as his facial scruff tickle the inside of my thighs.

"What in the world are you doing?" I laugh.

"Showing you I mean what I say."

"You're going to stretch out my dress."

He pokes his head out from under my skirt and looks up at me with those kind green eyes. "I can't wait to show you off tonight. I have the hottest wife on the team."

"How do you know? Have you met the others?"

He shrugs. "I've met a few of them in passing. They seem nice enough, but you are definitely hotter than any of them."

I'm grateful and lucky to have a husband who often reminds me that he thinks I'm beautiful. I lean down and kiss him, covering his lips in red lipstick. "I love you to the moon and back, Quarterback."

After a few more kisses, we leave and head for his teammate's home. I haven't met many of the guys yet but know of most of them through watching them play on television. I'm nervous to meet the other players and their significant others. It's never easy to be the new kid, even as an adult.

When we arrive at Devon and Kirstyn Douglas' home, Bryant reaches over and squeezes my thigh. "You're going to do fine. Everyone will love you as much as I do."

"I doubt that," I reply, but I appreciate the sentiment just the same.

As the wide red front door opens to the home, a tall blonde comes into view. Her long hair is pulled back in a ponytail. It's so tight, it might be working as a facial lift as well. She's wearing a hot pink bikini top and a black sarong around her waist. She's a knockout.

"Bryant! We were wondering where you were. The girls were just saying how we need our quarterback."

Not once does she look at me as she invites my husband inside.

"Am I invisible?" I ask him.

He blinks at me, not understanding the situation. "Of course you're not."

The Amazonian woman in front of us sways her hips. It's blatant enough to make me want to gag and punch her in the face at the same time. She leads us outside where five other couples congregate around a long outdoor table with drinks and plates in front of them.

"That is not your wife," one of the men says. "She's entirely too hot for you, Hudson."

Bryant places a finger to his lips and shushes the man. "I'm grateful she hasn't figured it out yet. Zhanna, this is Devon Douglas, left tackle."

I reach out to shake Devon's hand and am instead pulled into a hug by the gargantuan man. "Come here, girl. I'm stealing you away from the rookie."

"I'd have to fight you over her. I barely convinced her to marry me."

"Let's introduce you to everyone," Devon offers and goes around the table.

I can't keep up with the names and faces, but there's Kirstyn, Livia, Rachel, Margie, Polly, and Priscilla, the blonde who answered the door. Color me intimidated as fuck. I grew up around football players. Being dropped into a snake pit of women doesn't appeal to me. Every single woman stares back at me, judging and picking me apart, not saying a word.

A beautiful woman with caramel skin and long black hair finally stands from the table and walks toward us with her hand outstretched. "Livia. The big, bald guy is mine."

Her husband joins us and shakes my hand as well. "Demarion Jefferies."

I become quite taken with the couple, and it takes me a moment to realize not one other couple bothered to speak to me. As soon as Demarion engages me in conversation, Bryant eases off toward the table to talk to Devon. I quickly find I'm comfortable with Demarion and Livia and lose track of Bryant for close to half an hour. When I look up, he's not anywhere near the pool or outside for that matter.

"Uh oh," Livia murmurs into her cup as she turns it up and looks toward the house.

"Leave it alone," Demarion warns her.

Livia smacks her lips and lifts a brow. "Excuse me, but somebody needs to warn the girl."

"It's not our marriage."

I'm not going to sit around and wait for these two to decide whether or not I learn whatever knowledge they have. I haul ass inside and Kirstyn—short, skinny, and also very blonde—steps in front of me with a huge, fake grin on her face. "Hey, Zhanna, right?"

"Move."

"I know it must be tough."

"Okay, I'll bite. What's that?"

"Knowing you're just the starter wife."

I think of a million things to say to her. I think about slapping her in her rude little mouth, but I restrain myself.

I take a step toward her, and ease into her face. "I know you don't know this, but I'm not the girl you want to fuck with. I give zero fucks about the damage I'm going to do to you if you don't get out of my fucking way."

I shove her to the side when she doesn't do as she's told and go inside to find my husband. He's alone in the living area with Priscilla, who's tracing the tattoos on his arm, giggling at everything he says. It looks really bad. She's touching my husband, and he's allowing her to do it. He's not stopping her from touching my tattoos. If the situation were reversed, I don't know if Bryant could maintain his cool, but it's exactly what I do.

After I unglue myself from the spot, I walk right past them. My own husband is so invested in the cleavage in front of him that he doesn't notice.

Outside, I grab my purse from his SUV, pull my phone from my purse, and use an app to call a driver.

I'm not going to cry. I'm not going to cry. I'm not going to scream or fight. I'll go home and let him wonder where I'm at.

Twenty minutes later, the car service arrives. I take one last look at the brick mansion behind me and flip it the bird before climbing inside the vehicle.

By the time I arrive at our home, almost an hour has passed and still no word from Bryant. In the past hour, my own husband hasn't looked for me to know I'm gone. He took me to a house where I know no one and deserted me for tits on a stick.

I dash away my tears, only to have more fall behind it.

Thirty minutes after I get home, Bryant calls my phone. I almost pick up just to tell him to go fuck himself, but I restrain myself. Let him figure it out, because if the tables were turned, he would've lost his shit. No man or woman wants to walk in on their significant other being touched inappropriately by another person.

After a few more calls, my husband begins texting.

> Bryant: Baby?

> Bryant: I'm getting worried. Where are you?

I don't feel completely bad for making him worry, but I put him out of his misery out of courtesy.

> Zhanna: I'm at home.

He calls. I immediately decline his call.

> Bryant: What the fuck is going on, Z? Why aren't you picking up your phone?

> Zhanna: Do I have your attention now?

False Start

> Bryant: ?

> Zhanna: I'll be in our bed if you decide you can unwrap yourself from your current company. Do not join me tonight. I don't want to see or speak to you. We'll talk in the morning.

> Bryant: What's this about?

> Zhanna: Don't you dare play coy with me.

I shut my phone off and crawl into bed without removing my clothing or makeup. I'm suddenly bone tired and hurt beyond imagination. It's like Bryant turned into someone else tonight. He's never been a discourteous or unthoughtful person. He's quite the opposite, but tonight, he disgusted me with the way he behaved with Priscilla.

As I'm about to drift off, Bryant barges into the house and slams the door. "Zhanna!"

I pull the cover over my head. I told him I didn't want to see or speak to him. I want to be calmer before I say something I don't mean out of anger.

"Zhanna! Baby!" he shouts as he rounds the corner to our bedroom.

I throw the covers back, pissed he isn't listening to me. "I said I don't want to speak to you."

"Well, tough shit. You hauled ass out of my friend's house with no explanation. You think we're not duking this out now? You've lost your damn mind."

I spring from the bed as red-hot anger courses through me. "Excuse me?!"

"You could've and should've told me you wanted to leave. I was so embarrassed I didn't know what was going on with my own wife."

"You were embarrassed? You didn't know what was going on with your own spouse?"

He puts his hands on his hips. "What the fuck does that mean?"

"It means I walked right past you on my way out the door. You were too fucking busy letting another woman put her filthy hands all over you to notice *your own wife*. And if that isn't bad enough, you tossed me to the wolves and took off to be alone with another woman. How fucking kind of you to worry about my comfort level in a brand new place filled with strangers I've never met before." I take a step toward him until I'm in his face and pushing my finger into his chest. "How fucking dare you come home smelling like her and accuse me of embarrassing you."

"Zhanna," he says and reaches for me.

I swat his hand away. "You are in the wrong here, not me." I walk past him, grab his two pillows, walk them back over to him, and shove them in his chest. "Now, you're more than welcome to stay the night on the couch, but you will not come to this bed after the way you behaved tonight."

"You're kicking me out of my own bed?"

"No, I'm kicking you out of our bed. Don't you dare act indignant. You would've flipped your lid if you'd walked in on me behaving the same way. If you ever put me in that situation again, I'll do the same thing I did tonight and leave. I don't have to be subjected to a bunch of catty bitches out to fuck my husband, and I sure as hell don't have to hang around and watch you allow them to paw over you like I'm not standing there."

"Your jealousy is juvenile and unbecoming. I appreciate you leaving before you acted like this in front of the others and embarrassed me even more."

If he'd slapped me, it would've hurt less. I open my mouth to respond, but the pain takes root deeply inside. My voice fails me as the tears come once again.

How am I the bad guy in this situation? How does he have the right to be mad? I close my mouth and turn on my heel before he hears the hurt in my voice. In three steps, I'm locked behind the bathroom door, where I fall to the plush rug beneath me and silently sob.

We've always gotten along easily and well. An argument has never had a chance to form between us because we communicate well and often. There was a major breakdown in our communication tonight.

A quiet knock startles me. "Baby, shit, I'm sorry. Come out and talk to me."

A quick apology isn't going to fix this. I want to murder him right now.

A light thud sounds against the door. "Fuck, Zhanna, please come out. I'm sorry I lost my temper."

"Go away."

"I'm not going away. You're stuck with me, so you might as well open up."

I let him sit on the other side of the door and plead with me to open it. I need a minute to catch my breath after being on the receiving end of his anger. I'm not someone who can pretend it doesn't feel like he sunk a dagger into my chest.

He eventually grows quiet, but I know he's still on the other side of the door, so I curl up on the rug and cry myself to sleep.

CHAPTER TWENTY

THEN

I HEAR BIRDS CHIRPING before I open my eyes and remember last night's events. Sunlight streams through the frosted windows of the bathroom, and a muted light falls across my face. I stretch out as long as I can, cramped and stiff from sleeping in a ball all night on the hard floor. All I want to do is hide in here for the rest of the day and avoid the hurt and pain already creeping back into my chest. After I gather my bearings, I stand and open the door. Bryant falls inside and on top of my feet, so I step over to get away from him.

"Baby?" he calls out in a sleepy and confused voice.

I'm not over how he behaved last night. I'm not one to pretend like nothing happened, so I don't say a word as I walk out of the room and down the stairs to the kitchen in search of breakfast.

"Zhanna," he calls again, this time from behind me and hot on my heels.

I once again ignore him and continue on my way as though he doesn't exist, much like he did last night when he was drowning in Priscilla's tits.

"Goddamnit, baby, I have to go to work. I don't want to leave things this way. Going to bed with you mad at me was hard enough. Please don't make me endure hours of misery with you pissed at me."

Inside the kitchen, I pull a bowl from the cabinet next to the stove and pour myself cereal and milk, sitting at the bar to eat.

He sighs loudly, coming to stand beside me and tucking my hair behind my ear. I almost cave because it's one of my favorite things in the world. But if I cave now, he won't learn his lesson. If I give in now, he won't understand how much it hurt me to watch another woman freely touch him the way Priscilla blatantly did. It was a bad look, and I'm not getting in the business of putting up with that shit.

"Go to work," I finally say and go back to crunching on oat squares.

"You're really fucking pissed."

"Yes."

"Babe, you realize we've never argued. You can't send me off to work without talking to me. I'm playing tomorrow, so I can't sleep here tonight. I don't want to sleep away from you for two nights in a row, and I sure as hell don't want to do it with you not speaking to me."

I drop my spoon as I grow angrier by the minute. "You're so worried about you, you, you. You weren't so fucking worried about me last night. So go to work. I'm sorry, but I'm not ready to act like you didn't cross a line. Let's be honest, if the tables were reversed, you'd be in jail for letting a man draw lazy circles on my arm. Now, if I was wearing a bikini top and sarong while he was doing it, i.e. half naked, how do you think you would've felt then? Or, better yet, what if I left you with a bunch of people you'd never met before to let a man touch me inappropriately while I'm half naked in another room and away from everyone else?"

His jaw tightens.

"Yeah, that's what I thought."

He reaches for me. "I fucked up, Z. I admit it. I fucked up, but you have to get along with these people. I know what you saw with Priscilla wasn't the best image, but she's just trying to get me to sign with her."

"Sign with her?"

"She's an agent."

"You like Charles."

"Priscilla thinks I could be raking in millions in sponsorships."

"Why don't you give Charles an opportunity to do the same for you? I think you owe him that much before you start talking about switching to another agent."

He nods in agreement. "You're right. I should give Charles the same chance. I'll call him on my way in."

"Great." I pick up my spoon and start eating again.

He takes the spoon from my hand and places it on the bar. "I'm not going to work without talking to you."

"Excuse me?"

"We're adults. We're going to talk this out before I leave. If it means I'm late, I'm late. I'll pay whatever fine Coach gives me, because this," he says as he points between us, "is more important than football. Can't play worth a damn with you all in my head anyway."

I abandon my cereal and Bryant in the kitchen, but he doesn't take long to catch up with me.

"Are you at least coming to my game tomorrow?"

Tomorrow is the first game of the season, and I don't want to miss his debut in the league, no matter how pissed off I am at him. "Yes."

He sighs again. "Okay. Good. Thank you."

Inside the bedroom, I dig through my dresser and then in my closet for a fresh set of clothes. I need a hot shower to release the tension in my stiff muscles. Bryant climbs in behind me as I step under the water, places his hands on my hips, and leans down to press a kiss to my shoulder. "God, baby, you're so fucking beautiful. How could I want anyone else?"

His touch, his voice so close to my ear, and the reverence in his voice almost breaks me. *Almost.*

I need a few hours without him to sort out my thoughts. I'll forgive him because I love him and because he's sincere. But I should be afforded the opportunity to process my feelings before I'm ready to put it behind me.

"I know you've never really seen me upset, but I need time to process before I can talk about what happened last night. Please give me that time. We'll talk when you get home from work before your curfew."

I quickly wash up and step out of the shower to allow him to do the same. I feel like lying around all day and being lazy. Maybe, it'll do the soreness in my body some good. Since graduate courses began last month, I haven't had a lot of down time to relax. So I get comfortable on our big, gray couch covered in a million pillows with cute sayings, and I turn on the television.

Bryant steps into the living room with his duffel bag thrown over his shoulder. "I love you."

One thing I'll never do is not tell him I love him because I'm angry.

"I love you, too. Have a good practice."

He pauses for a moment before he finally walks across the room and leans down to press a kiss to the side of my mouth. "I love you more than life itself."

Then he's gone.

I sleep for most of the day, spent by the toll of my emotions and self-doubt. While Kirstyn was harsh in her little assessment of my relationship with Bryant, she pushed a button with her comment about me being a starter wife. It was as if she was blocking my entrance to protect Bryant and Priscilla, or at least Priscilla. As far as Priscilla goes, I don't buy the agent line. I think Bryant believes the woman wants him as a client, but I saw the way she touched him knowing anyone, especially me, could walk in at any moment and find them. I don't trust the woman as far as I can throw her. Also, who pulls their hair that tight without catching a migraine of epic proportions? Maybe her face is just naturally pinched tightly.

Calling my mom, I fill her in on the events of last night. I don't make it a habit to share our personal business, especially disagreements, but Mom has experience in the industry as a WAG (Wives and Girlfriends). She also had a successful marriage to a career professional athlete and coach. I'm sure she has a thing or two to say on the matter.

"Hey, sweetheart, how are you?"

"Hey, Mom," I say, immediately breaking down in tears.

"Oh, no. What happened?"

I manage to blubber my way through the story. I feel both better and worse for reliving the tale and crying it out with my mother. Nothing makes a girl feel better about boys than her mother.

"Priscilla Pavers," Mom says as she scoffs. "Watch that one, sweetie. She's got snakes coming out of her head, and if she had her hands all over Bryant, she wants him as more than just a client."

"That's what I said. So you think I read the situation correctly?"

"A woman has to trust her gut, and yours is screaming at you to protect your man. The best piece of advice I can give you is to remember Bryant is young and having fame thrown at him left and right. Unfortunately, fame entails women throwing themselves at your husband in hopes that he'll make them the next Mrs. Hudson after booting you to the curb."

"Did I make a mistake marrying him, Mom?"

"No, darling, not at all. You're just going to need a thicker skin for the world you now live in. That's okay. The best way you can fight them is by showing them how strong you and your husband are together. Show them you're a team and how in love are. How can they compete with love? And it'll chap their asses to see you happy."

I giggle. "You're quite manipulative, Mother."

"You have to fight fire with fire, sweetheart."

I feel better after my conversation with my mom, and when the call ends, I see a few missed messages from Bryant.

> **Bryant: You've been on my mind all practice. I hope you're having a relaxing day.**

> **Bryant: You being mad at me has to be the worst thing I've ever experienced.**

> **Bryant: I love you.**

> **Zhanna: I love you, too.**

At half past five, Bryant walks in through the kitchen door via the garage. "Baby!"

"In here!" I say from the couch.

When he rounds the bar and comes into view, he stops and smirks at me as he puts his hands on his hips. "Have you moved today?"

I grin back at him. "I tried not to."

"Can we talk?"

"I think we should."

His face falls. "Zhanna, baby, it won't happen again. Swear to Christ, I'm not ever letting another woman so much as hug me."

I frown. "I think that's a bit rash, however, you need to be a bit more selective with who you allow to touch you. Just because you didn't touch her doesn't mean you weren't wrong for not stopping it. I hope you put yourself in my shoes and imagined how it would feel to be where I was last night."

He comes around the couch and has a seat next to me. "It's what I've done all day, and I'm sorry. You're right because if I'd been in your shoes, I wouldn't have exited quite so gracefully. I know I said things last night, but I want to thank you for not causing a scene. It's more than I think I could've done in the same situation."

I slide my hand on top of his, ready to forgive and forget. He's sincerely apologetic, and I can't stand the rift any longer. I need to be closer to him and mend us until we're whole. "Thank you."

He reaches out and cups my chin in his hand and rubs his thumb over my lips. "Do you still love me?"

"To the moon and back, Quarterback."

"Come here, woman," he says and leans in to kiss me.

His kiss is desperate and hungry as though he can't get close enough or deep enough. Long, deft fingers tangle in my blonde hair as I leave my seat to straddle him. His right hand leaves my hair and travels to my hip to push down. I moan at the friction against and smile at the hardness beneath me.

Bryant breaks the kiss and opens his pale green eyes and searches mine. "I need you, Zhanna."

We've had intimate moments, and we've made love, but I've never been as wrapped up in his energy as I am right now.

"Hold on tight, baby," he warns, lifting me into the air.

I lock my legs around his waist and throw my arms around his neck. He takes us upstairs and down the hall to our bedroom, laying me on the bed before sliding over my body. We take our time exploring each other's bodies with our hands. I love the soft skin of his back and by contrast, the roughness of his hands.

When we're lying completely naked, I trace the script of my name on his chest and place a kiss to the spot. When women throw themselves at him, I need to remember he loves me enough to keep me inked on him permanently. I need to remember I'm the one he's coming home with.

"I love you," he whispers as he lines himself up and pushes inside. "I'm yours, and you're mine, and we'll be that way until the end of time, in this life and the next."

"I love you too, QB."

***

I'M ANXIOUS ALL DAY for the game. Late games are the worst on the nerves, especially when it's a big game. Today is most definitely a big game. I can't believe my husband is going to debut in the league as a starting quarterback tonight. It's surreal to be here on this journey with him.

When I arrive at the stadium, a security guard checks my ID and smiles. His name tag reads Marlon. "Mr. Hudson has been impatiently waiting for you to arrive. If you'll follow me, I'll take you to him."

"He's nervous," I say.

"Quite, but understandably so."

When we reach the locker room and another slew of guards, Marlon addresses the next guard. "Mr. Hudson requested his wife be brought down before the game."

Moments later, Bryant slips out with a huge smile on his face. Before I can ask him how he's holding up, he leans down, picks me up, and squeezes me tightly. As he tucks his face into the side of my neck, he whispers, "My good luck charm is here."

I can feel a slight quiver beneath his muscles, a sure sign of his anxiety over the game.

I squeeze him back. "You're nervous."

He chuckles. "Yeah, babe, a little, but I'm better now that you're here."

"You're going to be amazing. You know how it is when you're on the field and in the zone. Everything except the game fades away. Four quarters will pass before you know it, and you'll put up your first big W of the season."

"You have a lot of faith in me, Mrs. Hudson."

"I have all the faith in you, baby."

Out of the corner of my eye, movement catches my eye. Priscilla saunters up to the guards at the locker room door but doesn't take her eyes off us. I pretend not to see her. I'm glad she's behind Bryant. I want her to see what my mom was talking about—us being in love. It's the best ammunition I have against the Priscillas of the world.

I couldn't write the scene any better as Bryant touches his hand to my cheek and leans in to kiss me.

"I love you." He turns to Marlon. "Will you see her to the box?"

"It would be my pleasure, Mr. Hudson."

"Please don't leave the box and wander by yourself. Take a guard with you. And no matter how this shakes out on the field, I want your face to be the first I see at the end of four quarters."

A huge grin splits my face. "I can do that."

He gives me one last kiss before Marlon walks me to one of the boxes reserved for wives and girlfriends of players. I look over my shoulder to see Priscilla glaring at me, so I smile and send a wink in her direction.

How ya like me now, bitch?

When I make it to the box, it takes me a moment to recognize the girl standing outside the door.

"Zina?"

She chuckles. "Yep."

"What in the world are you doing here?" I ask as I hug her.

I miss my sister.

"Your hubby thought you could use some company. He wanted you to have a familiar face in a sea of WAGs."

Tears prick my eyes as it dawns on me Bryant isn't so unperceptive after all. While he was fighting his anxiety over the game all day, I was slaying my own dragon in regards to how I was going to handle the wives and girlfriends today. I'm not sure if any of the ladies from the other night are here, but I'd like to avoid them if they are. I hope other women are more welcoming than the clique I've previously met.

"Are you crying?" Zina asks.

"Yes."

"There's no crying in football."

"How did he know?" I wonder aloud how he could possibly know about the clique.

"Because he called me yesterday to tell me he's a dumbass. I agreed with him seeing as he fed you to the sharks and went off with another woman you don't fucking know."

"He called you?"

She nods. "He was beside himself and knew he fucked up. Wanted to know how to make it right."

The tears spill over. "He's so perfect."

My sister rolls her eyes. "Clearly. Can we watch the game now?"

I beam at her. "Can you believe he's here? That he's playing in the league?"

We both burst into fits of giggles at the idea as we jump up and down and hug each other.

Only the sound of Priscilla's voice stops the good times. "Children, you're blocking the door."

And in true Zina form, she takes another step toward the door to further block the woman. "Did your parents not teach you manners?"

Priscilla rolls her eyes and looks to the guard for help. "Do you mind?"

The guard steps forward to interfere with Zina, but I stop him in his tracks. "She isn't a wife or girlfriend, therefore, she doesn't have access to the box. There are plenty of other boxes for you to watch the game from."

"I always watch it from this box."

Zina snorts, not having a clue what's going on, but she picks up on the vibe pretty fast. "There's a new sheriff in town now, Betty Sue."

"Like I said, there's plenty of other spots where you can watch the game. Perhaps, you could find a place where your counterparts cavort. I assure you they aren't behind this door."

"Cavort?" Zina asks.

"It's on my Word-of-the-Day App."

Priscilla bats her eyes after the shock wears off. "I've been around a lot longer than you, honey. I'll be back in the box before the end of the game."

I bat my eyes back at her. "Not as long as I'm the one fucking the quarterback."

"My sister is a savage," Zina sing-songs as she crosses her arms over her chest in her best 90's hip hop dance move.

Shock once again crosses Priscilla's tight face, but she recovers quickly. "I think we got off on the wrong foot, Zhanna. I need to apologize for how I behaved the other night. Between drinking and the excitement of trying to win Bryant as a client, I behaved inappropriately. I hope you can forgive me."

And, just like that, I know I'm the one in control of the vehicle again. I feel stronger, more connected to my husband than ever before. There will be a thousand Priscilla's throwing themselves at Bryant. I have to trust him until he gives me a reason not to, and I have to trust that he'll always come home to me.

CHAPTER TWENTY ONE

NOW

BRYANT SITS BESIDE ME in an olive-green armchair as we sit across the desk from a strange woman. My ex-husband's idea of a first date is attending a therapist appointment.

Mary Acres appears to be in her early forties with slight graying at her roots. Her black-framed glasses make her crystal blue eyes pop as loudly as the white of her teeth against the thin red line of her lips. "Thank you for coming, Zhanna. Bryant and I spoke briefly over the phone when he made the appointment, so why don't you bring me up to speed on what's going on with you two."

"We're divorced," I start, laying out the obvious.

The news doesn't shock her. "Well, that's okay. Did you attend therapy before the divorce?"

"No, but I went to individual counseling. Zhanna wasn't ready to forgive me enough for us to attend therapy."

"Nobody says I'm ready to forgive you now," I reply, scoffing at him.

He reaches over and gently places his hand on top of mine as he continues. "I cheated. It's why we're split up."

Mary focuses on me. "Do you want to work things out with Bryant?"

"I don't know. You know the saying, 'Once a cheater, always a cheater'."

"Yes, I'm familiar with the saying, but I have to disagree. People cheat, and people cheat for different reasons. It doesn't always have to be because their significant other is lacking. Yet, it's very personal to the person cheated on."

"Yes," I agree.

"Did it make you feel unworthy and unloved?"

"Yes."

"Did it affect your self-esteem?"

God, I hate to admit it aloud. I don't want him to know how low I really fell when he cheated, so I don't answer her.

Thankfully, she moves on. "Bryant, have you two spoken about why you cheated?"

"I don't have an elaborate excuse for cheating. It's simple, I made a very big, drunken mistake."

Mary jots down notes as she continues. "Do you have a problem with alcohol?"

"No."

"Zhanna, do you think he has a problem with alcohol?"

"No, I think he has a problem with fame."

"Okay, I understand. Let's table the fame discussion for just a moment. Has there been any alcohol or drug dependency in the past?"

"No," we both answer.

"Do you drink now?" she asks him.

"I have a one-drink limit."

The knowledge surprises me. I didn't know he'd made the commitment. "Since when?"

"Since I made the biggest mistake of my life. My therapist thought I should reevaluate my stance on inebriation if I'm apt to make life-altering mistakes when I drink without my wife."

I allow the wife comment to slide and remain quiet. He's serious about making changes, it appears, but is it too little too late?

"Zhanna, have you thought along the lines of your expectations of Bryant if the two of you should reconcile?"

"My expectations for him have not changed from the moment we started dating. I don't ask for much."

"She's right. She's easy to be around and supportive in every way. I took advantage of her always being there. I took advantage of her being a good wife."

I snort. I was such a great wife that he went and cheated on me.

"You don't agree, Zhanna?" Mary asks.

I turn to Bryant. "Do you know how hard that is to hear? That I was a great wife and you cheated anyway? How in the hell am I supposed to trust you won't do it again if I didn't do anything to warrant it in the first place?"

"I don't think many situations warrant cheating," Mary explains. "To put it frankly, shit just happens sometimes. I know that isn't the psychological explanation you need or want to make you feel better about what happened. The truth is the only thing that will make you feel better about it is time and working on healing the fractured relationship between the two of you. Bryant has a lot of work ahead of him, but you're both here. It tells me you still love him, Zhanna. It also tells me Bryant is sincere in his quest to gain your trust again."

Both things are true–my love and his sincerity. But again, is it enough?

"May we start from the beginning? Tell me how you met and fell in love."

Bryant does most of the talking as he tells our love story. He starts at the fire at Hale's Row and brings her up to speed as quickly as he can. He ends on a low note, where he cheated, and I lost my shit and went to jail for assault and battery. He doesn't leave out the fact that we've been sleeping together since we split.

"And you're both in New Orleans now? How did that happen?"

"He orchestrated a trade behind my back to be close to me."

She blinks for a few seconds. "One could either call the move tenacious or lacking in boundaries."

"Exactly as I thought," I agree.

"I can't win her back if we're living 2,000 miles apart. I call it intelligence."

Mary smirks at his remark. "Touché. Well, folks, that's all for us today. Zhanna, are you interested in returning for a single or couple's session?"

Bryant squeezes my hand.

"Yes, I'll try at least one more session." I don't know why I agree so quickly, but maybe it's because I'm feeling nostalgic at the mention of so many good memories.

"Then I'd like to give you homework."

"Sure. I guess it's okay," I say.

"Go do something fun and spontaneous together that doesn't involve sex. It doesn't have to be grand or expensive, just fun and spontaneous."

Bryant pays the woman's secretary, and we meet at our cars.

He reaches out, placing a hand on my hip and bringing me in closer. "Thank you for coming. It means a lot to me."

"You're welcome. I think I'm going to head home."

"Have dinner with me? We both have to eat."

"Okay, but nothing too heavy."

"We're already in the Quarter. Why don't we walk from here and see what we happen upon on our journey?"

"Sounds good."

We walk in silence for a bit, but not uncomfortably so. I think we've known each other too long to ever really be really nervous. I break the silence when I catch him staring at me out of the side of my eye.

"What is it?" I ask and for some reason, I suddenly feel a little shy under his gaze.

"Nothing. I just... I just... guess I," he sputters and comes to a stop on the sidewalk before placing a hand on either shoulder and turning me to face him. He searches my eyes, takes another step closer to me, and tucks his hand under my chin.

When he lifts my gaze to his, I discover unshed tears there. "Listen, baby."

I reach out with my other senses and filter through the Quarter's many sounds until I first hear the melody and then the words. Inside an open-air cafe on the corner sits a man with a guitar on his lap. I can't distinguish his features from here, other than the curly brown hair and black fedora over his head, but he sounds an awful lot like Eddie Ved-

be with him in the moment as I let my guard down long enough to give it to him.

Bryant croons in my ear.

He rubs his thumb underneath the hem of my shirt on the sensitive skin of my lower back. If I wasn't so aroused, this would lull me to sleep—being in his arms, hearing his voice, and having him touch me intimately. Long after the man in the cafe moves onto another tune, we continue to sway to the song we danced to on our wedding day.

It isn't until Bryant abruptly pulls the hem of my shirt down and stiffens against me that we stop. "We have company."

I come back down to earth and reality. "Fans?"

"Appears to be. Want to make a run for it?"

I don't want anyone to see I've been crying, so I nod and bury my face into his chest for a moment before wiping my face.

"You're crying."

I keep my head tucked down to prevent anyone from seeing the evidence. "Can we get out of here?"

His fingers interlace with mine as we turn to the street closest to the therapist's office and make a run for it.

"That's him!" A man shouts.

"Bryant Hudson!"

False Start

"Shit," I say as I pick up the pace until I'm in a full sprint through the Quarter with my 6'5 football player of an ex-husband dragging me behind his long legs. "Slow down."

"Speed up, baby! They're going to maul us."

"My legs don't go any faster, you freaking giant!"

We round the corner to the parking lot of the therapist's office when Bryant pauses to stoop down, pick me up, and throw me over his shoulder. Then he takes off running again until we reach his SUV where he deposits me at the passenger door and quickly rounds the front of the vehicle. I narrowly escape the grabby hands of a fan as I crawl inside the car.

Bryant makes it inside in the nick of time and turns the ignition over before he backs out. A few minutes later, he stops at the gate to his house and looks over at me with concern in his eyes. "Are you okay? Did they hurt you?"

"No, I'm okay."

He pulls into the drive as the gate slides shut behind us. "I can have someone deliver your car."

"There's no need. I can call an Uber to retrieve it in a few hours."

After exiting the vehicle, I follow him inside the back door of the home which opens into the large kitchen. "Stay. I'll order us dinner. We can watch television while we wait, and the coast should be clear by the time we've finished eating. I can drop you by your car then."

I hesitate, not sure what I'm doing with him anymore. I'm going to therapy with him, dating him for at least fourteen dates, and having dinner with him. I'm dancing with him in the middle of the street to Elvis songs, and I'm feeling things.

"You have to eat," he says.

"Sure, I'll stay. What are we watching?"

We trek into the living area now sparsely filled with new furniture. The old drapes have been brought down and retired. In their place are thick white sheer curtains designed to allow light into the space while also providing adequate privacy. The brown leather couches are oversized. The walls have been painted a bright marigold yellow.

"Leslie has outdone himself," I slowly spin to take in the empty new floor-to-ceiling bookcases.

"I like the space a lot better now. It's much more comfortable even if it doesn't quite feel like home yet."

"It's big, but it's cozy. And it's not obnoxiously big like the place in California."

He clears his throat. "Have a seat wherever, babe. Make yourself at home."

It feels strange for him to tell me to make myself at home. We used to be each other's home. I take a seat on the edge of the couch and try to relax.

Bryant takes a seat beside me. "What's wrong?"

"Nothing."

"You look like you're ready to bolt."

"I'm not ready to bolt, Bryant. It's just, it's a little strange for you to tell me to get comfortable in your house."

"You mean because it's not our house?"

"It's just that we have different spaces now, and I suppose I'm still not accustomed to it after living with you for so long."

"Same. I still reach for you in the night, babe. I forget you're not waiting at home for me after a long day on the practice field. I forget you're not mine anymore. And it hurts every time I have to be reminded."

I let my walls down just a few inches and let him peek over the top. "I want to be able to forgive you, not for you, but for me. I don't know how to do that or where to begin, but I'm willing to go back to therapy with you if it will help me find peace."

His face lights up with excitement. His eyes dance back and forth as a dimple appears on either side. "What changed your mind?"

"I'm tired of being angry at you."

CHAPTER TWENTY TWO

NOW

"**W**ERE YOU ABLE TO complete your homework earlier this week?" Mary asks from her lone black wingback chair.

"Yes," we both answer.

"I'm curious, Zhanna, will you tell me the spontaneous and fun thing you did together?"

Bryant reaches across the small space between us, gently squeezing my hand.

"After our last appointment, we danced in the middle of the street not far from here."

"How wonderful!" She claps her hands together, a smile spreading across her face. "Whose idea was it?"

"It wasn't so much an idea as fate. We were walking along and I heard a song that carries meaning for us. We danced to the song at our wedding." Bryant explains.

"Love Me Tender," I offer.

"It's a beautiful song." After a pregnant pause, during which time she jots notes in her brown, leather binder, Mary says, "I know the story of how you met and fell in love, but I don't know why you're sitting in front of me today as a divorced couple. What changed? What do you hope to accomplish in therapy? It's pretty clear Bryant is here to reconcile, but what about you Zhanna? What motivated you to attend not only one, but two sessions?"

"A loaded question. I honestly don't know the answer to it. He came over the other night with beignets and coffee, and we connected in a way we haven't in a long time."

"And how did it feel?"

"It's a lot like relief. I'm still angry at what he did, but I'm not consumed by it anymore. It was a very sudden shift, one I can't quite explain."

"You're entering a new stage of grief. You've left the anger stage, and you've moved toward acceptance. It's great. It's progress. You're in a good place to be in therapy to assist in transitioning from the bouts of anger you may struggle with to perhaps trusting again."

The thought of putting my trust in Bryant again in that way is scary. "I don't know. Maybe."

"Maybe what?" Bryant asks.

Shrugging my shoulders, heat creeps into my cheeks. Therapy requires raw honesty, and I don't know if either one of us is ready for that level of brutal honesty.

Mary intervenes. "Talk to us, Zhanna. Tell us what you're feeling and thinking. Learning to communicate again is vital in learning to trust."

I stand from the couch and make my way over to a floor length window covered in white sheer curtains and burgundy drapes. Beyond the glass is an entire world coming and going to and fro, and their worlds go on when things happen and circumstances change. If I'm honest with myself, I'd admit I haven't exactly done that. I'm stuck in a pattern of sleeping with my ex-husband while my misery consumes me. I'm miserable with him but also unhappy without him. "Something has to change one way or another. I can't continue hooking up and living half in and half out of something with him. We need to see if this is worth salvaging."

"May I ask how and why you ended up agreeing to therapy almost two years after the divorce?"

I follow a blue bird outside as it flies from branch to branch on a cherry blossom tree. "I agreed to the fourteen dates I promised him when we first began dating. We moved quickly in our relationship together, and with his football schedule we didn't always have the opportunity to date in the way most couples do. He feels as though he never had his fourteen dates, and my best friend, Leslie, advised I owed the dates."

"He's on the side of love." Bryant snorts.

"I'm sorry?" Mary asks.

"Leslie, her best friend, is on the side of love." Bryant seems proud of the fact.

Mary appears a bit confused. "Your best friend is an advocate for your reunification?"

I roll my eyes at Leslie butting into our business. "My best friend has a crush on Bryant. His opinion is biased."

She has a good laugh. "It's good you two have support from a loved one. How many dates do you have left?"

"After today, I have eleven."

"Do you plan on using all of the dates to attend therapy?"

"I thought it would be a good idea to start each date off on the right foot. I'd like to make sure we're progressing toward something other than sex."

"You're sexually active?" she asks.

I nod. "Yes."

"Do either of you have any other partners?"

"No," we answer at the same time.

"Are these planned acts of intimacy or in the moment experiences?"

"In the moment," I reply.

"Do you use sex as a way to connect or is it a way to deal with your problems?"

"Both, but I've suggested we stop for a little while," Bryant replies.

"Before or after you connected the other night over beignets and coffee?"

"Before. We connected this last time, but I still think we should give it some time."

"And you, Zhanna? Do you think it's wise to abstain, at least for the next little while."

"Z," Bryant starts as he comes up behind me at the window, "let's do this. Let's do eleven more sessions as dates. No sex. See if we can find our way back to each other."

I know what he means, but I never lost my way to him. Even now as a divorced couple, we're the flame and the moth, although, I'm not sure who is which in the analogy. I'm terrified we could reach the end of eleven more dates and realize we were never meant for each other. Then what do we do?

"You're sacrificing eleven dates for therapy sessions?"

He presses a kiss to the back of my head as he reaches for my hip. "We'll do something after—something low key that will give us a chance to talk and spend time with each other."

I hesitate. It's hard to swallow pride and forgive. It's equally as difficult to let go of the familiarity of the anger I've held onto for so long. What will I have once it's gone? Vulnerability?

"Baby," he whispers, "give me a chance to make you fall in love with me again."

Love or being in love with him has never been the problem, but I'm not ready to admit it aloud. "Okay."

"Wonderful!" Mary claps her hands together again. "You've made real progress in such a short amount of time."

Bryant and I leave the view of the window and take our seats across from the therapist again.

"I think it's imperative you set healthy boundaries. As we delve deeper into therapy, there will be topics which hurt more than others. It's important to continue to communicate in a healthy manner. It's equally as important to know when to take a breather." She pauses and smiles at us both. "That's it for us today, but I want to give you homework again. Marriage is about teamwork, and I'd like to see the two of you work as a team on a project together. Paint a room together in Bryant's house or plant a garden at Zhanna's. Just do something together that requires you to work toward a common goal."

He squeezes my hand again. "We'll come up with something." As we leave the office complex on the edge of the French Quarter, he reaches over, takes my hand in his again, and brings it to his lips to press a kiss to my knuckles. "Let's pick up takeout. It's late, and practice wore me out. I want to fill my belly, have a beer, and relax on the couch with you."

It's been a long day at work for me as well, so his plan sounds perfect. Still, I'm shy to tell him so. I don't want to give him too much hope therapy will work. We've yet to address his infidelity in detail, and I don't know how I'll feel or act when we do. I've been known to fly off the handle when it comes to the topic.

Instead of ruining the good vibe with my thoughts, I agree. "Sounds good."

We drove separately to the session, so we meet at my place after he picks up Chinese food. Once I arrive home, I take the extra time to change into shorts and a tank to beat the heat. Bryant knocks at my back door about half an hour later.

"Come in!" He comes in with a plastic bag in one hand and a creature in the other that might resemble a cat. "What are you holding?"

"It's a kitten, woman."

"Why are you holding a kitten?"

"I found him outside the Chinese restaurant. He meowed at me."

The little thing can't be six weeks old. I'm pretty sure his coat is supposed to be white, but it's dirty and from here I can tell it's also smelly. Debris of some sort is caked into the area around his nose and mouth.

"Poor little guy. What made you pick him up and bring him with you?"

"He looks sick, Z. What kind of person would I be if I left a defenseless kitten out in the streets?"

"He does look sick. We should find an after-hours veterinarian to check him out."

We decide to eat our Chinese in the waiting room of the local vet's office as we pass the kitten back and forth.

The doctor looks him over, determines he's around four weeks old, and prescribes him antibiotics for a respiratory infection. "Bathe him in Dawn soap when you get home to take care of the fleas."

"What should we feed him?"

"My nurse will provide you with bottles and formula to get him through the next few weeks. He can eat soft kitten food as tolerated."

Bryant hands me his wallet to pay for the bill because he doesn't want to put the kitten down. It's adorable that he's concerned for the animal. I take the wallet and open it to find he still carries a picture of us from our wedding day inside. It tugs at my heart as I reach for the card to pay the cashier.

Inside the car on the way home, I listen to the kitten meow as I drive Bryant and him back to my house. "We can call a few local organizations that will help find him a home and someone who can care for him while he's on formula."

"I have a lot of money. I'll just hire someone to help me."

"You're keeping him?!"

"Sure, why not?"

"Cats can live forever. It's a huge commitment." When I park the car in my drive, I reach over and pet the kitten's head. He meows at me, and I can't help but smile at the sound. "He's cute. Why are you keeping him?"

"Everyone deserves to live their best life and be loved while they do it. This little guy is our homework. With teamwork and a cat sitter, we're going to make sure he has a great life and all the love he could ever want. We both have a lot of love to give, babe, and I think we need this."

I pull my phone out and snap a picture of Bryant and the kitten. "He needs a name."

"I already have a name."

I smirk at him. "You do?"

"Punter."

"Aww."

"Shut up, woman."

I pull up the picture of Bryant and Punter on my phone and quickly post it to his social media with the hashtags #bigbadquarterback #PuntertheKitten #TheresACatSomewhereUnderneathTheDirt #NewOrleansVoodoo.

"What did you just do?"

"Posted a picture of you looking super macho on social media."

"Come here," he says, crooking his finger at me.

We meet in the middle of the car at the console and kiss over the smelly kitten. "No offense, QB, but Punter needs a bath before we can kiss over him."

CHAPTER TWENTY THREE

NOW

AFTER WORK THE NEXT day, Bryant walks into my office with a big smile on his face. Since he found Punter last minute, we weren't able to find a cat sitter. I brought the kitten to work with me in a shoe box and hid him in my office all day. Zina and I took turns feeding him with a bottle while Bryant was at practice.

"Where's the little guy?" he asks as he rubs his hands together, eager to get them on the kitten.

"Nice to see you, too." I huff.

"Babe, I'm always ecstatic to see you, but you've been playing with him all day while I've been pouring sweat in the Louisiana August sun. I haven't had a shower, so I'm not trying to get in your space. I just wanted to hold him for a minute before I hit the locker room."

I grin at him. "You're adorable."

He grins back and two dimples make an appearance on either side of his full lips. "Glad you think so. Hand over the kitten."

I take a step back and tuck Punter in the crook of my arm. "This kitten?"

"Don't make wrestle you to the floor and take him from you," he threatens with his hands on his hips.

My thoughts turn naughty at his threat.

No sex, I remind myself.

"Don't do that," he says.

"Don't do what?"

"Lick your lips and give me 'the' look."

"'The' look?"

"Baby, when you want my cock, you lick your lips and get this hungry look in your eyes."

I snort. "I do not."

He gets back to the issue at hand. "Zhanna, hand over the cat."

"Meow," the little traitor in my arms says as though he's crying out for Bryant.

"Fine," I say and give him Punter.

He baby talks the little guy and asks him how his day was before he hands him back over and heads to the showers.

He's back in my office in less than twenty minutes with loose, wet hair hanging past his shoulders. "I need to hit the pet store close to my place. He hasn't had his shots yet, so can you watch him while I go inside?"

"Okay, sure. Why don't I meet you at your place? I'll stay there with Punter until you get home."

"Sounds perfect. Here," he says as he reaches into his pocket and produces a single key, "I've been meaning to give this to you. Please don't take it the wrong way. You live closer to me than anyone else. I may need you to check on Punter or something while I'm on the road."

I take the key without a word. Before a few weeks ago, I would've fought it. Hell, I would've fought pretty much anything to do with Bryant.

He touches his palm to my cheek. "Thank you for taking it."

I lean into his touch, loving the smell of his expensive body wash. "I'll meet you there."

Bryant kisses my cheek as he pets Punter's head, before he's out the door. Zina sticks her head in a few moments later while I'm still standing there looking at the empty door.

"What are you smiling about?" she asks.

I wipe the smile from my face.

"Aww, look at the wittle bitty fella!" she says like she hasn't already stopped by to see him fifteen times today.

"No time for cuddles. I'm taking him home."

"Your home or Bryant's home?"

170

I roll my eyes. "I'm taking Punter to his home."

"If I'd known all it would take is an awkward-looking cat to bring you two back together, then I would've adopted all the stray kittens in New Orleans years ago."

"We're not back together, and Punter is Bryant's kitten, not mine."

"I'll come with you two. I don't have anything else to do tonight."

I'm reminded about Bryant's two guests, who I've yet to lay eyes on. I'm also reminded their move to New Orleans has slipped my mind with everything going on with Bryant. "Probably not the greatest idea."

She frowns. "Why not? I used to hang out with you guys all the time."

I take her by the hand and pull her over to the two chairs in front of my desk. "I've been meaning to tell you something, but it's slipped my mind for the past few weeks. I apologize in advance for it."

"You're pregnant," she blurts out.

"God, no."

"I give up."

"After one guess?"

She starts talking with her hands, a sure sign of her anxiety. "Are you telling me or what?"

"Ben is back in town."

"Okay?"

"For good."

"He lives in Detroit."

I reach over and pat my hand on top of hers. "Not anymore."

"Oh my God. Did he retire early?"

I close my eyes and take in a deep breath before I blow it out and jumble all my words together. "Ben is signing with the Voodoo."

She stiffens beside me. Shit.

The longest moment passes before she speaks. "Well, okay."

"Okay?"

"It was a long time ago, Zhanna. We've both moved on with our lives. He's married and has a son now."

I don't know much about Ben's life in the last few years, but Bryant and I were together when Ben married and divorced.

"Zina, Ben hasn't been married for three years."

Her face pales when she realizes him being a married man may not play into her perfect little scenario where they'll be good, old friends. Him being single scares her. "Oh."

Yeah. Oh. "But Bryant would love for you to come over. I think it'd be great to have the whole crew together again."

She quickly stands, shooting up from the chair like her ass is on fire. "I think I'll pass. We'll see each other soon enough."

"Zina…"

She gives me an unconvincing smile. "It's fine. I'm going home to crash. It's been a long day."

"Okay"

As soon as she's out the door, I dial Leslie and ask him to hang out with her until I can pass Punter off and join them.

I take my time driving to Bryant's place, stopping along the way to purchase a chai latte at my favorite coffee shop. When I arrive at Bryant's, he's already there with ten giant pet store bags.

"He's a four-week-old kitten. What in the world did you buy?"

Bryant bounces around like a young child excited for his first pet. "Toys, food, treats, and look at this little collar," he says as he holds up, touching the little green bell on the collar.

The grin on my face nearly splits me in two when a familiar face rounds the corner of the den. "Ben!"

I hand Punter to Bryant and take off across the room for my old friend. He catches me in the air and spins me around. "Coach!"

When he puts me down, I notice his son, Ansel, beside him. I haven't had the pleasure of meeting Ansel very many times. Ben is a single dad, and he's super protective of his son. When Ben divorced, he pulled away from everyone. Even after Bryant and I divorced, I made many attempts to check in on him, but he never returned my calls.

"Hi, Ansel," I say to the adorable child with Ben's amber brown eyes and Cupid's bow mouth. The little boy has his mother's jet-black hair.

He sticks his hand out. "Hello, I'm Ansel."

"You wouldn't remember me, but I've known you since you were born."

"I was born on March 4th at 10:03 a.m. in Detroit, Michigan."

I love his word vomit. "Yes, you were. I remember very clearly the morning you were born. It snowed the night before, and your Uncle Bryant and I were almost late arriving at the hospital in time for your birth."

"You knew me when I was born?" he asks, surprised by the information.

"Of course. I've known your dad a long time."

"Are you Uncle Bryant's girlfriend?"

Why does a simple, innocent suggestion make me feel slightly violent? "No, sweetie. We're friends."

Ansel looks at Bryant with big, wide eyes. "I don't think I want a girlfriend either, Uncle Bryant. They cry a lot."

I do my best to hide my smile from him as do the other adults in the room.

"They smell really good, though," Bryant argues. "And I like their silky hair."

"Yuck" Ansel tugs on Ben's hand. "Do I have to have a girlfriend?"

Ben ruffles his hair. "No, son. You're a bit young for that right now. You have more than enough time to worry about it."

"Can I see the kitten?" the little boy asks Bryant with hopeful eyes.

"Of course. Why don't we sit you on the couch so we can place him in your lap?"

"It's a boy cat?'

"Sure is, buddy. His name is Punter. Here you go. Will you hold him still while I put his new collar on?"

"Yes, sir."

I watch my ex with our friend's son and feel a pang of loss. He would've been a good dad to any child we brought into the world. I didn't have long to dream that dream before it was all taken from me in a divorce neither of us saw coming. Love is far more fragile than any of us realize.

I clear my throat, slightly thick with emotion. "I should go. I need to check on my sister."

Bryant's head whips around at my announcement. "You're going?"

I incline my head toward Ben. "She just found out."

He stands, glancing down at Ansel. "Can you and Daddy watch Punter for me while I walk Ms. Zhanna to her car?"

"Yes, sir."

"Got it," Ben says.

Bryant takes me by the hand and leads me through the den, foyer, and kitchen to the elegant brick mudroom. Outside my car, he presses me against the driver's door as one hand goes to my hip and the other dives into my hair. "I wish you didn't have to go."

"I told Zina about Ben before she left work. I didn't want her to find out from someone else. I sent Leslie over to her apartment until I could get there. She didn't look all that okay when she left my office."

"Do you need me to go with you?" Bryant loves my sister like she's his sister, even though we're divorced. It's one of the reasons I fell in love with him in the first place.

"I think this is a sister's duty. You know, Ben probably should've been the one to tell her, not me."

"Yeah, I agree. I hope it's not awkward and tense at work."

A sigh escapes me. "Me too."

"Hey," he says and pulls his hand from my hair to rub his thumb across my lips. "Be careful going to Zina's. Will you text me when you're safely inside?"

"Yeah."

"I'm going to kiss you now, babe."

"Okay."

He smirks before he presses his lips to mine. His masculine scent, soft lips, and hard planes have me standing on my tiptoes to kiss him back. I grab a fistful of his shirt to bring him closer to me. Scraping my teeth against his bottom lip, he groans in response. "Fuck, baby."

He presses four more kisses to me before he finally breaks it for good. He leans his forehead against mine and sighs, and we stay that way for a long while, slightly swaying with the sporadic sweet kiss.

The cicadas chirp around us for a long while as the sun slowly dips in the sky on a late summer night. We continue to stay wrapped around each other for half an hour before my urgent need to go to Zina's place resurfaces in my mind. "I should go."

He closes his eyes briefly, a clear sign he's unhappy with being reminded of the news. Then he kisses me again, long, and deep. "I know you're not ready, but I love you, Zhanna. Please be careful, and let me know when you make it safely inside."

CHAPTER TWENTY FOUR

THEN

"COACH!" BRYANT SHOUTS AS he comes through the garage door into the kitchen.

"Right here, Quarterback," I say, standing in front of the stove.

He skids to a halt on the other side of the bar as he takes in my outfit. "Fuck me, Zhanna."

I suddenly feel self-conscious. "It's stupid."

"Nuh-uh. Nothing about garter belts, corsets, thongs, and fuck me heels are stupid, baby." He starts for me.

"Nope." I hold my hand up to stop his progress. "You stay on that side of the bar while I finish cooking your dinner."

"Fuck the food. Let's go upstairs."

I cast a smirk in his direction. "Happy anniversary."

He starts for me again.

"Nuh-uh. I've been planning this meal for weeks. You're eating this food."

"And then I'm eating you," he replies as he heads for me anyway. He wraps himself around me and buries his face into my neck. "I have a surprise for you."

"Yeah?"

He unravels from me and bops me on the end of the nose. "You'll have to wait until after dinner."

"Will you pour the wine?"

He works on opening a bottle of red wine while I finish sautéing the green beans and pull a casserole from the oven. "Can you believe we've been married three years?"

"Yes, it's seemed like an eternity."

He laughs. "Hardy-har-har. She's got jokes. But you're half naked, so I'll let it slide."

We make a plate and take it to the dining room, where we rarely eat, but it's a special occasion. I can't believe we've been married three years. All jokes aside, time has flown by because being with Bryant is easy. We've only had one big argument in the four years we've been together, and the makeup sex was worth it.

As usual, Bryant eats off both of our plates. His appetite is bottomless being such a big guy and all. "Ben called. He's proposing to the girl he's dating."

"The one he just started dating?" I ask.

"Yeah. Wendy. She's preggers."

I drop my fork. "No!"

"'Fraid so. I think I'm still in shock that he's having a kid before us."

"No kidding. How does he feel about it?"

"Hasn't hit him yet. Wants to do the right thing by the girl."

"Babies shouldn't always equal marriage though. He can be there and support her and the baby without putting a ring on it."

"You know Ben, babe. He's always wanted a big family. Somewhere deep inside, he's over the moon about this even if it isn't the most ideal situation to bring a kid into. Anyway, he's coming to town and wants to do a quick bachelor party this Friday night. Are you cool with that?"

"Sure. Will you be making it rain?"

It earns me a grin. "Yes, baby, we're going to the strip club."

I grew up around a lot of men, and deep down most of them are dogs who want to objectify women. I accept it for what it is and only ask him to follow my one rule. "Please don't drink and drive."

"Have I told you how amazing of a wife you are today?"

"Nope. You're really falling down on your game there, QB."

We play footsie under the table and enjoy the duck with an orange glaze I prepared especially for our anniversary. It's one of his favorite dishes.

"I love you, Zhanna," he says, pushing back from the table and throws his napkin on his plate. "The duck was wonderful. I'm afraid I'm too full to take you upstairs and have my way with you."

I drink the rest of my wine before standing and walking over to him. "Who said we need to go upstairs?"

"Naughty, naughty Coach."

"Hmmm, I suppose we shall see." I throw a leg over his lap to straddle him. His hand goes straight to my hips as he pushes me down and thrusts up at the same time. He's hard as a rock. "I thought you were too full to have your way."

"Babe, I think you're having your way with me right now, and I'm enjoying every single moment of it."

I lean forward to kiss him, but he winces. "What's wrong?"

"This isn't the greatest position for a new tattoo."

"You have a new tat?"

God, I love his dimples. "Yeah. It's my surprise."

"Show me. Show me. Show me!" I shout.

He laughs and pats me on the ass. "You'll have to move for a minute."

After I move, he stands up to unbutton his pants. He pushes his pants and boxers down and raises the hem of his shirt to display new artwork just above his pubic bone. It takes a moment to make out the big, ornate letters. "What on earth is that? CZ ∞ QB?"

"Coach Zhanna and the Quarterback are forever."

I start grinning like a loon, leap into the air and jump onto my half-naked husband. "You're the sweetest man in the world."

"I love you more than life itself," he says before he leans forward and presses a kiss against my lips.

"I love you to the moon and back, Quarterback."

178

***

THE WEEK AFTER OUR anniversary, Ben flies into town to spend a few days with us. It never felt right that he and Zina aren't together. I always thought they were the perfect couple. I can't imagine the woman he's marrying can hold a candle to my sister, but I'm a little biased.

We enjoy a nice lunch and dinner before the groom-to-be and his best man head out for the strip club in a rented limo stocked full of football players and enough alcohol to inebriate an army.

After a midnight text from Bryant, I crawl in the bed and grab a little shuteye before my big test tomorrow. Graduate school isn't easy. I never expected it to be, but the coursework load doubled in size from undergrad. Fortunately, I'm in my last semester. I can't wait to graduate in May and sit for my physical therapy board certification exam.

I ease into sleep and dream of Bryant and I holding a little baby. It's an odd dream where I'm so busy trying to determine the gender of the baby that I fail to bask in the enjoyment of holding who I assume is our child.

"Coach!"

"Z!"

"Zhanna!"

The sound of glass shattering has me sitting straight up in bed.

"Baby!"

"Uh-oh," Ben slurs.

"Your wife is going to kick our asses," replies an unfamiliar voice, and then it sounds like an entire football team laughs at the joke.

I snag my robe from the bathroom and make my way down the long hallway to the grand staircase. Looking down into our foyer and living room, I find at least half a football team in it.

"Your wife is fucking hot."

"I know," Bryant slurs to the large man next to him. "She'sssss the hottessst."

"Dude, your crib is dope."

Bryant waves his arms in the air as he introduces me to the team like I don't know them. "Zhanna, this is the team. And team, this is my hot wife, Z."

I press my lips together in an effort to hide my smile as I begin down the steps. "Feeling toasty, Quarterback?"

He moves to the bottom of the steps and waits for me to meet him there. "There's glass, baby. I don't want you to cut yourself."

"What happened?"

"I broke a lamp." Then he gives me the biggest grin he can muster. "I'm a little drunk."

"Where's Ben?" I ask.

Bryant crooks his thumb over his shoulder to the living room behind him.

I look around my husband to discover Ben passed out on the couch. "Is he alive?"

The entire room erupts in masculine laughter.

"Doubtful. He overdosed on naked women and too much booze," Bryant replies.

He carries me over to our friend so I don't step on glass. I check him out to make sure he's breathing and bring him a trash can, water, and aspirin. Ben is such a great guy. I can only hope Wendy knows and cherishes him as Zina would. I'm glad he had the time of his life tonight. Every guy and girl should have their night out on the town with friends before they tie the knot. Bryant and I never had parties because we rushed to Vegas to elope. I never missed what I didn't know. But someone in a more traditional type of ceremony should definitely enjoy an evening all about them.

"How is he?" I ask Bryant when the house is quiet, and the players begin to split off to the guest rooms.

"I don't know, babe. Couldn't get a read on him all night. He doesn't seem like himself though."

"I've yet to break the news to Zina." The thought of it causes anxiety to fill my chest.

We crawl into bed with Bryant reeking of bourbon.

"She'll be okay. It's what she wanted."

I'm not so sure my sister knows what she wanted two years ago. I think she was scared of losing him to the league like so many college girlfriends do. Bryant doesn't understand it because he's not a woman.

"Night baby."

"Night, Quarterback."

CHAPTER TWENTY FIVE

THEN

"IT SEEMS LIKE THE longer we live in Los Angeles, the more party invitations we receive."

"What are we invited to this time?" Bryant asks as he pulls the vehicle away from the mailbox and curb.

I open the envelope to discover an elegant black script on a shimmery gold invitation. Beautiful. Someone dropped a mint on the invites. "We are cordially invited to a fundraiser for the Los Angeles County Special Olympics. Awww, you should do this."

"We should. I hate going to those things without you."

I usually have to push him out the door so I can study while he plays the football star.

"I can't go. It's the night of my study group."

"You can't skip your group this one time?" he whines.

I giggle at his inability to be by himself. "This close to my boards?"

He reaches over and squeezes my thigh. "You're right, babe. I'm sorry. Just hate going without you."

"No, you don't like being by yourself."

"No, I don't like being without you. I feel better in your company. I always have."

I turn and smile at him. "You're perfect. You know that?"

***

THE NIGHT BEFORE MY boards, I crawl into bed without Bryant again. Since the season has ended, he's been going out to events more and arriving home late smelling of liquor. His star has really risen in the last year in the league due to the numbers he put up this past season. He didn't win a ring, but he was only one game shy of entering the Super Bowl as a contender. Plus, he's young and gorgeous, and he's been gracing covers of style magazines in his recent outings to fundraisers and other events. Bryant always comes home to me, if slightly inebriated, but he comes home to his wife. So I climb into bed with my phone on the nightstand, in case he calls in need of a ride, and I close my eyes to find rest.

The next morning, I scoot across the bed to Bryant's chest to snuggle for a minute for good luck on my boards, but his side of the bed is cold. I turn over and find it empty. The sheet was never pulled back on his side.

What the hell?

I roll over and pluck my phone from the nightstand, but I don't find his usual text message telling me he's on his way home. He always messages to tell me he's on his way home. Maybe he forgot. I get up and put my robe on and then search the house for him, but I come up empty.

I call his phone.

He picks up immediately, heavy sleep in his voice. "Hello?" he croaks.

"Where are you?"

"What?"

I look at my phone in frustration and then put it back to my ear. "Where in the fuck are you?"

"Baby?"

"Yes, this is your wife."

"Shit," he grumbles. "What time is it?"

"Six in the morning. And it appears you didn't come home last night."

"I didn't?"

I swear I'm going to throw my phone across the room.

"I have to go," I seethe, hanging up the phone.

I jump in the shower and rush to get ready for boards as my mind goes to dark places about Bryant being out all night. He's never given me a reason not to trust him, so I need to stop wondering if he did the unthinkable. When I emerge from the shower, my phone buzzes and dances across the bathroom vanity. I'm sure it's my husband, but I don't have time to talk to him. I need to get my head in the game and focus on boards. I can't believe he'd stay out all night the evening before something this important. He's not even here to wish me good luck—something he always does the morning of a big test.

Rushing to dress and blow-dry my long hair, I apply very little makeup to my blue eyes before I'm out the door and headed for the testing center. Bryant continues to call and message. I roll my eyes and turn off the phone. I'm so mad at him right now I could spit fire. This is one of the biggest days of my life, so I have to get my head in the game. I can't screw this up.

I park at the testing center, rush inside, and find my seat in the nick of time. Tests in general make me anxious. It takes me a long moment to calm my mind and focus on the material in front of me, but after twenty minutes, I'm in the zone. I have five hours to answer 250 questions and become a certified physical therapist.

Delving deep inside the test, I start with the first question and take my time moving through each item. I read each question twice before scanning the answers twice, then mark each correct answer. The longer I sit for the test, the more confident I feel about my answers.

Just under four hours later, I come to the last question and almost shout with glee. My eyes hurt from staring at a computer screen for a small eternity. I collect my personal belongings from a locker inside the testing facility. A big sigh of relief leaves me as I walk out to my car. Hopefully, I passed. If not, at least I know what to expect next time.

I turn on my phone as I turn the engine over to head home. My phone chimes about fifty times when it powers on. Bryant and Zina have both been blowing up my phone. Not bothering to read the messages or listen to the voicemails, I head for a local coffee shop and hide for a few hours.

I need a minute to process Bryant not coming home last night. I'm not ready to see him yet. I don't even know what happened, but I'm already disappointed in him for not bothering to call or text.

I'm a pretty understanding wife. I don't care if he goes out without me as long as he comes home to me. It's not too much to ask my husband to come home every night, with the exception of away games.

Bryant and Zina continue to message and call. I put them out of their misery.

> Zhanna: I'm out of my test, but I need a minute before I come home.

> Bryant: I'm sorry, baby. Please come home, and we'll talk.

> Zhanna: I'll be home by dinner.

    I shut my phone off and order a chai latte and decompress over my test. While I break it down question by question, I people watch from the corner of the little cafe. And then my thoughts travel to Zina. I should let her know I'm okay, so I power on the phone and message her.

> Zhanna: You okay?

> Zina: Yes. Are you? How did boards go?

> Zhanna: Boards were brutal. Clocked in under four hours.

> Zina: And Bryant? I hear he didn't come home last night.

> Zhanna: Nope. I'm not happy.

Zina: He's freaking the fuck out. Scared you're going to leave him.

Zhanna: Jesus.

Zina: LOL

Zhanna: I'll put him out of his misery in a bit. He needs to realize how bad he fucked up first.

Zina: Poor guy already knows, sis.

Zhanna: I'm not rushing home to him just because he's feeling guilty.

Zina: Fair enough. Love you. Call me if you need me.

Zhanna: Will do. Love you, too.

I ignore the thirty-four messages from my husband and tuck my phone into my purse. It's not okay to not come home when you're married. It's definitely not okay for him to not call his wife if he isn't going to be able to make it home for an unforeseen reason, and there aren't many of those that are going to fly in my book.

I remain tucked in the small cafe for most of the afternoon. When the summer sun begins to warm in color in the later part of the day, I drive home.

My head is full of test questions and self-doubt over my answers, and my heart is full of concern for my husband's recent actions. Between school, football, and all the damn events he's invited to, we don't see each other as much as we used to. I didn't realize we'd grown apart to the point where he can so easily dismiss his own wife when he's drinking. Or, at least, that's what it feels like.

Our home has a gate at the entrance to the neighborhood and another gate at our long drive. When someone pulls through it, a chime sounds inside the house, so Bryant is already standing in the garage waiting for me when I pull inside. He's shirtless and covered in ink. And my God. I never grow tired of looking at him, even when I'm pissed off. His long brown hair hangs past his shoulders now. Blue gym shorts hang low on his waist and show off the sharp V of his hips.

He walks over to my door. Opening it, I don't immediately emerge. There's concern etched across his face and a plea in his eye. "Baby, please come inside and talk to me."

Moving from the car to the kitchen with his hand at my back, I try to pull away once we're inside. He prevents me, spins me around and presses me against the door, his forehead pressed to mine.

He peers deeply into me, and my resolve starts to melt. "I fucked up. It won't happen again, Z."

The tears I've held at bay all day finally come. "You didn't sleep next to me last night, so who did you sleep next to?"

"No, baby. No. That isn't what happened," he says, smirking. "I slept beside Demarion, and he snores like a beast. I kept thinking it was you. Imagine how confusing my dreams were when I kept reaching for a much larger version of you."

A snicker escapes me. "Yeah? Should I kick his ass for trying to snuggle with my man?"

"Most definitely." He reaches down, picking me up until I wrap my legs around his middle. With one hand on my hip, and one at the back of my head, he softly kisses me. "I think he tried to come on to me last night. Maybe my hair began to look a little too much like Livia's?"

I snort, but then refocus and bring the attention right back to the issue at hand. "If you can't come home, and there aren't many reasons in this world that you can't come home, all I ask is you call and give me the courtesy of knowing where my husband is—the same I think you would ask of me."

"It won't happen again. I'm so sorry you were worried. Do you still love me?"

"To the moon and back, Quarterback."

The next kiss is slow, deep, and it means everything. I feel so connected to him through it, more than ever before. His hunger is evident in his kiss and from the hardness beneath me.

He carries me upstairs, lays me on our bed, and begins to remove my clothing piece by piece. His lips caress every inch of my skin, the tips of his fingers leave goosebumps in their wake as I part for him. I open up to my husband again and forgive him for his minor transgression. We've never been a couple that argues. We much prefer to make love. It's exactly what we do as his mouth meets mine again and he slides inside.

Slowly, he moves on top of me, pushing my legs open to allow him to move his hips in wide circles. He pulls his lips from mine, moving down until his teeth scrape against my nipple. When he sucks the pink flesh into his mouth, my back arches in response, a loud moan escaping me.

God. He's so good at this.

"I belong inside you," he whispers against my lips and slows his thrusts until he stops completely and looks deeply into me. "We've been together four years, Z. Let's have a baby. We're good. We're solid. We're ready."

"We don't have to rush it."

"Babe, I want to see you pregnant with my baby. I want to hold your hand and cheer you on while you give birth. I want all the sleepless nights, diaper changes, feedings, burpings, baths, and newborn cries. I also want to nibble on chubby baby parts and blow raspberries on their bellies. And I want to do it all with you."

He's serious, sincere, and very much wants to be a dad. "It could take us months after I stop taking my birth control."

"That's okay. It'll give us time to fix up a nursery."

The word "nursery" tugs at my heartstrings. Thinking of my husband holding and loving our child fills me with such joy that tears begin to leak from my eyes. The beautiful thing about Bryant is I don't have to explain my tears to him. He gets it. He understands it. He leans down to kiss them away as we both erupt around each other.

CHAPTER TWENTY SIX

THEN

AFTER NINE MONTHS PASS with no signs of pregnancy, I start to worry. Bryant says he isn't concerned at all, and we'll get pregnant when it's meant to happen. I try to stay positive and upbeat about it, but it's difficult at times. Once I decided I wanted a baby with Bryant, I became baby crazy and very impatient.

In two weeks' time, Bryant will enter the Super Bowl as a contender with the Los Angeles Spartans. He's worked hard and becomes the leader I saw in my father. I'm proud of the man he's become on and off the field.

I'm standing in the room we've begun decorating as the nursery when Bryant wraps his arms around me from behind. He nearly scares me to death, but I quickly relax at the scent of his cologne, snuggling into him.

"Z," he croaks which has me twisting in his arms to see what's wrong. "I need to go back to New Orleans."

His face is full of a pain I've never seen before. "What's wrong?"

"Mom called. Dad fell over at the dinner table tonight and had a massive heart attack."

"Oh my God. Is he okay?"

His lips thin into a line as he closes his eyes and gives a slight shake of his head. "No, baby. They couldn't resuscitate him."

"Oh, Bryant, I'm so sorry." I don't know if there are words in the English language that will bring him comfort at this moment, so I wrap my arms around him and hold him tightly instead of saying more. He sinks down to his knees, taking me with him, and quietly sobs for his father.

When my father died, I was in shock for days. I couldn't believe he was gone. I didn't know how to relay the sentiment to all the people who were sorry for my loss. I was lost in my own head for weeks after we'd buried Dad. On the week anniversary of his death, it hit me he wasn't coming back. It floored me that he was gone so suddenly, and I was still so young. I still needed my dad.

So, I don't pressure Bryant to speak more than he feels he's up to in the days leading up to the funeral or the days that follow. I stay close and wait for the moment it hits him. When it hit me, I'd come home to tell my father something exciting that had happened to me moments before. I opened the door to his study, his stale scent hitting me in the face doubled me over. I've never felt something so painful before or since. The realization that life has forever been altered by their permanent absence is a jagged pill to swallow.

Bryant is strong for his mother. I'm proud of him for holding it together, but once we've buried his father and flown back to California, I grow more concerned for him. He's quiet. Bryant isn't a motor mouth, but he's not quiet. I stick close by to make sure he knows I'm here when he's ready to fall apart. I'll pick up the pieces for him and put him back together.

As the days pass and we grow closer to the Super Bowl, he doesn't say anything at all. During the night, he still reaches for me as he cries in his sleep.

The night before the big game, he's required to stay in a hotel with a 10 p.m. curfew. I toss and turn in our bed without him, hoping he's okay without me there. He just lost his dad, but he had to go right back to work. He didn't have the luxury of having time off to grieve, and I'm worried he's holding it all in until he explodes.

The next morning, I rise around eight and dress in my Hudson Spartan jersey. At ten, Bryant sends his first message of the day.

> **Bryant:** I love you.

> **Zhanna:** I love you, too. How are you?

> **Bryant:** I missed you last night.

> **Zhanna: I missed sleeping with you. I tossed and turned all night.**

He doesn't say anything else. I don't see or hear from him until I arrive at the stadium. This year, we happen to be slated to play the Super Bowl in Los Angeles. Taking a limo Bryant sent, I head to the stadium and wait for my favorite quarterback.

Priscilla, who I met years ago at a party, saunters into the box reserved for Bryant's family and friends.

"Zhanna," she greets, offering a kind smile.

"Priscilla, how can I help you?"

She takes a seat but leaves two seats between us. "I'm sorry for the loss of your father-in-law."

"Thank you, I appreciate it."

"I'm not one to beat around the bush. May we speak candidly?"

I wave a hand out for her to continue.

"Charles isn't doing all he can do for Bryant. He's the top quarterback in the league right now. He's favored to win tonight, and it means big things coming down the pipelines."

"Sponsorships."

"Charles has only gotten him relatively mediocre sponsorships. Bryant is worth so much more than he's currently receiving."

"Let me guess, you can get him much bigger paychecks?"

"Of course."

"Why aren't you talking to Bryant about this?"

"Bryant isn't in a great place right now. He's not thinking in the future, or at least not past getting a ring tonight. If he's lucky, he'll play until he's 40? Brady and Brees have done it, but it's not always likely in football. You know they have the shortest careers out of professional sports. He can set himself up for retirement now and not be stressed if he's taken out of the game by injury."

"What do you want from me?"

"I have a video game company interested in him if he wins tonight. With a ring on his finger, the offers will pour in. Do you want someone who will do a mediocre job, or an agent who'll give you and your family a big future?" She hands me her business card. "Talk to him. Convince him the move is in his best interest. He won't make the move without your support."

I turn her card over in my fingers. "I'll think about it."

As she's leaving, Bryant opens the door and walks inside. He frowns at her.

"My deepest condolences," she says. "I was giving Zhanna the same."

"Thank you" He steps back outside to open the door for her.

Once she's gone, he steps back inside and makes his way to me. "What the fuck did she want?"

"She wants to be your agent."

He leans down to kiss me, lingers there for a moment, and looks deeply into me. There's so much pain there. I'd do almost anything to make him feel better.

"I'll pass. She caused one of the biggest fights between us we've ever had. I'm not the same young, dumb kid anymore."

"No, you're not, but she has a point, and she did apologize for it. Charles isn't doing all he can do for you, not when your star has risen so quickly in the last few years. You're on the brink of having a ring. I agree he should be doing more."

"You think?"

"Yeah, QB, I think if you don't go with Priscilla, you should go with someone else, perhaps even someone younger— someone more on the edge of what's hot in the league."

"You should be my agent."

I laugh. "I'll stick to being a physical therapist and your wife. It's what I'm good at."

False Start

Bryant takes the chair next to me, turns to face me and leans forward to put his head in my lap.

"Talk to me."

"I just need to be close to you," he whispers.

For the next twenty minutes, I run my hands through his long hair. He'll tie it back before he puts his helmet on, but for now, it flows down his back. He moans here and there, letting me know he's enjoying this. I love touching him and bringing him comfort. I focus on his tense shoulders and rub knots out of his throwing arm.

"Feels amazing, Z."

"You have to go soon."

The stadium will soon fill up with fans and industry people, and he's the man of the hour. He likes a nice quiet place to find his calm before the chaos of a game ensues. Between the media and playing four brutal quarters, he won't have another minute to himself until we're in the car headed home after the game. We won't have a moment alone until then either.

It's when he leaves me for the locker room that I begin to feel nervous. I've been anxious since I rose. It's a big game, and he just lost his dad. For the first time in probably the entirety of our relationship, I don't know where his head is at. I'm worried about him. The weight of the world is on his shoulders, and all he likely wants to do is crawl under the covers for a few weeks and cry.

He sits up, pulling himself from my lap, and leans forward to kiss me. "I love you, Zhanna."

"I love you, too, Quarterback. Go out there and get us a ring, baby."

His sad smile breaks my heart. He's about to have the chance to win the Super Bowl, but his heart isn't in it. It's bruised and battered by grief. "I'd rather go home and bury myself inside you."

"If you can manage to stay awake after the game, you can do just that as soon as we get home."

He kisses me again. "I'm holding you to it."

***

THERE'S TWO MINUTES LEFT in the fourth quarter. The Spartans are only up by three points. There's enough time for North Carolina to tie it up with a field goal or score a touchdown to take the lead on their current possession. We'd have to score again if they were to tie us or take the lead, but with only two minutes left, North Carolina could eat up the clock and leave us scrambling without enough time to make it back down the field to answer.

There's nothing Bryant can do from the sidelines as he watches the Spartan defensive line push back against the offense, trying to hold them down the field. I watch him through the television monitors as the cameras pan to him every so often, and I worry. I don't know if he can take the crushing blow of not winning this game after losing his dad two weeks ago.

With forty-two seconds left on the game clock, North Carolina scores a touchdown and an extra point and takes the lead by four. Now we need a touchdown to win by two, and our field position starts us at the twenty-five-yard line. Bryant and the offensive line take the field against North Carolina's defense.

The center hikes the ball to his quarterback on the first play of the drive. Bryant steps back as the men lock against each other like battering rams in a battle for control of the ball. The offensive line spread out to protect Bryant as his wide receivers run down field to catch the throw. He fakes left, then center, then he goes back to his left, but his man has double coverage.

I stand up and ball my hands into fists. He's running out of time. "Throw the ball, baby!"

He quickly looks down the right side of the field and finds his man. He launches the ball just in time to avoid being sacked while still in possession. He goes down when he's hit by a linebacker but rolls away and jumps to his feet just in time to see the tight end jump in the air and catch the ball, but he's covered up by the defense as soon as his cleats hit the turf. We gain twenty yards, taking us almost to the halfway mark of the field. Our boys have thirty-five seconds left to deliver the ball into the end zone fifty-five yards away.

Bryant steps behind the line of scrimmage and calls out the next play. The center hikes the ball again, Bryant catching it and dipping way back to look down the field, but no one is open. I look at the clock. There's twenty-eight seconds there. Glancing back to Bryant, I see the moment he makes the decision to do it. In all the years I've seen him play, I've never seen him barrel down the field toward the end zone with the football gripped in his large hand. Some quarterbacks will run the ball, but most will not in order to prevent injuries. My husband isn't a runner, or at least he wasn't until the Super Bowl was on the line.

My heart beats against my chest wall as I watch him dodge football players, jump over fallen men, and gracefully dance down the field like he does it every damn day. The moment he steps across the pylons, I start screaming and jumping up and down.

Oh my God. Oh my God. Oh my God! We won the Super Bowl!

I take a seat for a moment and try to catch my breath as I watch Bryant celebrate the victory with his teammates. The men pick him up and carry him across the field to his coach, who they also hoist up. The two men hug it out above the rest of the players.

I don't know what Coach says to my husband, but emotion crosses Bryant's face for just a moment before he locks it down and nods. They shake hands before they're put down and encircled by the Spartan army.

Security shows up moments after the end of the game to escort me to Bryant. I anxiously speed walk to get to him as quickly as possible. On the field, he turns to me, smirks, and sprints toward me. He picks me up, spins us around, and lowers me to kiss him as my feet continue to dangle in the air. He's sweaty and gross, but I couldn't care less.

God, He won the Super Bowl. His dad would be incredibly proud of him. I hope his mom, who understandably couldn't make it to the game, can see her son on TV and is cheering him on from home.

"What did Coach say?" I ask.

Bryant presses his forehead against mine as his green eyes meet my blues. There's moisture in them. "He said Dad was with me."

"Yeah, babe."

"You think?"

"You think your dad would miss his son playing in the Super Bowl?"

He chuckles through his tears. "No. He's probably talking your dad's ear off though."

I love the thought of our dads being together. "You know those two were arguing the entire game."

    We share a quiet laugh.

    "Do you love me, Coach?"

    "To the moon and back, quarterback."

CHAPTER TWENTY SEVEN

THEN

GRIEF CAN BE A deep, black hole of misery and pain. In the months following his title win, Bryant sinks into that hole. I don't know how to help him. It's hard to stand by and watch him drown in a sea of alcohol. He's partying all the time. At times, I hold his hair while he pukes over our toilet at all hours of the morning. I strip him down, bathe him, and put him to bed because I love him. I'd do just about anything to make him feel better.

"I love you, Coach," he slurs.

I turn my head to stave off the stench of bourbon. "I love you, too, Quarterback," I reply, tears streaming down my face.

He has to pull it together before preseason begins. I just hope the game will help him refocus on our dreams of having a family. For now, I've put our baby dream on the back burner. I started taking my birth control again because he's not ready. He needs more time to process his father's death before he can center his attention on creating a family.

I manage to grab a few hours of shuteye before work the next morning. I leave Bryant in bed to recover from his late night out with some of the other players who live in Los Angeles during the offseason. He says they most often remain indoors at one player or another's home, but sometimes they do go out.

On my drive into work, Priscilla calls which isn't entirely unusual since Bryant signed with her the day after his win. His daily hangover and recovery leave him out of touch before noon each day.

"Good morning," I greet.

"Sorry to bother, Zhanna. I tried to reach out to Bryant first, but there's no answer."

"He had another late night."

"Did you get a chance to talk to him about therapy? I think it would do him some good."

"Not yet. He's been irritable, and I haven't found the right time to broach the subject."

While Priscilla and I got off on the wrong foot when we initially met years ago, she's become somewhat of an ally in the effort to get Bryant back on track before the preseason begins in two months.

"I have three video game companies vying for his attention. I need him up and dressed in an hour when I'll be over with the first group of techies. They want to give Bryant a gazillion dollars for using his image and name."

Fuck. I'll have to call out of work again today. It's become more common since the Super Bowl win. I fear I'll lose my job if I miss any more unexcused time. Bryant's job is crazy important, not more important than mine, but there's a lot on the line if he fucks up his career. So I call into work and cringe when my boss compassionately advises that I should take a leave of absence for a few weeks to straighten out my home life. I'm thankful for the time, but I know I'm skating on thin ice.

I rush home and rouse Bryant from sleep. He looks at the clock on his nightstand. "What are you doing here?"

I take a deep breath and audibly release it. "I took the day off again. Priscilla needs you up and dressed. The video game creators are coming to schmooze you."

I leave my seat on the side of the bed and begin to change out of my scrubs.

"You're mad."

I'm so glad he takes notice of something other than the bottle.

"My boss told me to take a leave of absence. I'm close to losing my job because of all the time I've missed."

"Shit. I'm sorry, babe, but I'm glad you'll be here today. You know when they're bullshitting me."

I roll my eyes, glad I'm turned away from him, and try not to cry. I hate disappointing people, especially my boss. I feel guilty each time I miss work.

I step into our massive walk-in closet, plucking jeans and one of Bryant's replica jerseys in my size from the rack.

False Start

He comes up behind me and wraps his arms around me. "Let's do something just you and me tonight. We need to spend some quality time together." He kisses the side of my neck and places a hand on my hip. "Fuck, I need to be inside you."

He places his dick against my back. Considering he hasn't wanted sex in the past few months, I'm rather surprised he's in the mood. He's usually too hungover or passed out drunk to want it.

"Priscilla will be here any minute."

"I don't give two shits about Priscilla hearing me fuck my wife in my house or anywhere for that matter."

Months without it and this is how he talks to me to get me in the mood? "You'll have to wait until the day is done."

I leave the closet in search of my flip flops with him on my heels. "I need you, Z."

The desperation in his voice reminds me of a terrified child.

It stops me in my tracks. "You have to stop drinking. Do you realize how long it's been since you've touched me?"

"I know it's been a few weeks…"

"Try over three months."

He has the good sense to look sheepish. "I didn't… I guess I hadn't realized it's been that long. I've just been in a dark place."

"I know, and I get it. I've been where you are, and I didn't have to play the biggest game of my life two weeks after. I can't imagine how awful it was when all you wanted to do was hide from the world and grieve, but alcohol isn't the answer, QB. Staying out all night and partying has to stop. You're a married man. I've tried to be understanding, but really, what wife is okay with their husband being God only knows where without her? Would you be okay with me doing the same four or five nights a week?"

His jaw tenses. "No."

"Something has to change."

He takes a step forward and touches his hand to my cheek. "You're scaring me."

"I'm not trying to. I think you should talk to someone about your dad, and please know I'm always here for you to talk to as well. But I'm not a professional. I can only tell you my story and hold your hand while you deal with his loss, but baby, you have to deal with it."

"I know. I'll find someone tomorrow after the gamers leave. I promise."

I release a breath it feels like I've been holding since his dad died. For the rest of the day, Bryant keeps me close. He's never handled me being upset with him particularly well. He touches me more than he's touched me in months. I can't help but bask under his attention after being starved of it for so long.

The third group of techies after Bryant's image bring a bottle of bourbon with them and insist on breaking out the bottle, even after I decline their initial invitation to open it. I don't think Bryant is an alcoholic, but he's certainly using alcohol as a way to deal with his problems. His poor liver needs a chance to detox after his three-month binge. He doesn't take the many hints I drop that he should put the fucking glass down. Nope. He continues to refill that bad boy until the six men in the room are all half drunk.

Priscilla's own smile is tight as she watches her drunk client sing karaoke with the nerds. As the night goes on, the louder the lyrics become, the tighter her smile grows.

I resign myself to going to bed alone tonight. I have a mind to lock him out of the room to keep him from stinking up the damn sheets, but I leave it open after I wish everyone a good night. Poor Priscilla has to stay up until everyone has had their fun. I don't envy her job one bit.

I don't often talk to my dad, but as I lie down at one a.m. I reach out and ask for help to protect the man I love and bring him out of the dark place his grief has opened in his heart. I hope like hell Bryant will get his act together before he ruins his career.

Not sleeping well, I dream of Bryant getting injured on the field because he's hungover. The heartache, even in my dreams, keeps me on the edge of consciousness.

The noises filtering from downstairs stop two hours after I lie down. I hope it means Bryant has told everyone to go home. I continue to doze lightly while I wait for him to slide in behind me and wrap his hand around my hip like he does every morning he stumbles in, but Bryant doesn't show.

False Start

I worry about him locking up the house after guests leave when he's been drinking. We live in a great neighborhood, but it's still Los Angeles, so I roll out of bed and make myself use the bathroom before I head for the first floor.

Downstairs, all the lights are off, but the moon shines through the many skylights and large windows in the home. I still love our home, but it's too big for us. It'll feel much more cozy when there's little ones taking up space.

"Fuck, yeah," I hear someone whisper as I quietly walk down the stairs. "That's it."

When I reach the large foyer at the bottom of the steps, I walk across the white marble floor, and flip on the light. I look to my right into the living room and find Bryant sprawled out on the couch. I blink once, twice, three times, and open my mouth to scream, but I can't manufacture any sound.

I stand there frozen to the spot as Priscilla sits between my husband's legs and bobs her head up and down on his dick. His eyes are closed with her back to me. Neither of them notices me or the foyer light.

I'm sleeping. I'm dreaming. This isn't happening, and yet, I can't stop watching or stop my heart from shattering into a million pieces in my chest. And, if this all isn't bad enough, Bryant's hand is on top of her head encouraging her up and down his shaft. He's just as into the act as her.

"Fuck," he moans. "Suck my cock, baby. Good girl." He throws an arm over his eyes and shoves her face down hard into his lap. "I'm coming. Drink it up, girl."

The choking sound that leaves me as chest pains simultaneously rip through my body alerts Bryant to my presence. He squints around the room. Priscilla either didn't hear me or doesn't care as she continues to slurp and gag. Bryant's green eyes are unfocused and bloodshot as he lazily searches the room. Before his eyes land on me, they close again. He relaxes as he enjoys his orgasm in another woman's mouth.

Somewhere in this world, another woman is feeling my pain right now. She's discovering the man she loves doesn't love her in return, or at least not enough to remain sober and faithful. I feel for her.

My soul suddenly feels empty as rage courses through my veins, replacing any rational thoughts in my head. I take a few steps to the center of the foyer to a large round table. In the middle of the table sits a huge, beautiful floral arrangement Bryant has brought in every few weeks. The crystal vase he insisted on buying costs more than most people's salary for a few months. It's a waste of money in my opinion. I remove the long-stemmed flowers and toss them to the floor. The soft foliage doesn't make a sound as it hits the marble, but the vase is another story.

Beyond the couch where Bryant sits are gorgeous floor-to-ceiling windows, and I can't think of a better place for the vase to be. I might be a woman. I might not have ever played professional football, but I'm a fucking Hale. I reach back with the large vase in my hand and throw it like a rocket as hard as I can at the massive windows behind them.

Large sheets of glass shatter and fall like rain. The resulting sound is louder than I imagined it would be. It's actually quite deafening, but I can't find it in me to flinch or give one fuck about anything but the anger I want to use to set the motherfucking house on fire.

Bryant and Priscilla disengage and cover their heads as glass skitters across the marble floor of the living room, reaching as far as the foyer. With bare feet, I walk across the shards of glass until I reach Priscilla cowering in front of Bryant. My husband looks up at me with shock in his eyes that morphs into absolute horror as I reach down, grab Priscilla by the back of the hair, and escort her to the front door.

"Let go, you crazy bitch!" She screams as she claws at my hand.

I twist harder, causing her neck to bend at an unnatural angle, and hold her that way until we reach the front door of the mansion. I open the door, yank her back for good measure, and whisper in her ear, "If I ever see you again, I'll snap your neck in two. Now fuck off." I push her through the door, slamming it behind her.

Bryant is swaying in the middle of the living room gazing at me.

"Baby," he singsongs.

I hold my hand up to stop him. "Don't."

"Is not what it wooks wike," he slurs and almost falls over when he holds a finger in the air.

This is not the man I fell in love with. The man I fell in love with would never do this to me or us. He would never compromise what we have for a fucking blow job. How far the mighty have fallen.

"I watched you come in her mouth. So save your bullshit for somebody else. Put your dick back in your pants. You make me fucking sick." I turn for the stairs and walk back across the glass.

"Your feet!" he yells, stumbling and attempting to put himself back in his pants.

"You're yelling about my feet with your dick hanging out of your pants? You're standing here talking to me about my fucking feet when your dick is still wet from another woman? You don't give a shit about my feet!"

I feel every slice in the bottom of my feet, but shards are everywhere and can't be avoided. Besides, the pain is nothing compared to excruciating ache in my heart. I need to get far away from him before I do something stupid. I need to leave this place and figure out how to breathe again before I completely fall apart. I rush up the stairs, take my nightgown off, and dig through our closet for clothes. I lock myself behind our bathroom door and pick the glass out of my feet before I dress.

Bryant knocks at the door. "Baby. We need to talk."

We don't need to talk. I'm done talking. He did the unthinkable.

"Z!!! Are you okay in there?"

No. I'm dying, slowly dying inside. Soon, there'll be nothing left of me, and I'll wither away until I'm numb and dead inside. I stand in front of the double vanity and watch the tears silently cascade down my face, one after the other.

A thud sounds against the door followed by another and another before the door comes crashing down into our large bathroom. Bryant stands on the other side swaying from side to side, disheveled and out of breath.

"You didn't say anything!" he shouts, but I can barely make out his thick drunk words. "There's blood all over the fucking house. I didn't know if you were okay or not. Fuck!" He pulls at his hair and grunts in frustration.

I walk past him, slipping my shoes on.

"Baby.' Bryant reaches for me.

I wrench my arm away from him which nearly knocks him over. "Don't you dare fucking touch me! Never again!"

"You don't mean that."

Leaving our room and taking the grand staircase two steps at a time. I need to leave here and get away from him before I hurt him.

"Zhanna. What are you doing?"

I round the corner of the kitchen and pick up my purse from the bar, digging through the contents of my bag in search of my keys to no avail.

"Where the fuck are they?" I murmur.

"Coach."

"No!" I scream at the top of my lungs and throw my purse at him. "Don't you dare call me that!"

It hits him in the nose as he shouts and grabs it. "Fucking shit, Zhanna!" Blood pours from underneath his hand as he reaches for a paper towel.

"Fucking shit, Zhanna, huh? Fucking shit, Zhanna? Fuck you! You're a piece of shit!"

I take two steps to the left, open the cabinet door, and pick up the first dessert plate my hand touches. I throw that motherfucker across the room at his ass. It feels so damn good when it hits him in the head and bounces across the way. In fact, I relish bringing the pain to him as I see red and start throwing plate after plate at him. When I run out of those, I reach for the appetizer plates. At first, he attempts to block the incessant blows that just keep coming.

"Fucking stop!" he howls.

"Stop? You want me to stop?' I ask as I reach for the salad bowls.

He dives behind the bar, but it doesn't deter me from my mission to cause him a fraction of the pain I feel inside all the way down to my bones.

"Baby, you have to stop. We'll talk. Let me… fuck!" He yells as he takes a bowl to the brow bone and ducks down below the bar again. "Zhanna, I'm drunk. Can we talk about this in the morning?"

"In the morning?!! I won't fucking be here in the morning!" I shout so loud my voice cracks. "Oh my God! What the fuck did you do?!! How could you do this to us?!!" I scream and sob through my hoarse voice. "You killed us!!!"

"No, baby," he says, his own voice heavy with emotion as he stands from behind the bar and almost falls over again. "We're never gonna be done."

I drop the large dinner plate and let it crash to the floor. It rolls across the kitchen and stops at the back door where it spins to a stop like a bottle top. The fight leaves me. I'm fatigued beyond measure, and my heart suddenly isn't in it anymore.

A knock sounds at our front door, but neither of us moves. It comes again, but I can't seem to move the muscles in my body. It's too painful to breathe. It simply hurts to be alive. I'd welcome death if it knocked on my door just to ease my excruciating pain.

The knock sounds again. Bryant moves to answer it, but before he does it opens.

"L.A.P.D.! Anyone home?" a male officer identified himself.

"Here," Bryant says, but he's around the corner now so I don't see.

"We have an assault complaint from an unidentified female. She claims to have been inside the home when your wife assaulted her... holy shit...What happened to your windows?"

"It was an accident," Bryant lies.

Who knows if his drunk ass truly knows what's going on.

"Sir, have you been drinking?" asks the officer.

"Yes."

"Wait, aren't you Bryant Hudson?"

"Yes. Listen, my wife kicked a guest out of our home, but she didn't assault her. Is there any way we can clear this up later this afternoon?"

Several flashlights shine across the living room to me in the kitchen. "Did your wife break the windows?"

"It was an accident."

"Where is she, sir?"

I step around the kitchen into their view. "Here."

"Mrs. Hudson?"

"Hale," I answer.

"Zhanna, baby, no." Bryant starts for me, but one of the five officers now in our home steps between us.

It seems like five officers turn into ten in a heartbeat. There's a flurry of activity around me, but I'm not here anymore. I'm somewhere deep in my mind where it's safe, where it doesn't hurt, where the world still makes sense.

I'm not sure how long I stare at my shoes before a set of hands gently grip both of my wrists and pull them together in front of me.

"Zhanna Hudson, you're under arrest. You have the right to remain silent."

CHAPTER TWENTY EIGHT

THEN

THE LOUD, OBNOXIOUS BUZZING of the jail door wakes me up. The sound of heavy footsteps grows closer with each step.

Otto stops in front of my cell. "I've heard the old saying 'Hell hath no fury like a woman scorned'. Never seen it until now. Don't like the look of it. So I imagine he did something pretty rotten to deserve that level of ire from you."

I can't find the words to tell him what Bryant did. I can't even bring myself to move from the cot.

He nods and looks away as though seeing me in pain is too hard for him. "Never figured him for that type of fella."

Neither did I, not in a million years.

"Let's get you out of here, sweetie. I don't like the look of you in this place."

I manage to pull myself together and follow my godfather out of the cell. He doesn't take me to the house I share with Bryant, but to a swanky hotel in the downtown area instead. Zina is waiting inside the suite with a man I don't know, but judging by the suit, he's a lawyer.

My sister immediately crosses the room and hugs my neck tightly. "I'm so sorry, sis."

The man in the room is indeed an attorney who introduces himself as Ned Combs. I miss most of what the short, stocky man with a barrel chest says. I'm lost somewhere in the scenes that continue to play out in my head from the moment I heard Bryant on the stairs until law enforcement placed cuffs on me.

This has to be a bad dream. Bryant, even drunk, wouldn't do this to me. He wouldn't sacrifice all we are and will be for Priscilla, or anyone for the matter.

"Zhanna?" Otto calls out to me.

"Yeah?" I ask, and my voice comes out quiet, meek, defeated.

"Mr. Combs asked how you'd like to proceed."

Zina reaches over and places her hand on top of mine to stop me from fidgeting. "I think the first step is taking care of legal matters. Relationship issues can wait until Zhanna has had a chance to catch her breath."

Apparently Ned is golf buddies with the presiding judge over my criminal case, and she happens to be a divorced woman in her fifties with a bad taste in her mouth from her last husband. He cheated. She might be forgiving, or at least, I hope she is. If I'm convicted, I could lose my physical therapist's license, and then I'm going to prison for murdering both my ex and his lover.

"I want a divorce. Quickly." I announce.

"It takes six months for a divorce in California if he doesn't contest it," Ned advises.

"How soon can you draw up the paperwork and have him served?"

"With his fortune?"

"I don't want a dime."

Ned chokes, coughs, and sputters. "There will be legal fees."

"I can cover your fees from my inheritance, or Bryant can pay them. After all, it's his fault we're in this mess." I stand and walk across the room to the balcony. For half a second, I think about opening the doors and jumping over the railing, but my suicide won't solve anything. "Also, I'll pay for the damage I caused to the house."

"It will go a long way in appeasing the judge."

The next day the Honorable Adele Kants dismisses criminal charges against me since Bryant nor Priscilla press the issue. Bryant turns down my attorney's offer to fix the home, and he insists on paying my legal fees. I don't turn down his generosity because it'd require me to speak to him, and I'm not ready. I don't have anything to say, not after he destroyed us.

But I have to face him to gather some of my belongings, and while Otto and Zina both offer to go with me, it's best they don't see the showdown it's likely to be.

False Start

A week after the incident, I return to our home alone. I don't call or ask for permission, and part of me hopes he's not here. Part of me hopes I can dissolve this marriage without making it any messier than it already is.

I don't pull all the way down the drive to the large multi-car garage. Instead, I park near the front door, using my key to go in that way. I've never used this door to enter the home, and I suddenly feel like a stranger walking inside. The tall, wooden door echoes as I close it, the sound of my boot heels bouncing off the walls. The house was always too big for us, but we made it work.

I walk past the grand staircase and stare at it like it personally harmed me. I'll never be able to be in this foyer or on those steps without remembering what he said to her. Beyond the foyer in the living room is a large wall of plastic sheeting where the glass windows previously existed. In the middle of the room is the white sectional couch where I found him and Priscilla.

Bryant comes around the corner from the kitchen. "I was in the garage. I thought you'd come through that way."

I can't bear to look at him, so I look down at his bare feet instead. "I parked out front."

Neither of us says a word as silence stretches between us. Never has the air been so stiff and tense between us, but tonight, it's suffocating and thick.

"Can we talk?" he finally asks, and when I don't respond, he continues, "I tried to bail you out, but Otto beat me to it. Zina asked me to let you breathe for a little while, but I've been leaving you messages to let you know I was worried about you and thinking of you."

Yeah, he was real fucking worried about me. I turn on my heels and head for the stairs. Looking at them makes me want to vomit, but I manage to climb them quickly enough.

"Zhanna!" he calls after me.

There's nothing to talk about. What's he going to do? Apologize? No, thank you. Apologies don't fix something of this magnitude.

I speed walk down the wide hallway to our bedroom, entering the closet before pulling out every bag I can find between us.

Bryant comes into the closet and takes the bags from me. "We're not divorcing."

As I pull clothes from hangers and drawers, I scream. "I can't fucking stand to look at you!" He comes closer, so I jab my finger in his face. "Don't you dare touch me, not after you touched her."

His voice cracks, broken and full of emotion. "Zhanna, baby, please don't go. We can work through things. It's me and you. We can survive this."

I shake my head. "No. Not this."

"How am I supposed to live without you?"

"I guess you should've asked yourself that when your dick was in another woman's mouth."

"I don't remember shit except you throwing the vase through the window."

"And why is that, Bryant? Why do you not remember anything? Because you were drunk? A-fucking-gain?"

He has the decency to look sheepish. "I deserve that."

I laugh. "You deserve so much more. You've fucked up everything."

I shove clothes into bags and suitcases before removing them from the closet. He follows me from the closet, through the bedroom, and out in the hall where I begin a stack of my belongings.

"Z, we'll go to counseling and work through it. I swear to everything holy, I'll never put myself in the same predicament again."

"It's too late. You can't ever fix this, Bryant. You can't take it back. You can't make it stop hurting. I can't stop seeing it on repeat in my head."

The images from that night assault me and nearly take my breath away. I push through, shaking the thoughts from my head as I head back to the closet for another bag. Then his words, *Fuck, suck my cock, baby. Good girl. I'm coming. Drink it up, good girl.*

Fuck. I can't breathe. My chest feels tight. I bend at the waist to pick the bag up, but it suddenly weighs a ton.

"Zhanna?"

False Start

I feel dizzy as I stand up straight and reach out for the wall to steady me.

"Baby, breathe." He touches my arm, but I fight against his contact. "Please sit down before you pass out."

Panic attack. I had one when my father died. Just one. It's all I needed to have to know I'm having another. I push myself from the room, waging a war against my anxiety, and pull away from him as he continues to try to help me. I have to get away from him. I can't be here anymore.

I abandon all of my clothing and hold onto the staircase railing for support. I can hear Bryant's pleas to get off the steps before I hurt myself, but he sounds so far away. When the front door is just in reach, I stumble, dizzy from hyperventilating.

Outside my car, I fumble with my keys as I try to escape the place that has quickly become my personal hell.

Bryant snatches them from my hand. "You can't drive like this."

"Give me my keys!" I scream and launch myself at him. I beat and pound against his chest as I reach for my keys, my freedom, my escape from this place and from him. "I hate that you did this! I hate that you let another woman have you!"

Tears roll down his face as his sad green eyes watch me fall apart in our driveway. He reaches for me, hand behind my head, and pulls me to his chest. "Shhh, baby. Come 'ere."

I fight against his hold, beat against his chest with my closed fists, and scream and sob at the top of my lungs. Nothing coming out of my mouth is coherent anymore. My pain has shut down parts of my brain. He's talking to me, but I can't hear him over the screams in my head. Grief and anger consume my tormented soul.

I deliver the final blow. "Your touch makes my skin crawl. Your voice makes me want to puke, and seeing you just makes me want to scream. I hope I never see you again."

"You don't mean that. You're mad, and you have every right to be, but we'll get through this because we love each other."

I close my eyes, take a deep breath, and steel myself. When I open them, I straighten my back and square my shoulders. "If I never see you again, it'll be too fucking soon."

The resolve in my eyes and the finality in my voice causes him to stiffen against me. He releases me and stumbles back, eyes unfocused and brows furrowed in disbelief.

"I hate you— the air you breathe, the ground you walk on, and your fucking name— I hate you."

Bryant swallows hard and attempts to speak but doesn't produce any sound.

I step over to him and snatch my keys from his hands. I swear if I pushed him, he'd fall over from shock. Now he knows how I felt the other night.

"Zhanna," he whispers and searches my eyes.

He can't believe it's really the end, and there's a small part of me still in denial as well.

"I'll send for my things."

I leave him standing in the drive. Pulling through the gate, I look back to see him on his knees with his hands in his hair.

CHAPTER TWENTY NINE

THEN

WHEN YOU DIVORCE THE Super Bowl Champ, the fans are going to choose a side, and it's most likely going to be his side. I've learned in the few months I've been home in New Orleans that Bryant Hudson will always be Louisiana's golden boy. While the details of our divorce have remained out of the news, the masses have speculated why two college sweethearts would suddenly fall out of love—him cheating is the number one reason most people have suspected. It's difficult not to confirm those suspicions when there are cameras in my face and reporters shouting inappropriate questions at me in public.

I don't leave the house. I can't even go to the grocery store without seeing both of our faces plastered all over magazines and papers. Every channel on the television seems to report it, and his face is on every fucking billboard in New Orleans it seems.

After two weeks of sleeping in Zina's guest room and moping around her apartment, I throw a little of my energy into finding a place of my own. I've always wanted to live in the Quarter. I'm drawn to its mysterious, historical nature.

It's impossible not to be reminded of the reason for the ache in my chest and the nausea in my gut. He tries to call every day, several times a day. Zina took care of having my things shipped to her place, and we left Los Angeles hours after I left him in the drive on his knees.

Zina, who loves him like the brother she never had, is hurting. She's devastated with the turn of events, but she's been my rock. My mom has also been equally amazing in supporting me. She's even offered for me to come home, but I'm much more comfortable at my sister's. I feel a bit more free to break down when I need to.

A loud, incessant knock at the apartment's front door diverts my attention from my tearfulness. I immediately suspect Bryant's on the other side. I knew it was only a matter of time before he showed up. I'm surprised it took him two weeks.

I creep quietly to the entrance and look through the peephole.

Bryant isn't on the other side of the door, but a large African American man is.

His deep voice makes me jump out of my skin. "Delivery!"

I open the door. "I think you have the wrong address."

He puts his hands on his hips and purses his lips in displeasure. His royal purple and yellow striped muumuu sways somewhere around his knees. "Suga, what are you wearing?"

I look down at my sweatpants, oversized sweatshirt, and mouse house slippers. I look back up at him and shrug. "I'm going through a divorce."

"Ew, girl. This is not the time to let your guard down." He snaps his fingers in the air to the left and then to the right. "You don't let a silly little thing like divorce leave you in this condition. It's time to get it together, honey child." He pushes past me into the apartment, spins around, gives me another perusal, and flares his nostrils. "How long have you been like… this?" He waves a hand in my direction.

"Two weeks."

Why is this dude in my sister's apartment?

"Did he cheat?"

I tear up at the "c" word. "Yeah."

"He cheated two weeks ago?"

My bottom lip quivers. "Yeah."

"Damn," he says as though he's resigned himself to something. "That's tough. No wonder you look like you've been hit by the ugly cry truck." He narrows his eyes at me. "Wait a minute… you're that girl!"

He pulls his phone from his pocket, taps on the screen with his long nails until his eyes widen, and holds the phone up to compare the photograph to me. "Yeah, it's you. Oooo-wee, Mr. Football Star did a number on you. Who did he cheat with?"

"His agent. In our house. While I was sleeping."

"You caught 'em?"

"Yeah." I sniffle.

"That's fucked. You need a drink. Shit, I need a drink." Then he's off to Zina's kitchen, opening and closing cabinets in search of alcohol.

"She keeps it in the freezer."

"Who is she?" he asks, heading for the freezer and plucking a bottle of tequila from it.

"My sister, Zina."

He locates two shot glasses in Zina's kitchen, pours us a drink, walks it over to me, and hands me the glass seconds before he clicks his own against the side of mine. "Leslie."

"Zhanna."

"Pleasure, Suga. Now, talk to Uncle Leslie. What are your plans? We need plans if you're going to move past this."

I shrug again. "It's only been two weeks."

Leslie takes my glass and places it beside his on the counter near the tequila bottle. "Nuh-uh. Universal breakup rules say you get a week for relationships lasting less than a year and two weeks for anything more. Then it's time to reinvent yourself and say 'fuck that motherfucker'." He places his hands back on his hips. "Now, let me hear you say it."

"Fuck that motherfucker," I muster.

His right brow nearly hits his hairline. "It just won't do. Give me more moxie than that. The motherfucker cheated on you in your own house. So. Let. Me. Hear. You. Say. It."

"Fuck that motherfucker!" I growl.

He shakes his head, clearly not impressed with my level of anger. His index finger is in the air signaling for me to hold for a moment. "We need more tequila. What's your tolerance like?"

"I'm a cheap date."

"Wonderful. Drink up."

We take two shots this time, warming my cheeks a few moments later. I feel a little better, a little number, and even a slight inclination to smile. Leslie takes me by the hand leads me to the guest room where he tells me to get into the shower. He could be a serial killer for all I know, prepping my body for torture and dismemberment, but I get in the shower and clean myself.

When I emerge with a robe around me, Leslie is looking through what appears to be all of my clothing in the closet and drawers.

"At least you have style."

"Thank you?"

He throws a pair of dark wash jeans at me, a black tank top, and a mustard cardigan. I turn around for the bathroom to change and talk to him through the door as I do.

"It's nice you have a sister to take you in. Will you stay here?"

I love Zina, but we both like having our own spaces. "No, I'll look for a place in the Quarter."

"I know of a place."

"You do?"

After I dress, Leslie blows my hair out, curls it, and uses my make-up to do things to my face that should be illegal. I look amazing when he's done. He's somehow hidden the dark circles under my eyes. "You clean up nice, Suga."

"There's a townhouse next to me for sale. Are you in the buyer's market?"

"Yes."

"I must warn you, the place needs a little TLC, but it has good bones and nice residents."

"I can do TLC."

He grins from ear to ear, quite pleased with his work on me. "Girl, you need to get laid and a good project to focus on."

Getting laid isn't high on my priority list at the moment, but a project seems promising. I send Zina a text message with Leslie's vehicle registration number as I leave her apartment with a perfect stranger and head for the Quarter.

On the way to what I hope isn't a dilapidated home, Leslie chatters. He talks about everything from the club he works at during the week as a performer to his friends at the club. Leslie loves a little drama.

When we arrive at his place, he lets us inside. His vibe is eclectic with a lot of animal prints and shaggy covered chairs. I have no idea how a man of his height and size can sit in the dainty chairs without them breaking. We walk through the living room into a large kitchen with an island in the middle.

Leslie opens a drawer, reaches inside, and produces a key. "I used to help care for the old tenant. She was elderly. Still have the key."

"Are we supposed to be in the home?"

"The place isn't on the market, Suga. The former tenant passed, and her son asked that I only show it to those who would be a good fit. Mrs. Brownstone didn't want just anyone living in her home."

He leads me through a courtyard to the other townhome. Inside the air is stale and musty from sitting vacant.

"How long has it been empty?" I ask.

"Mrs. Brownstone has been gone just over a year."

I can tell from the hitch in his voice that he loved the woman and misses her dearly.

I explore the home with him, going upstairs to check out the three bedrooms, and downstairs for the master bedroom and bath, kitchen, and den. There's a sunroom off the kitchen where I can curl up and read a book as I bask in the rays. I can see myself here. I can see Leslie being my neighbor.

"I love it."

"You do?"

"Yes. The floors need to be redone and the carpet ripped up. The cabinets in the kitchen and the tile in the bathrooms need updating. It needs a lot of paint, more love, and elbow grease, but I'm in love with it. If you think I'm a good fit, I'd love to have it inspected to make sure the bones are solid."

Leslie, a man I don't often think smirks, smirks at me. I imagine it must be lonely living next to a vacant home where a deceased friend lived. "Suga, I think you need this as much as I do."

***

IT TAKES A FEW weeks for the inspection to come back. Mrs.

Brownstone's townhome has good bones, but needs updated electrical and plumbing, something I suspected before the inspection was complete. It's an old place. The former owner's son flies in to complete the sale a few weeks later, and I begin moving my things inside the townhome the next day.

I manage to have a bed delivered for my first night, and Leslie insists we shop the next day for furniture. By day he's an interior designer. He's actually quite sought after in the area, so I gladly accept his help to fill my home with furniture and decor. I decide on a French Country style for the house, and we hit markets and stores for weeks until every room is brimming with the pieces it needs to make it comfy and homey.

When the house is decorated and full, I have nothing else to focus on. On a Friday night when my new neighbor and friend is working at his night job, I climb the stairs to the second floor. I stand in the hall, looking into each of the perfectly arranged rooms, and I feel empty inside. I feel alone in this world. I miss Bryant. I miss our love and our relationship. This house should be full of him and children.

There's no one to hear me cry as I silently hit my knees and sob for all I've lost. It feels like I need to rip him from my soul to finally get away from him, but I don't know how. I don't know how to separate him from me because he was a part of me for so long. I'm not sure how long I sit on my knees and cry, but I eventually calm myself to a sniffle before I take the stairs back down to my room and climb under the covers to hide from the world.

***

"ZHANNA!" LESLIE AND ZINA both yell.

"I'm coming in!" Leslie shouts.

The two of them pop inside my room moments later.

I really need to get the key back from Leslie.

"Suga, we've been calling. Something wrong with your phone?" he asks as he dials my number on his phone.

I only know it's my number he dials because it dances and rings on my nightstand.

"Mmmhmm. I see. Well, it's time for an intervention. You stink. You're not answering your calls, and my beautiful ass should never be ignored. It makes me gassy."

I cover my head with the duvet and groan.

Zina rips the covers off. "Leslie is right. You have to do something other than sleep all day."

It's been a few months since I moved in. I haven't handled the breakup all that well. I'm trying, but every morning when I wake I find I'd rather stay in bed, so I do. "I'm tired."

"No, Suga, you've got the blues," Leslie sings.

"Otto's on the way over. Says he needs to talk."

"I don't feel good. Tell him to come back tomorrow." It's not a total lie.

Leslie puts his tough face on, slings his dreads behind his head, and shakes his finger at me. "You a sad sack of shit. You want to be a sad sack of shit for the rest of your life?"

I frown at him and whine. "No?"

"Well, you're gonna be if you don't get your ass out of the damn bed." He paces back and forth by my bed. "I can't do this no more, Suga. I can't watch Mr. Football Star tear you down like this. You know what you need? You need a shower, tequila, dick, and a job."

"In that order?" I ask.

He stops pacing. "Yes, girl, in that order. Now go get your narrow behind under the water and put some soap on your ass."

"Fine!" I shout. These two aren't leaving me alone until I'm clean and talk to Otto.

I shower and when I emerge, Otto's in my living room waiting for me.

He stands to hug and place a kiss on my cheek. "You've lost weight."

"Have I?"

He frowns at me until Zina clears her throat.

It seems to jolt his words loose. "You look great. Listen, we had a therapist turn in his notice this morning, and we have a game Sunday.

He needs to fly out to train with a new job, and we need a PT on the sidelines. The position is yours if you want it."

For the first time in a few months, I feel hopeful. "Work for the Voodoo?"

"Yeah. You're a Hale, girl. The Voodoo loves Zane Hale, and they're jumping at the chance to hire both of his daughters."

"Both?" Zina asks.

Zina works as an athletic trainer at an elite club in New Orleans. She also has several athletes she trains as her personal clients, but her dream has always been to work as a trainer in the league.

"I can't offer one of you a job and not the other," Otto replies.

I launch myself off the couch and throw my arms around Otto's neck. Soon, Zina follows suit, and we double team him. He chuckles at our affection, and eventually we allow him to breathe again.

"One thing, Zhanna, we're playing the Spartans Sunday."

My whole soul feels heavier the moment he mentions it.

"Perhaps this isn't the best position for me."

"No, nuh-uh, nope. I'm not going to sit by and watch you ruin this because you might see Mr. Football Star. I hope you do see him, and make sure if you do, you show him how good you're doing."

He's right. I can't hide from Bryant forever. I need to start the process of moving on with my life. Fake it until you make it even.

"Okay. I accept."

CHAPTER THIRTY

THEN

AS I ANXIOUSLY WAIT for Sunday to approach, I think of all the possible scenarios I can likely come into contact with Bryant. I don't know if I can hide from him, but Otto's advised the staff to let me tend to injuries in the tent on the sidelines to keep me out of view. I appreciate it. I know I can't hide from him forever, but we haven't seen each other in two and a half months. Game day isn't the most ideal place for us to reunite. It's too public. The sports world and beyond are worried enough about our divorce.

I remain in the tent and out of view for most of the game. There are no injuries in the first half. I wait for the players to leave the field and enter the locker room before I leave the tent at half time. Pulling my hat down, I sneak out through the crowd still milling around the sideline and head for the locker room to check if any of the players need to be taped.

After the break, I follow the team back out to the field with Zina beside me. "He looks terrible."

"I don't care, Zina. I don't fucking care."

I'm livid she still cares for his well-being after what he's done. Rationally, I know I still care too. I wish I didn't. You can't just stop loving someone at the drop of a dime, but I'm faking it until I make it.

I hide inside the tent for the third quarter and tend to a hamstring injury during the latter part of the quarter. The last quarter of the game brings in three injuries in a row.

With three minutes left in the game, someone yells, "All hands on deck."

My direct supervisor, Brandon, pokes his head inside the injury tent. "I need you on the field, Hale."

I don't hesitate but for a second, but my hesitation could cost the player dearly. I feel guilty and horrible about it as I make my way to the field beside Brandon. A tailback is on the ground, unmoving, and images of my father lying on the field unmoving resurface. I shake the thoughts from my mind and focus on the player I kneel beside.

"He's been out since he went down," a paramedic reports.

There's not a lot I can do with the man being unconscious, but I can monitor and assess to assist the process of removing him from the field. When he's put on a board with his neck and spine protected, we lift him to a gurney and wheel him off the field. It's rare that a player leaves this way. It's every mom's and wife's nightmare, but it does happen.

"Zhanna?!!" I hear my name distantly, but I know who it is.

I hold my head down and continue to the Voodoo side of the field until I make it to the tent. I almost have a panic attack waiting for Bryant to come through, but he never does. I remain inside the tent until the commotion of the Voodoo win allows me a moment to escape the field undetected.

I make it through the game and the hours after as I help a few players with exercises to relieve pain, but I do it on autopilot. I'm going through the motions as the sound of my name on his tongue continues to haunt me. I've not heard his voice in months, never realizing the effect it has on me until now

"Zhanna." Otto sneaks up, scaring me.

"Yeah?" I ask, turning around.

"Our tailback is gonna be alright."

Walking out to the employee parking lot with a few players and coaches to be safe, I drive home. It seems like every song that plays on the radio reminds me of him. I welcome the reprieve of silencing it. At home, I slip inside the dark house and undress in the moonlight of my bedroom windows. I want to crawl between my sheets and go to sleep so this day will be over.

The bell at the front door rings. I suspect it's him at this late hour. He has the resources to find me if he really wants to, and I've not gone through the trouble to hide my location from anyone.

I open the door in my silk robe and look into his beautiful, pale green eyes.

"Zhanna…," he starts with wide eyes, "I didn't think you'd open."

God. Why is he still so gorgeous?

"It's late." I pull my robe tighter.

"It was you on the field."

"Yes."

"You're working for Otto?"

"Yes."

A pregnant pause has me looking away from the pain in his eyes. I can't let it affect me. I have to be strong.

His voice is raw. "I'm dying without you, Coach."

"No!" I shout and stand on my toes to get in his face. "You don't get to call me that. My name is Zhanna to you now."

He swallows hard as a tear leaks from his eye. "Baby, you've lost weight."

The rage has lain dormant for months now, suffocating underneath the weight of my depression. Now that he's here, I can't seem to contain it. It curls around the base of my neck, heating my face and blood.

"Yeah? It's probably because you broke my fucking heart. You did more than that. You obliterated my entire soul and left me empty. You did that. So I don't have much of an appetite because I still can't seem to stomach what you did to us."

"I'm in therapy. I've stopped drinking and partying. I know I put myself in a bad position that night, but you can rest assured it'll never happen again."

"No, I can't. And that's the problem. I can't be sure of anything. I was sure—the surest wife there was—that you'd never cheat and look where we ended up."

"I put myself in a bad spot, Z. I know I did that to us, but let me spend the rest of my life making it up to you."

"I can't do this with you." A sob breaks through as I turn to go inside.

His hand snakes inside the crook of my elbow. "Wait! Please don't go yet. I haven't seen you in months, and I just need…"

"You need? You need what?!! Because I don't owe you shit, not after what you did."

He holds his hands up in surrender as he pleads, "Please just listen, baby."

"I'm not your baby anymore."

He reaches for me, wrapping me in a bear hug as I fight against his hold. "Baby, stop. Just listen. I love you. Okay? I know you're hurting, and I know I'm the cause of it. I'd give anything to change what I did. Anything to hold you again, so please just give me a minute to do that. Then I'll leave you alone."

I wish I weren't crying and sniffling. I wish I weren't falling apart in front of him, but it all hits me at once. Him being here in New Orleans is what pushes me over the edge. If he's here, it's real—the separation and divorce. So I hold onto his shirt and sob against his chest, and he shakes as he cries with me.

"God, I'm so fucking sorry, Z."

His voice sounds like home. His cologne smells like every good memory I've ever had. He feels like the only man I've ever loved. The man I was supposed to spend the rest of my life with. It's all gone.

I yearn to feel something other than the deadness inside me. I want something to replace the dull ache in my bones.

"Show me." I pull away and gaze up at him.

He searches my eyes for my meaning and quickly finds his answer. Desperation rolls off him in thick waves. "Baby, we shouldn't do that. We need to sit down and talk. I can find someone to counsel us tonight if you're willing. We can find our way back from this."

We can't, and one day, he'll realize he fucked our future up when he allowed her to put her mouth on him. He'll realize he went too far and we reached a point of no return.

"Take it or leave it, Quarterback."

He considers me for a long moment, bites on his lip, and attempts to speak a few times before he does. "You know I'll take whatever scraps you throw my way, but for the record, I…"

I cut him off when I wrap my arms around his neck and lift myself. He catches me around the waist as I lean forward and press my lips to his neck.

"Fuck, Z."

He thrusts against my center. It's the first thing that's felt good since we split. I crave more and devour him like a starved woman.

"Z, come here," he whispers, asking me to turn my head to kiss him.

The thought of my lips on his…it's too much too fast. I unwrap my legs from his waist, ready to run away. I shouldn't have let it get this far.

He pulls me back against him and thwarts my escape. "You can't kiss me?"

I turn my head away from him and refuse to answer. I swear I can hear his heart break. I wish I had the emotional capacity to empathize with him, but he gutted me and left me empty. There's nothing left. I manage to get away from him and drop my robe, pulling my matching silky purple nightgown over my head. "Here are the scraps. We can do it my way or not at all."

He inches toward me, shy and unsure. With unsteady hands, he reaches out to touch my breast. His hand travels up to my cheek. "Let me kiss you."

"Take it or leave it." I show him my back as I take a few steps toward the couch and bend over with my ass in the air.

"Fuck." He reaches out and caresses both of my cheeks with his hands before he squeezes both sides. His right hand travels to the center of me and his index finger slides up my middle. "Baby, you're so fucking wet."

I hope he doesn't back out. I need this and don't want to go find a random person at a local bar. It seems like a lot of work and risk for a relatively low payoff.

He unzips his pants and presses the length of himself against my ass.

"You need a condom," I tell him, suddenly nervous about having sex with him after spending not only our separation without it, but every day since the Super Bowl.

"Zhanna, I don't own condoms," he says with a bite in his tone. "For fuck's sake, I'm not having sex to need condoms."

I shouldn't believe him. I know, but I do, so I back up and reach between my legs to hold him in my hand. God, he feels good. I line him up at my entrance and push back.

"Jesus fucking Christ," he hisses and immediately stops my progress. "Babe, it's been a minute. You're going to have to go slow."

I can't go slow. I can't let it be that intimate, so I keep an even tempo and listen to him moan my name. I feel him jump inside me and know he's close, but I'm not. I stop and give him a reprieve.

"Thank you," he says, out of breath.

He leans over my back as his hands travel up my sides and over to my breasts. He peppers kisses along my shoulders and the back of my neck. Tears well in my eyes at the tenderness of it. I'm grateful he can't see my face.

"I love you, Zhanna," he whispers.

Then he begins to torture me with slow, long, deep thrusts. If it didn't feel so fucking good, I'd make him speed up. As usual, he plays my body like a fiddle and brings me to the edge of bliss time and again before he finally allows me to crash over. The wait is brutal. He doesn't want it to end, but it has to. I can't keep guarding my heart against this and hope to stand a chance.

I increase the speed. At first, he tries to fight it by grabbing my hips and holding me in place, but I win.

"I'm going to come," he warns.

He begins to meet me thrust for thrust, hard and steady, deep, and long. His hand weaves through my hair as he pulls my head back and presses his lips to my ear. "Feels so fucking good. Are you coming for me again?"

"Yes," I murmur, barely able to form words as I come closer to the cliff of ecstasy.

"That's it, baby. Come for me."

I dive over the cliff, taking him with me. He pulses inside me, filling me with his seed, as he continues to fuck me through my orgasm. I hate that it's the best orgasm of my life. I hate that I can't stop falling apart around him.

When I come down from the stratosphere, he's still hunched over my back, breathing hard to catch his breath. He's still inside me as my shame washes over me. I pull away, step around him, and find my nightgown and robe.

He's still standing in the middle of my living room hanging out of his pants. "Zhanna…"

"Get out."

"We can't just fuck and not talk."

"We very well can because it's all I have left to offer. You ensured that when you came in that bitch's mouth. Now, get out."

He pulls himself together. He tries to lean down to kiss me, but I turn my head. "We're not done, Z."

"We were done the minute the vase went through the window. Lock the door behind you, and for fuck's sake, sign the divorce papers," I say and head for my bedroom to effectively end any further conversation.

I shut my bedroom door, sink to the floor, and cry.

CHAPTER THIRTY ONE

THEN

I'D LIKE TO SAY the last time I was intimate with Bryant was the first night I saw him after we split, but I can't.

How am I supposed to know if a man will take the time to find my G-spot like Bryant seems to do every time we're together? I hear other women talk. I know most men aren't as talented as my ex in the bedroom.

"You've got that look on your face again," Leslie says as I stare into the distance, lost in thought.

I came home from an away game late last night. Leslie always misses Zina and I when we're gone for work.

"What look?"

"Regret. You and Mr. Football Star did the hokey pokey last night."

I roll my eyes. We so did. "I don't know what you're talking about."

Leslie smacks his lips. "Lyin' ass ho."

Zina snorts from across the courtyard as she lounges in a hammock. "She looked like he'd rode her hard when she showed up at the airport. Hard to believe you two have been divorced a year the way you still go at it like rabbits."

"Ew," Leslie says. "Airport bathroom sex?"

I shrug. It's better I let them think it's the only disgusting place we screwed yesterday. I'm ashamed of myself.

"The Holy Spirit has come down and spoken to me, and it has advised me the two of you are bringing your narrow asses to my show tonight. Be cute." He snaps his fingers back and forth, pursing his lips. "Feel yo' self. I go on at 11:00, so have a drink in your hand and your rear end in a seat near the stage by 10:45."

Leslie grills us hamburgers before he takes his ritualistic afternoon beauty nap— his routine before a big show. Zina and I curl up in our respective hammocks and take a nap. I enjoy the quiet of the courtyard Leslie and I fixed up when I first moved here over a year ago. It's nice to have a place in the middle of the city to call my own.

At around six, Zina and I order takeout and shower. By nine, we've had dinner and we're out the door headed to Sparkle— the club Leslie performs at Thursday-Saturday.

I teeter in my heels toward the door of Sparkles and pull at the impossibly short dress Zina insisted I wear. I love being sexy, but there's a way to be classically sexy without looking like a slut. I'm unaccustomed to such attire, but try to appear more comfortable in my own skin than I really am.

Inside at the bar, we start a tab and share a celebratory shot. Leslie and his best friend, Reeva, join us for a few more shots just before the show begins at 10:00.

Leslie rallies us together. "Let's get you to the table."

Reeva, who's much shorter than Leslie, hooks her muscular arm through mine and leads the way. "Move it, bitches."

When we're deposited at our table, we all have one more shot before Reeva and Leslie depart for the backstage area. We wish them luck in their performances. Leslie is the headlining act most nights, and Reeva goes on before him, but we cheer all the guys and girls who come out to sing and dance for us.

"Don't look, but there's a guy in the corner who is staring straight at you," Zina says between Reeva and Leslie's performance.

"It's really hard not to look!" I say over the music.

She chuckles. "He's hot. Oh, shit. I think he's coming to say 'hello'."

I giggle at her words and start to blush. I haven't spoken to a man in years, not since college, not in this way.

"Excuse me," comes a baritone voice. "Can I buy you ladies a drink?"

I turn around with a smile on my face, but my jaw nearly unhinges itself and drops to the floor. A man approaches us with a kind smile and beautiful hazel eyes.

"I think we can pour you a drink," Zina says and nudges me.

"Hi!" I wave. "I'm Zhanna, and that's Zina."

"Dalton. You must be sisters."

I laugh. "Yes! We are!"

He laughs back. He's a very attractive guy. I offer him a seat at our table and soon, Leslie comes out and sings five songs as the headlining act. He dances and sings like a professional as he wins the crowd over.

When the show is over, Dalton invites Zina and I to his table in the back corner. Zina passes to go back to the dressing room to hang out with the performers

"I'm going to the ladies."

I squint one eye as I make my way through the dim, smoky club and eventually find the women's restroom. I have no idea how I make it inside to use the facilities without breaking my neck in these heels, but I manage. After I wash up, I leave the bathroom. I'm thankful I emptied my bladder because the set of hands grabbing me scares me half to death. My back hits a wall outside the women's restroom, and lips press against mine.

I push against my attacker and see it's Dalton.

"Sorry." He smiles sheepishly. "I thought you saw me."

I wipe my mouth with the back of my hand. "What are you doing?"

He touches his hand to my cheek. "You're so beautiful. I just wanted to kiss you."

It's been a long time since another man has told me I'm beautiful. Dalton may not be my type, but I want him to be. I want to like him. I wish I wanted to rip his clothes off. He's a nice guy. He's been attentive all night.

I grab a handful of his shirt and pull him to me. I close my eyes and try my best to get into it, but he's just not Bryant. It feels odd and unfamiliar. I don't like the way he kisses or touches me.

"Zhanna," Zina says from behind Dalton. "It's time to go home."

I break the kiss and take one last look at the man I wish I'd wake up and regret in the morning. "Sorry. She's my ride."

"I can take you home," he offers.

I press a kiss to my fingertips and then to his lips. "It was nice to meet you, Dalton. Thank you for a wonderful evening."

His hopeful face falls. "Damn. Okay. It was nice to meet you too. I hope to see you again."

"Yada, yada, yada." Zina rolls her eyes and pulls me down the hall.

Leslie stands at the end of the entrance to the hall with his hands on his hips and disappointment on his face. "Tequila was about to make your clothes fall off, girl."

In the backseat of a hired car with my sister, my thoughts drift to Bryant. If he was near, I'd choke him for fucking up my life. I send him a text to let him know how I feel.

> Zhanna: I hate you. I wish I'd never met you.

> Bryant: Baby.

> Bryant: Are you okay?

> Zhanna: No.

> Bryant: I'm calling Zina.

> Zhanna: No!

> Zhanna: I kissed another man tonight, and I hate you because I couldn't enjoy it. I've never loved someone the way I loved you.

> **Bryant: I'm calling.**

I jump when the phone rings.

"Who is calling you at this hour?" Zina asks.

I answer. "I hate you. I hope you die a slow, painful death."

"Jesus," Zina replies, and then she leans over closer to the phone. "Hey, B!"

"Hey, Zina!" my ex says in my ear.

"I'm hanging up."

"No! Please don't."

"I kissed another man," I admit.

I swear I can hear his jaw grind through the phone. "Zhanna, please don't do something you'll regret."

"You'd know all about that, wouldn't you?"

He sighs. "Yes, baby, I would. But since… since that night, I haven't touched anyone but you and my hand. Also, I'm telling you that going to the place where it's numb and everyone is smiling is not the answer. I would also know all about that."

"He was a good kisser."

He growls. "Are you trying to piss me off and make me jealous, because it's working!"

I don't reply, but instead play the scene with Dalton over in my head again. What was so wrong with him? I can't put my finger on any one thing that turned me off.

"Zhanna?"

"What?" I snap.

"I love you."

"I can't," I say and nearly choke on my emotions like I do every time he tells me.

"I know."

It's all I can do to kiss him now, and the act took some time for me to fall back into. I sure as hell can't tell him I love him.

"But I love you just the same."

CHAPTER THIRTY TWO

THEN

MY HAND RESTS ON the door to the Country club for a moment too long. I think of turning around and heading back to Louisiana where I belong, but I came all this way. I received a wedding invitation for a sweet guy we went to college with, Amos Terry, who also played on the university's team with Bryant. While I was never close to the bride, I helped rehab a particularly grizzly injury for him when he followed Bryant from college to the Spartans. He swears I saved his knee, but Amos did all the hard work. I couldn't say no to the invitation because he's always been such a kind person.

I unsuccessfully attempted to coax both Zina and Leslie into being my dates, but neither were available for the weekend. It sucks to be here alone because Bryant will be here. He called to tell me, but I haven't seen nor spoken to him in the six months since I last talked to him and half-drunkenly told him I kissed another man. It's not for lack of trying for contact on his part, but I've remained radio silent.

I've done nothing to move past him in these six months, and I'm afraid everyone inside will know as soon as they look at me. It's a ridiculous notion, but one that causes me anxiety, nonetheless.

"Are you going inside, or did you dress up to stand outside of the party?" Ben Slate asks.

I turn on my heel with a smile on my face and launch myself at my old friend. He happily catches me and spins us around as we both laugh. "Ben!"

"Damn, woman. It's so good to see you."

"It's been too long. How have you been?"

He holds his left hand up to show me his empty ring finger. "Divorced. Single dad."

"I'm sorry to hear that."

He shrugs. "Shit happens, Z. Just hate it happened to you."

"Yeah. He did a number on me."

"Any chance I can talk you into falling in love with me?"

I laugh and punch him in the shoulder. "Zina would murder us both in our sleep."

His face softens at the mention of my sister's name. "How is she?"

"She's good. Still working for the Voodoo."

He offers me the crook of his arm. "What do you say we go inside and give 'em hell?"

"Sounds like a plan." I sound unconvincing, even to myself.

Once we're inside, Ben leads me to the bar in a room filled with fancy circular tables and gold-covered chairs and orders us a few shots of tequila.

"One for courage, and one love."

I snort. "Fuck love."

"Here, here," he says as he holds his full glass in the air. "Fuck love."

"We should probably take our seats. The ceremony will begin soon."

Ben and I choose to sit on the bride's side of the aisle since Amos' is full of massive, bulky football players who look like oversized cartoon characters in the folding chairs they occupy.

I catch my first glance at Bryant as he walks behind Amos to the altar. Even after all this time apart, he still takes my breath away. His long, dark hair is down which surprises me since he's wearing a suit—black with a mustard yellow tie. As if he senses me, he turns his head in our direction but not quite far enough to see us.

"Fuck, Z, if you and B can't make it, who can?"

He has a point. Bryant and I were the couple all other couples wanted to be. Even when we'd been married and together for years to the point of comfort, we were still head over heels in love.

"I can't figure out how to forgive him. I can't get the images out of my mind."

He shakes his head, disappointment clearly written across his handsome face. "What the fuck was he thinking?"

"He wasn't. He was drunk."

"Doesn't excuse it."

"No."

Bryant turns around on the platform, faltering in his step when our eyes meet. A pained expression stares back at me. I can see him swallow from here. He looks down at his shoes, continuing his way to where the rest of the wedding party congregates as they wait for the event to begin.

"You okay?" Ben asks.

No. I'm not okay. When am I going to get over him? How long will it take? How long can this thing possibly go on between us?

I barely remember the ceremony as memories of mine and Bryant's wedding surface in my mind. At the end, I chance a look at Amos and find Bryant standing right behind him as the best man. His eyes are locked on mine, green forces of steel willing me to look back at him, but they want more than that. They want me to submit, to give my heart back over to him, and I can't ever do that again. I can't open myself back up to bleed that way again.

"Zhanna?" Ben calls and snaps me out of my daze.

I tear my eyes from my ex and give my friend my attention. "Yeah?"

"I asked if you wanted another drink?"

I look up to realize the ceremony is over and Bryant is no longer standing at the altar. In fact, it's completely empty of the wedding party. "Yes, a drink would be wonderful."

I make it through the motions of smiling, clapping, and being happy for the couple. I dance with Ben and a few other players I know, including the groom, and I catch up on the latest gossip amongst the WAGs. I'm intensely aware of Bryant's every move. I can feel his eyes on me, watching me from across the room.

When I smell his cologne, I turn around to see him dancing with the bride. He's pulling away while smiling at her, clearly ready to leave the dance floor, but she's pleading with him to dance. How can you say "no" to the bride? Amos dances by with the bride's grandmother, spins the elderly woman around, and claps Bryant on the back. My ex gives in, hangs his head still smiling, and dances with the star of the evening. I catch myself smiling across the room at the scene, but when he settles in to dance with her, another emotion fills me.

Bryant dancing in a tux brings back so many memories, memories of our love story, of the way we were the day we married. I can still remember the way that love felt. It was deep, authentic, and all-consuming. It completed me. The scene is quite bittersweet because while it reminds me of a beautiful part of my life, it also reminds me those chapters are in the past. The book is forever closed on us.

"Zhanna?" Ben comes from behind me as his hands come to my shoulders.

I look over my right shoulder and plaster a smile on my face. "Hey, you."

He's frowning. I must've let my emotions play out over my face. "You okay?"

"Yeah."

He's not buying my bullshit. "Let's get some fresh air."

"You know? I think I will, but you stay here and enjoy the reception. I'll be back in a second."

"Are you sure?"

"Positive."

I pat him on the arm and weave through the many bodies in the room until I reach the back of the venue. Stepping onto a rocking-chair front porch with black chairs, I breathe in the clean air. It's not as humid as New Orleans. I suck in a lung full of oxygen and stroll along the sidewalk around the building. My walk takes me past several fountains, koi ponds, beautiful landscaping, and eventually, I arrive at a garden.

The garden contains tall shrubbery cut into a cute little maze ending at a white gazebo filled with string lights. The music from inside softly plays on hidden speakers in the garden. The cicadas are singing, and there's a slight breeze tonight. It's serene out here in nature, away from everyone else. It's been a while since I've been to Hale's Row to enjoy the simplicity of Mother Nature.

A seat is built into the sides of the gazebo, so I take a chance to rest my feet from the high heels I've been dying in all night. They're the first thing I'm taking off when I get home before I climb in the bath and have a good cry.

"Zhanna," he says so softly I barely hear him, but there's no mistaking his voice. I'd know it anywhere.

I slowly spin around.

God, it hurts to look at him. He's still so beautiful, and in a tux to boot.

I clear my throat. "Hey."

He climbs three steps to the gazebo and steps just inside it. "You look beautiful."

I smile. "Thank you. You're very handsome yourself."

He looks down at my feet and smirks. "Still hating heels?"

"I'm not sure if I'm correct in my assumption, but I'm pretty certain a man invented the high heel. Women don't invent torture devices. That's man's work."

He laughs, and it sounds good to hear it. I've missed the sounds he makes from singing to grunting. It's taken some time for me to adjust to the quiet of living alone, and I'm not sure I've completely accomplished it.

He leans against the entrance to the gazebo and slowly loses his smile. "How are ya, Z?"

"I'm okay. But look at you! Another Super Bowl! Your career is already one for the history books."

He shrugs like it's no big deal, but the corner of his mouth twitches with the beginning of a smile. "Yeah, but I couldn't have done it without the wisest words spoken by a professional football coach."

"Oh?" I ask, curious as can be.

"Throw the damn ball."

I look down at my feet for a moment to escape the intensity of his green gaze. "I'm so happy for you." It sounds flat, even to me.

"Thanks. Football is all I have left. I might as well try to be good at

False Start

at least one thing. I was a shit husband."

"It wasn't all bad, Bryant. Some of my best memories are with you. We were good together, until we weren't."

Neither of us says anything for a long moment. I'm lost in thought trying to figure out exactly when we weren't good together anymore. When is that moment in time when it changed?

"Thank you for remembering the good. Thank you for remembering the love," he says as he places a hand over his heart.

What do I say to the perfect response?

"We should go back inside."

"Listen, baby," he says and points to the speaker in the gazebo.

Can't Help Falling in Love with You is playing over the speaker. A gasp leaves me as a chill spreads over my skin.

"Of all the places in the world, of all the moments in time, we both ended up here with our song playing. You know what I call that, baby?"

"Fate," I whisper.

"Yeah," he whispers back. "Come dance with me, Z."

I hesitate, consider him for a moment, and quickly decide I don't want to let this moment pass me by. I strap the shoe back on my foot and stand from the bench. He waits patiently for me to make another move. I look down at my shoes, watching them move under me as I meet him in the middle of the gazebo.

His finger goes underneath my chin until I'm looking into his beautiful eyes. He takes my hand in his and places it over his heart. Taking my free hand, he drapes it around his neck before going to my hip. We sway with each other, lost in another place of our making, and we let Elvis sing to us. The entire world disappears from my mind as we glide around the gazebo. All I can see, hear, smell, and feel is him. He's everywhere, and for the first time in a long time, I just exist in this moment with him. I let it go. I let it ride. And I can breathe for the first time in ages.

I'm reminded of the first dance we had after we married—the way the orchids and lilies smelled in my hand. The unshed tears in his eyes remind me of the way we were both moved to tears during our first dance. As the song, our song, comes to an end, the world comes crashing down around me. The cicadas and the other sounds of the night are louder than they once were. The music from the speakers also seems higher.

The bass of Bryant's voice is deeper and reverberates through my core. "I love you, Coach."

I swallow around the lump in my throat and pull away from him. "I can't," I croak.

"I know, baby." He reaches for me as I step toward the entrance. "It's okay."

It feels like he's telling me it's okay to go, as if he's giving me permission to run from him again. So I wipe my eyes, take a deep breath, and walk away. I duck through the venue and stay to the outside of the room until I escape to the front of the property. And I hold back what feels like a tsunami threatening to break loose at any moment. When I reach my rental car, I climb inside and fall apart.

CHAPTER THIRTY THREE

NOW

"ZHANNA, DO YOU STILL love Bryant?" Mary asks after Bryant finishes relaying the last two years of our estrangement.

"Yes." Admitting I still love him aloud feels both like I've lost the battle but also like I've shed twenty pounds of baggage.

He lays his hand on top of mine. "I told you at a previous session that I've stopped drinking. I have a one-drink limit at social events, never drive when I do, and I refuse to keep alcohol in the house. I know trusting me is hard to do, but I'm not where I was. I won't ever make the same mistake again because I'm not going to drink and ever put myself in the same position.

"I learned through therapy I had a drinking problem that began around the time my dad died. When things got too tough, I turned to alcohol instead of dealing with it. I just thought I was having a good time, but when I got a blow job from a woman who wasn't my wife, I knew I'd gone past just having a good time."

They say when you hold onto anger it's much like holding onto a hot coal. It burns you at first, but the anger I have has become a friend to me. If I don't have it, I might return to feeling numb and dead inside again. I don't want that. I don't want to fade away. I'm too damn young to be stuck in limbo with my ex-husband. I have to either release him or forgive him.

I don't even know what forgiveness really is. What does it look like? What is it supposed to feel like? I can't forget, but forgetting and forgiving aren't the same thing.

I leave my chair and walk to the floor-length window. I enjoy looking out of it during therapy. It gives me a moment to focus on something other than the heaviness in the room.

"Zhanna, is there something you have in mind that could aid Bryant in gaining your trust again?" Mary asks.

Nothing comes to mind. There's no magical solution to our problem. There isn't a list of steps to mend what's broken. It takes a huge leap of faith.

"There are things I don't understand. Things that I need answered before I can figure out if I can move past it."

"I'll answer anything."

"I know you were drunk. I know you were in a bad place. But I want to know how it happened. And I want to know what was going through your mind while it was happening with Priscilla."

"Z…" he starts and stops. "I was very drunk. I don't remember a lot of that night."

"Do you remember me going to bed?"

"No. I remember walking a few people to the door and crashing on the couch. The next thing I knew…" He stops, and I turn around to see him rub his hands over his face in frustration, likely with himself. "I thought it was you, Zhanna. Fuck, I didn't know it was her, and that's the God's honest truth. I'd never fuck around on you. Even in my grief, I wouldn't stray. Even drunk, I have no interest in other women. You're it for me."

"Why would you think she was me? Surely being with her was vastly different than being with me. Shouldn't you have noticed something?"

"She called me 'QB'."

I blink once, twice, thrice. My mouth opens and shuts several times. Words fail me. That fucking bitch Priscilla is going to choke on her own teeth next time I see her. The gloves are off when we meet again. She was close enough to us in the months after the Super Bowl to know I affectionately call him "QB".

"Well done," I murmur.

I nod, anger coursing through me as I remember how I'd suspected her motives in the early days. I'm livid I ever trusted the woman. I feel like the biggest fool. I believe him, but the pain in my chest and stomach is more than I can bear.

"What?" Bryant asked, confused, and worried.

"Nothing, I wasn't talking to you. Why didn't you tell me before now?"

"I did tell you the night in the drive when you left California, but you weren't in a place where you were listening to anything I had to say. Swear to Christ, babe, it's the truth."

Mary allows a moment of silence to fall in the room before she speaks again. "Bryant have you been in contact with Priscilla since the night of the incident?"

He shakes his head. "Yes, I fired her immediately. She quit sports after I had her blackballed from the league. Last I heard, she moved back to Canada where I hope she stays."

Hearing her name hurts more than I wish it does. I wrap my arms around my middle. "I don't want to do this anymore."

"You don't want to do what, baby?"

"This," I say and wave my hand around the room. "Therapy. I don't want to do this anymore."

Mary sympathizes. "It's hard. It's hard to talk about what happened. Remembering can take us back to the place and time where we were traumatized. Anger is a natural reaction to your memories. Anger, in small doses, is also perfectly natural and healthy, but not when you're holding it to the point of exploding. Therapy is hard, and it can make us hurt a little before it gets better, but it will get better. You're in a fragile, vulnerable place. Trust is hard for you with Bryant, but it is possible to forgive and trust him again. I think the first thing we have to address is your inclination to run away and let your fear rule you."

"I'm sorry?" I ask defensively.

"You've been afraid the relationship would end from the very beginning. While you feared another specific event would tragically end your relationship, it ended in another way, and you walked away."

"What the fuck was I supposed to do? Stay with him? Let it slide? Pat him on the back?"

"If I recall, your first real argument as a married couple resulted in you leaving a party alone without speaking to your husband about your departure. When you found him with her, you acted out of rage, and then you left the state and filed for divorce. You didn't let him explain or try to make amends. You didn't give it time to see if it could be worked through before you dissolved the marriage."

"I..." I begin and stop.

"You never wanted to be with a football player. And I get it, babe, with your dad and all, but for once, even when I fucked up, I wanted you to stay and fight. I feel like I'm the only one fighting for us."

"I feel like I'm being villainized because you cheated."

Mary smiles gently. "Not at all, Zhanna. But if we're going to work on the relationship, we have to work on all sides of it to make it a successful and loving relationship again. Part of the equation is communicating when it's difficult and not running away from the conflict. There's disagreement in every healthy relationship, but communication is key in dealing with issues when they arise.

"That leads me into my next point about communication— I've noticed a tendency for both of you to use sex as a band-aid to your problems. While sex after an argument is very normal and natural, it's important to communicate about the disagreement before you become intimate. Put issues to bed before you engage."

She's 100% correct. We use sex to deal with our problems, and I'm honestly not sure who's worse, me or him.

Maybe she's also right about me running away. Maybe I've always had it in the back of my mind that Bryant wouldn't always be around. I expected something else, much different and much more permanent than infidelity. He's still here though. He's not become injured on the field and left me. My worst nightmares didn't come true, so perhaps my worst fear didn't come true. I thought infidelity was it, but his death or tragic injury is the worst possible scenario in my world.

He thought it was me. Something shifts inside me, but I can't quite put my finger on it. There's a million thoughts swirling around in my mind, but I do feel a bit lighter in my soul for having learned he thought it was me that night.

"This brings us to an end for our session today, but I want to give you homework until our next session. I want you to think about how you will cope differently as a couple now when a conflict arises. What can you do instead of running away and/or using intimacy to sweep over the disagreement?"

We leave the office in silence and head to his car. I hate that I rode with him today. I need distance and perspective. I apparently have personal issues I need to also deal with in addition to our issues as a couple.

I don't say anything as he drives us to the other side of the Quarter until we come to a crossroads to either go to my place or his.

"Can you take me home?"

He glances over at me. "Baby, what's going on in that beautiful head of yours?"

"I just want to go home for the night. I have a lot to sort out, and I think I need to do it alone."

I can tell it hurts him to hear it, but his eyes are full of love and compassion. "Okay. I'll take you home. Do you need anything on the way?"

"No, thank you."

When we pull into the drive, he parks the vehicle and reaches over to presses a kiss to my cheek. "I'm just a call away, Z."

"Thank you," I say and exit.

He idles in the drive until I'm tucked safely inside.

CHAPTER THIRTY FOUR

NOW

I TAKE THE REST of the evening to decompress and sort through my thoughts. The thing I keep coming back to is the fact that I do indeed still love him, very much. Also, I'm miserable without him. I hate that I'm miserable without him, but I can't help it. A long time ago, at Hale's Row, he stole my heart and never gave it back. I thought he'd ripped it from my chest when I found him with Priscilla. I thought it ceased to beat, but there's still life left in there yet.

How different would things be if I'd known Priscilla had basically pretended to be me while my husband was drunk and nearly passed out? It's not lost on me that I didn't stick around to give him a chance to let him finish his explanation, and I also cut him off every time he tried to explain. In my defense, I was mortally wounded and running for cover. My fight or flight kicked in and I chose to run. I have to stop running.

The next morning, I remain in bed longer than I should. I call into work and take a personal day to reset myself. Zina, Otto, and Bryant call and message to check on me, so I let them know I'm okay and go on with my day.

"My beautiful ass is coming in!" Leslie shouts from the side door that leads in from the courtyard. When he comes into view, he takes me in and purses his lips. "Why are you wearing all kinds of regret on your face?"

"I messed up."

"Well, that's okay, Suga. We all mess up from time to time. I mean, not me, obvs, but most people. It's okay to be normal."

"Thanks?"

"What I'm trying to say is you're human, and we're faulty creatures. No need to stay in your pajamas until two in the afternoon about it. But, those pajamas are fabulous, girl."

"I don't know what to do."

Leslie tosses his long dreads over his shoulder and comes around the couch to have a seat across from me. He crosses his legs at the knee and places both hands on the top one, leg bouncing away. "Tell Uncle Leslie all about it, boo boo."

"I walked away too soon...from Bryant."

"Oh, no, honey child, no, no, no. You aren't taking that weight on your shoulders. I love me some Mr. Football Star, but he messed up. Had his wanky in another woman's mouth."

"She pretended to be me— Priscilla, his old agent, she pretended to be me, and I didn't know until yesterday."

"Oooo," he singsongs as he shakes his head. "And you didn't give him a chance to tell you before you hauled ass to New Orleans?"

"He told me. I didn't listen."

He cringes. "Girl."

"Yeah, I know."

"I don't know. It's a hard thing to watch your partner be unfaithful with someone else, regardless of the circumstances. I get it. I understand you running and getting the hell out of there, but at some point, could you have listened to the man?"

My expression relays how much this hurts.

"My girl is feeling this."

"Yeah."

His eyes dance back and forth and sparkle with excitement. "You know what we need? We need a night at the club."

I cringe this time. "I wasn't on my best behavior last time."

He pulls a wad of cash from the top of his muumuu and unfolds the green lump. "I want you to go down to that new fancy spa down on Royal Street and have a day on me. Get the works, girlfriend. I'll meet you back here at seven. Oooo-weee, I can't wait!"

Then he's out the door before I can argue back. A spa day doesn't sound awful, especially when I'm so weighed down with depression.

I spend the rest of the day at the spa Leslie recommended and enjoy every last second of being pampered from my head to my toes. Since I arrived late, they keep it open a bit past closing to finish my nails.

I barely manage to make it home in time to meet Leslie.

Leslie is a makeup and hair artist genius, and he's the only man I know that can dress a woman better than she can. By the time he's done with me, I have a new outfit I didn't buy, and I look like a million bucks. I'd definitely do me.

The club is in the Quarter, but it's too far to walk, especially in heels. Zina and I order a car and head on over around 9:30. I love to see the entire show, and Leslie is usually the headlining act at Sparkles.

Reeva is checking ID's at the door and smiles from ear to ear when she sees us. "Hey, there are my favorite sisters." She waves us in, kisses both sides of our cheeks and gives us a squeeze. "So gorgeous. All this blond, and you look like a million bucks," she says to me. "Look at all that leg on display!"

Reeva calls a bouncer over to take over her duties, escorting us to the bar to grab a cocktail and a shot. She then deposits us at the table front and center of the stage. "This is the best show ever!"

"She's excited tonight," I say when she walks away.

I love Reeva. She's easily excitable and her happiness is always infectious.

Zina and I cheer on all the guys and gals in the show and have a damn good time. Leslie was right about coming out tonight. I needed a night here amongst his friends, live music, and easy laughter. For the first time in a long time, I wish Bryant was here. I wish he was right beside me soaking up the show.

"Going to the ladies'," I say as I leave Zina holding down the table for us.

I pull out my phone to call Bryant, but it goes straight to voicemail. I think of leaving a message, but I chicken out at the last minute and hang up.

After I use the ladies' room, I make my way back to the table and frown when I notice the lights are down. You can hear a pin drop; the entire place is radio silent. A single spotlight clicks on Leslie in the middle of the stage. He's probably seven feet tall in his long, deep v-cut, sequined, hot pink dress. He's wearing a black wig that cascades

False Start

down his back and strappy silver heels on his large feet. My friend is gorgeous.

The crowd cheers for him.

"Thank you. I love you too," he says. "Tonight, I wanted to do something a little different for y'all. I've had the opportunity to play Cupid, and y'all know I couldn't turn it down. Lawd."

More shouts go out for Leslie.

"So, I invited a friend here to show his lady how much he loves her."

"Awww," Zina says.

Leslie turns to the side of the stage and waves someone over. "Suga, don't be shy. Come on out here. Y'all give him a round of applause now."

The crowd goes wild.

A large man dressed in an emerald sweetheart cut gown, broad chest, and long brown hair curled in ringlets steps into the spotlight as he teeters on heels.

"Oh my God," Zina says and laughs.

"That's…" I start. "No way."

"Baby," the man says into the microphone.

I'd know his voice anywhere.

"No," I say, slapping my hand over my eyes while my sister continues to cackle next to me.

"Baby," he repeats and shields his eyes from the light to look into the crowd. "Fuck, I can't see shit," he says. He pulls the mic from its stand and teeters down the short catwalk of the stage to stand in front of us. Bryant grins down at me when he catches sight of me. "Coach, I love you. I'm sorry for all the shit I've done, and I'll do anything to have another shot at making you happy."

A second spotlight shines further down the stage on Leslie who's sitting at a piano with a second mic in front of him. My best friend and ex-husband play and sing Whitney Houston's I Will Always Love You with Leslie singing backup and Bryant's beautiful voice singing lead.

I can't help or stop the tears that form and cascade down my face, because regardless of all the times I've run and all the times I was afraid or angry, he never gave up. He never gave up because he loves me. Zina throws an arm over my shoulder and pulls me in a little closer while I look into Bryant's green eyes, complete with a full set of faux lashes and a beautiful smokey-eye as he serenades me like a diva.

I look behind Bryant to see Leslie's face also full of tears as his voice starts to quiver singing backup for Bryant. "Sing it, Suga," he sings into the mic and shakes his head back and forth like he's Stevie Wonder.

As Bryant nears the last verse, he begins to pump his fist, belt into the microphone, and shake his ringlets all around like he's Beyoncé. His large hands move around like he's conducting a symphony. He makes very interesting expressions as he digs deeper into the song.

Zina leans over. "I'm not sure if he's doing this to impress you or himself anymore."

I laugh but shake my head. "I don't care. Color me impressed. Look at him in drag!"

"This has Leslie written all over it."

I nod in agreement. It sure does, and I love both men for going all out to bring us back together.

When Bryant drags out the last note for maybe a little bit too long, the lights die down, and the crowd goes wild. When the lights flash-back on, Bryant is kicking his heels off and headed for our table. I stand in my seat, and we collide as soon as he steps off the stage. His long, fake fingernails dig into my thighs as he picks me up. I lock my legs around him as we kiss. The crowd grows louder, and their cheers only encourage the man.

He marches us through the club with me attached to him like a spider monkey and takes us through the long dressing room off the side of the stage. We head straight to his SUV's back seat where he presses my back to the seat.

"Your feet," I remind him when I remember he kicked his shoes off.

"Fuck the shoes, baby. Got other things on my mind."

"Yeah?" I smirk. "Like what?"

He pushes my dress over my ass and pulls at my panties. "I need you naked."

"You're dressed in drag."

He stops and hovers over me as his face softens. "Yeah, baby. There's not much I wouldn't do for you." I start to cry. "Shhh, don't cry."

He kisses me as I claw at his dress. When I feel a bra underneath, I break the kiss and start to giggle. "I've never taken a bra off someone before."

He cracks up laughing. "Leslie insisted I put all of my effort into my role. He thought it might help me win you back, so I gave it a shot."

I reach down and pull his dress over his head and chunk it in the trunk. Next, I remove his bra, running my hands along the smooth skin of his chest. He leans down to pull a hand from his chest and place a kiss atop it.

"I'm so hard it hurts."

"Mmmm," I moan in response.

"No, babe, you don't understand. Leslie practically strapped my dick to my asshole."

I snort. "Sounds painful. Should I free you?"

"If you never do another thing in this world for me, please release my dick."

After I untuck him, he really begins to struggle with his height and the width of the vehicle, so we maneuver until I'm straddling him in the middle of the seat. He unzips my dress and pulls it down to expose my breasts, but leaves the rest of me covered. His mouth covers my nipple as he gently licks and sucks. I start to grind on him, making both of us moan in response.

His hands snake into my hair as he thrusts into me with a masculine grunt. Then his mouth crashes onto mine as we war with each other for control. I reach between us and pull him from his boxers before I line him up and sink down on him.

"Fuck, baby," he whispers against my lips.

I give myself a moment to adjust before I rock against him, taking both of us higher and higher as we inch toward the finish line. My fingers find their way to his perfectly curled hair and tug. I get so lost in him. I allow myself to let go for the first time in years. Our hands wander as our lips connect.

    I forget we're in a parking lot half naked and in view for anyone to see. I forget the entire world exists as I lose myself in the beautiful act of love we're sharing. I'm so turned on by his performance and him putting his heart on the line for me that I drag it out. I could've erupted around him moments after he first entered me, but I don't want it to end. I don't want this bubble we're in to pop. I just want to dive inside him and never come up for air.

    As his teeth scrape against my chin, I arch my back and finally come undone around him. He follows and pulses inside me as he wraps himself around me and holds on for dear life.

    "I love you more than life itself, Zhanna."

CHAPTER THIRTY FIVE

NOW

THE NEXT DAY, MY off day, my phone rings at eight in the morning. I groan and roll over to see who would dare call me on my day off.

Bryant.

"Hello?"

"Something is wrong with Punter's eye," he says frantically.

"Huh?"

"Baby, I don't know what to do. I've never had a cat."

I groan again. "Okay. Can you meet me here in thirty?"

"Coach, what takes thirty minutes? This is an emergency!" He shouts into the phone.

"If you yell at me again, I'm going to hang up. Is Punter's eye hanging out of its socket?"

"No."

"Then it can wait thirty minutes."

"How can you be so sure?"

I sigh. "I'm hanging up now."

I answer the door to Bryant and Punter. I frown at the cat, lying on its back, cradled in Bryant's arms like a baby. "He looks fine."

"I was staring into his eyes this morning when I woke and noticed they look different. One is really blue, and the other one is lighter. I think he might be blind in one eye."

"Aww, poor guy." I pet the little guy's head and grab my keys to drive us to the local vet.

I've never seen a cat rest on its back for as long as Punter very happily lounges in Bryant's big, beefy arms, but there it is. Bryant and

I have never had animals before, so I've never seen him with one. His concern is adorable.

At the vet, Bryant very reluctantly allows the veterinarian to examine the tiny kitten. He's very skeptical of the doctor, but I manage to assuage his fears with all the medical degrees on the wall.

"Punter has heterochromia iridium," Dr. Grant says.

"That sounds terrible. You don't suspect blindness?" Bryant asks.

"Not at all. It just means he has two different colored eyes, and both pupils respond to stimuli or light on both sides."

My ex releases a sigh of relief. "Okay. Thank you."

We pay the vet for their services and head home. Punter sleeps tucked against Bryant's neck as we drive across town to my townhome. When we reach my place, Bryant asks me to come over and see Ben and Ansel who have asked after me. Bryant thinks Ansel has a small crush on me. I think it's cute as can be.

"I haven't had coffee yet, and it's still early yet for Ansel. Why don't I come over for lunch?"

He smiles at me, happy with my answer. "Yeah, sounds good."

He kisses me on the top of the head before he and Punter take off for his car.

I head inside and instead of fixing a cup of coffee, I decide to take a short nap. I send Bryant a message to let him know I'll be over a little later than expected and doze off as soon as my head hits the pillow. Except I sleep the day away, and when I wake, it's three in the afternoon.

Shit. I guess I needed the rest more than I realized.

After a cup of java, I head for the shower, taking my time to pamper myself a bit. I opt for comfortable jeans and a Voodoo tee. By five, I'm in the car headed to Bryant's. I hope I'm not too late for dinner. It would be nice to have dinner with the three men.

I turn the corner on Dauphine and before I pull up to the gate I see Bryant leading someone up the front steps to his house. Odd. He usually uses the back door that opens into the kitchen. As I drive closer, I also notice it's a leggy blond he's leading into the house.

False Start

My heart drops into my stomach, and shooting pain rips through my chest. I hit the brake and grip the steering wheel so hard I swear I almost break it off the column. My first inclination is to run. It's my defense mechanism when it comes to Bryant. It seems easier than standing there and hurting in front of him again.

A voice in my head whispers, He wouldn't do that to you, not again. I close my eyes and breathe deeply. I'll give him a chance to explain. I pull up to his gate and push the call box button for entrance, and I'm immediately granted access.

My heart beats wildly in my chest as I exit my vehicle and enter the house through the kitchen door.

Bryant walks into the kitchen a second after I do with a huge grin on his face. "Hey, baby." He leans down to kiss me, and it's hard to kiss him back when there's another woman somewhere in the house—a woman I don't know. "You're just in time to see Leslie have a panic attack."

"Huh?"

He laces his fingers through mine and leads me through the house until we come to one of the dens where Leslie, Ben, Ansel, and the blonde stand. I eye the woman but try not to be obvious about it. When I hear her laugh at something Leslie murmurs, I realize I know the laugh. It's very loud, a little obnoxious, feminine, and dainty.

"Girl, what is Mr. Football Star up to? The anticipation is killing me. Me and Ophelia have been standing here for a minute waiting on your slow ass."

Ophelia. That's Leslie's friend's name. I haven't seen her in a while.

"Hey Ophelia," I greet.

"Hey, girl. Looking beautiful as ever."

"Ditto." I grin at the woman.

I can't believe I almost ran away because Leslie brought a friend to Bryant's.

Bryant releases my hand and rubs his together. "Are you ready to see Punter's new toy?"

"This is about the cat?" Leslie asks, brow raised.

256

"He's not just a cat. He's family." Bryant leads us into another den.

"What the fuck did you do to my masterpiece?!!" Leslie shouts, hands on his hips and shock on his face.

"Whoa," Ansel says of the 'toy'.

In the corner of the room is a large tree. I'm not sure what it's crafted of, but it's as high as the high ceiling.

Ben snorts. "That's not a toy, bro. That's a treehouse inside a house."

"The little guy needs a dose of the outdoors. Cats like to climb trees, but I can't let him outside unless he's in his stroller."

"You bought a motherfucking stroller for a cat?" Leslie asks. "Something is seriously wrong with you, Mr. Football Star. You're taking shit too far."

"He's never had a pet." I defend him.

As if on cue, Punter saunters lazily into the room and rubs himself against Bryant's legs. Bryant scoops the kitten into his arms, scratching his head. "That's a good boy." He puts him down and Punter races to the tree, climbs all the way to the top, and sticks his cute little head out of the top of the tree.

"See how happy it makes him?" Bryant asks with pride.

He'd be a wonderful father. I love that he's quite taken with the kitten. It just shows how big of a heart he has, and it's one of the many reasons I fell in love with him.

We watch the kitten climb all over the tree for a few more minutes before Bryant announces he's bought steaks for everyone. We spend the rest of the night playing card games and eating a great meal.

When it's time for me to go home for the night, I find I don't want to leave Bryant. We've had a wonderful day. I realized I can trust him. It feels like the weight of the world has been lifted off my shoulders.

CHAPTER THIRTY SIX

NOW

THE FIRST GAME OF the season is always full of hope, and every team dreams of a win for the opening matchup. A victory is always a hopeful indicator of the season to come. It's also Bryant's regular season debut as the Voodoo quarterback, and the football-crazy city's energy has been on high all week.

I haven't bothered Bryant before games because he has a lot on his plate, but when he messages a few hours before the game, I meet him in an empty conference room in the stadium. I'm surprised to find him already waiting there for me.

He smiles, appearing a bit anxious. "Hey, thanks for coming."

"Yeah, no problem. Are you okay?"

He blows out a big sigh and laughs nervously. "I've won two Super Bowls, but I don't think I've ever been this nervous. Playing at home in this crowd is just madness."

Our stadium is known around the country as being the loudest. Our fans are known as being some of the craziest.

"This was always the dream, Quarterback," I remind him.

His face softens. "Playing for the Voodoo under your dad was the dream, babe. Being married to his daughter is an even bigger dream, one that came true for a little while."

I reach for his hand and lace my fingers through his. "You're going to play just fine. You're the best QB in the league."

He grins at me, and waves it off. "You're just saying that because you've taken my bra off. I think you're a little biased."

I giggle. "You're probably right. The bra is what really pushed me over the edge of seduction."

"I knew it," he jokes and leans in, whispering against my lips, "You used to give me a kiss for good luck before a game. Think I could talk you into a little one?"

I look up as I pretend to think hard about his request. "Well, I suppose it depends on how small we're talking."

"The teensiest."

I smile as I lean forward and press my lips against his. "That's all you get until you bring home a win."

I pull away, drop his hand, and head for the door, but he scoops me up from behind. "You didn't just tease the fuck out of me and walk away, woman."

He tickles my ribs and gets a few shouts of laughter from me. "I give up!"

Bryant spins me around in his arms and leans his forehead against mine. He licks his lips. "I think you can do better than that. As a matter of fact, I know you can."

"Yeah?"

He reaches between us and grabs himself. "Yeah, baby."

I close the small gap between us and softly bite his lip before sucking on it to make it all better. I almost tell him I love him, but shy away before I can spit it out. "Please be careful out there."

He kisses me. "I always am. Will you be there after the game?"

"I work here, silly."

He shakes his head. "No, Z, like you used to be there after the game."

He wants me to meet him on the field and be the first to congratulate him on a win or console him over a loss. It's a big step for us.

"Yeah, Quarterback. I'll be there."

He searches my eyes for a moment before he grins, cradles my face in his hands, and pulls me to him for a kiss. "I love you, Coach."

I panic and stiffen against him. Fuck. It's been so long since I've uttered those words to him. They feel foreign. There's a heaviness to those three short words. I close my eyes and turn a perfectly great moment into a shitty one.

"Z, baby, it's okay." He presses his forehead to mine as I cry and shake my head.

"It's not okay. I'm sorry, I'm just not ready." I try to pull away, but he holds me tightly.

"Don't run. Let's talk about it, baby."

I freeze in my tracks. I'm running. I do it without thinking. It's my response when I get scared, but I have to stop sometime.

"Okay."

"Listen, I don't expect everything is going to go back to being the way it was. Honestly, I don't want it to go back to being the way it was. I want to be a better husband and man for you. I've been working on that for two years, but you need time to adjust to it. When you're ready, you'll say it back. I know you love me, Zhanna, and that's what keeps me going."

I do love him, and it warms my heart that he knows it. I told him as much in therapy without outright saying the three magical words. Saying them simply because he said them first isn't how I want to tell him I love him for the first time in two years.

He pulls me into a big bear hug and kisses the top of my head. "I've got to get back before Otto comes looking for me."

I snicker thinking of Otto finding us in an empty conference room together. "Yeah, you do."

We walk out together and part ways before we run into cameras. Our relationship isn't their business. I don't want to explain where we're at in it right now.

***

THE DOWNSIDE TO WORKING for a professional football team is missing the game from the fan's perspective. I spend four quarters watching for and treating injuries. There's little time to keep up with the game on a play-by-play basis. I love watching football as much as I love being on the sidelines treating the players, so it's a trade-off.

I keep an eye on Bryant and how he's playing during the game as much as I possibly can. He's having a fantastic first game as the Voodoo quarterback. The fans are deafening with their screams and cheers. I swear half of them already have a Hudson jersey on their backs. Their college hero returned home, and they're ecstatic about it.

Ben also makes his premier as the starting Voodoo tight end. I can't tell who is happier about being back on the field together, Bryant or

Ben. There's lots of high-fives and celebratory dancing, with the crowd eating it up.

Early in the fourth quarter, we're up by four touchdowns. Otto puts in the backup quarterback to give Bryant a break. When he jogs off the field, he heads straight for me as he pulls his helmet off. There's just something about the man when he's in a football uniform.

I grow nervous as the cameras follow his every move. I'm not ready for people to put together the fact that we both work for the Voodoo seeing as no one outside the organization has made the connection. Instead of stopping and talking to me by the water cooler, he winks at me and pulls a water bottle from the table, jogging off and leaving me smirking like we're back in college again. I smile for the rest of the quarter.

With two minutes left in the game, Bryant takes the field again to finish what he started. He passes the ball off to Ben on the first play, giving us twelve more yards. The offense lines up at the line of scrimmage, the center snapping the ball on the second play of the drive. Bryant drops back, looking for a man down field, but the defensive end is able to make it past the left tackle. He heads straight for Bryant.

Bryant realizes he's in trouble and throws the ball to the nearby cornerback, but he's not fast enough to stop the sack. The defensive end tackles Bryant to the ground, but he hits him so hard Bryant goes airborne.

Every cell in my body freezes. I wait with bated breath for him to move as the defensive end rolls off him. Bryant doesn't move. He doesn't roll over in pain or jump up ready to play again. We're signaled to come to his aid, and I'm across the field before anyone else can get there.

I kneel beside him. He's out cold. I make sure he's breathing and has a pulse before I move on to assessing other injuries. Usually when a football player goes down and he's unconscious, he wakes up within a minute, but Bryant isn't waking up.

The cold realization that he could never open his eyes again punches me in the gut. I don't remember the last thing I said to him, but I didn't tell him I loved him. If he doesn't open his eyes, I may never have that opportunity again. Because I do love him. I can't live without him anymore, and I don't want to.

"Baby, please wake up and let us know you're okay."

Precious seconds turn into minutes as shouts fade into the background. I place my hand on his chest and wait for the rise and fall. If it were a cold night, I'd be able to see his breath, but it's humid. He's not breathing deeply, if at all.

"Please," I quietly sob to him. I want the opportunity to tell him that I forgive him. I want the chance to tell him I still love him. I need the peace I've been looking for since he cheated two years ago. "Please."

He doesn't wake and give me a second to tell him anything at all because the paramedic comes and loads him onto the gurney to transport him off the field. Holding his hand the entire way, I'm terrified for him, for me, for us. I talk to him. I have no idea what I say other than I need him to wake up. I'm busy trying to keep up with his injuries and what the medical staff is doing to him.

Zina walks into the facility where we're checking him out, throwing an arm around my shoulder. "Let them work, sis. You just focus on being there for B."

I lean down, whispering the three words I should've said earlier to him. I've never regretted something so much. "I love you. Please come back to me."

His eyes open and dart around, confused, and unclear. I start to cry tears of relief. When he finally focuses on me, I cry harder.

His voice is hoarse. "Shit. That hurt."

As soon as the medical staff realizes he's awake, chaos ensues. I hold his hand through the entire thing while he answers neurological questions and gives them an update on how he's feeling.

When a football player goes down like Bryant did, they have to carefully remove the helmet, ensuring there's no spinal injury before they can allow him to move. But once he's able, he sits up on the bed with a little help from us.

As he recovers his wits, he begins to laugh and joke, putting us all at ease. He likely has a concussion, but he's not having memory issues—a huge positive. We monitor him for some time and keep the press updated on his condition.

Late in the evening, once most people have left the stadium, I help Bryant to my car. He's too sore to drive himself, and I don't want to risk it with a possible concussion. I pull onto the interstate and head for the Quarter. A light snore comes from the passenger seat. I smile over at him.

When I reach a stop light, I take in his beautiful face. His gorgeous green eyes are missing, but still, he's beautiful inside and out. He made a huge mistake, but good people make bad decisions sometimes.

I pull into my drive and take another moment to watch him rest. I hate to wake him, but he'll be cramped if he sleeps in here much longer.

"Hey, Quarterback," I say and touch his face.

His eyes flutter open. "Yeah, Coach?"

"We're home."

He looks out the front windshield. "We're at your place."

"I'm not letting you out of my sight for the next 24 hours, not with a possible concussion."

The corners of his mouth twitch with the beginnings of a smile. "I know you're worried. It's one concussion. Okay?"

"Why are you smiling?" I ask.

"I'm not."

"It's a half-smile."

"You being worried about me is all. It just feels nice."

"Of course I care, Bryant. As a matter of fact, I more than care."

"Yeah? You saying you love me, Coach?"

I lean across the middle of the car. He meets me there with a smirk on his face and then presses his lips to mine.

"I love you to the moon and back, Quarterback."

EPILOGUE

BRYANT

WHEN I ASKED ZHANNA to marry me again, it was our fourteenth date. I lit a fire at Hale's Row and got down on one knee. It was across from a huge bonfire that I first saw the woman of my dreams. I knew the minute I saw her sitting on the back of a tailgate sipping beer out of a red solo cup that she was the one. When she called me a chicken shit while giving me the best advice I've ever received, I had to have more. She was a football princess made to be my football queen.

As I stand at the makeshift altar in the middle of a field at Hale's Row, I look over to the officiant, Leslie, and silently thank him for all the times he's had my back, pushing Zhanna and I together. There was never a question of who would marry us. We both agreed that it should be our friend and cheerleader from the very beginning, and he gladly accepted the honor, wasting no time in becoming ordained online.

Zina walks down the aisle in a hunter green floor-length gown with lace sleeves. Her blonde hair is up in a complicated style, and her blue eyes shine with joyful tears. She carries a bouquet of white lilies with her as she walks toward me and my best man, Ben. I wish Zina and Ben would follow our example and reunite. I miss the foursome we were.

A horse and carriage brings Zhanna from the cabin, just atop a hill, down a path that leads to our location. As I look across the wide-open land, a bittersweet feeling overtakes me, watching the candles flickering in the four empty chairs we left at the front. There's a candle for my dad, her dad, Grandma Rose, and Phillip. We felt Rose and Phillip helped us fall in love, and we wanted to honor their contribution.

When the horse stops at the end of the aisle, Otto waits to open the door and help Zhanna step down. She steps onto the aisle in a boho, ivory, lace dress with bell sleeves and a flowy skirt. Her blond hair is curled. Her makeup is perfect. In her hands is a bouquet of lilies and orchids. She's gorgeous.

Otto walks her down the aisle to me, and with her mom, they give her away to me.

"Dearly Beloved, we are gathered here today to witness the union of Bryant and Zhanna," Leslie starts as Zhanna and I hold hands.

I miss most of what he says until I'm to repeat after him. I'm so lost in her that it's hard to breathe. The ceremony goes by as I stare deeply into her and remember all the things it took to get us here today. There was a lot of pain, most of it caused by me, but in the end, we came out stronger and better for everything we've gone through. I couldn't ask for a better woman. I couldn't ask for a better wife. I'm beyond grateful for her.

Zhanna and I still have moments where we struggle. Sometimes, she's insecure. I do my best to reassure her that she's the only woman I'm remotely interested in. Trust isn't easily earned back when it's shattered into a million pieces, but I often put myself in her shoes. She handles the hard days better than I would if the roles were reversed.

With the help of continued counseling, we've learned to communicate, not just on the easy days, but on the hard ones too. It's made us a stronger couple than we were before the divorce. I think it's taught us to be grateful for each other every day. For my part, I've learned to tell her everything and involve her in all of my decisions. I ensure we're always a team.

For her part, Zhanna is no longer a runner. When she's feeling insecure or having a hard time trusting, she asks questions. I do my best to reassure her. She's really embraced the open communication we've established.

"You may kiss the bride, Suga," Leslie says, and I snap to it.

I smirk at Zhanna, and she grins back. It's time to show anyone who's watching what Zhanna and Bryant Hudson are about. I pull her to me, press my lips to hers, and kiss her softly. Then I press my hand between her shoulders and dip her back as I kiss the hell out of her. The guests cheer me on, so I go for it. Zhanna breaks the kiss by laughing at me and the crowd, so I set her to rights. There'll be plenty of time to kiss my wife, although I'm quite impatient to be inside her again as her husband.

Leslie turns us to the crowd and introduces us. "I present to you Mr. and Mrs. Bryant Hudson."

We walk down the aisle to congratulatory cheers and hugs. Then we wait by the horse and carriage on Ben and Zina.

I kiss my wife again. "I love you, Coach."

"I love you too, Quarterback."

Beside the altar and ceremony area is a huge tent ready for a party, and we do just that. We eat, drink, and dance. By midnight, Zhanna is dead on her feet and holding her lower back like it's killing her. I speed the goodbyes along and get my baby out of there.

Tonight, we'll stay at the new cabin we had built at Hale's Row. It's much bigger than the smaller cabin we've spent years in. It'll allow us to grow and all be here at once. We spend a lot of time here in the offseason, but we're still in the Quarter at the house Leslie renovated within an inch of its life for us. Plus, I spent a mint on a giant fucking tree for Punter. Zhanna has grown accustomed to its large, looming presence.

"I have a wedding present for you," she says as we pull up to the new cabin in the horse and carriage.

"I have one for you as well," I say and waggle my brows.

She giggles at me. "Then I have two gifts for you. Would you like to open it now or later?" She asks and I can tell she's really hopeful I'll say now.

"Definitely now."

Once we're inside the cabin, she leads me to the bed in our downstairs bedroom, and she reaches underneath it to pull out a wrapped t-shirt box. Zhanna is a thoughtful person, so I can't wait to see what she bought or made for me.

"Dig in," she says as she hands me the box.

"You didn't have to buy me anything. Marrying me a second time is more than enough."

She leans down to press a kiss to my lips, and then I start ripping the gift paper. Inside the box, underneath white tissue paper, there's a little cat onesie that reads "Hudson" on the back and "Future Quarterback" on the front.

"You bought Punter a shirt! But, babe, I think it's a bit too big for him."

She puts her hands on her hips and sighs. "Keep looking, QB."

Underneath another piece of tissue paper, there's a pink onesie with "Hudson" on the back and "Future Coach" on the front. I look up my wife with confusion and maybe a little hope. She's bouncing up and down on the balls of her feet in excitement.

"Baby?"

"Yeah?" She nearly squeals.

"Really?"

"Keep looking."

Underneath the last piece of tissue paper is a sonogram of a little bean-shaped baby.

"I'll be damned," I say and start to feel a little weepy. And then I leave the bed and find my way to my knees in front of her. I place both my large hands on her belly and lean forward to press a kiss to it. I can't wait until there's more to kiss. "I love you more than life itself, Coach. Thank you."

"And I love you to the moon and back, Quarterback."

If you enjoyed this book, please consider leaving a review. Indie authors depend on word of mouth to find new readers. Thank you for reading.

Sasha Marshall

Please visit this website for more information about Sasha Marshall

Linktr.ee/SashaMarshallWrites

Experience Sasha's other titles:

Linktr.ee/SashaMarshallWrites

(Please continue reading for more information about the author)

ACKNOWLEDGMENTS

After six books, I still find it most difficult to write this section of the book. It takes a tribe to put together a book. The words are mine, but the heart and soul of a book is pieced together like patchwork by the hands of not only women, but also a man and his cat.

Sandy, this book would not be possible without you. You're my left hand, as you say, and one of my very best friends. I look forward to coming to work each day because you're there. Our adventures, however fictitious, are the heart of my day. Thank you for being your wonderful self. Love you.

Derek, thank you for your infinite football knowledge and for lending me your support any time Sandy hands you the phone. I must also show my gratitude for allowing me to monopolize your wife's time with my crazy ideas and antics.

Samantha & Sethery, my second family, you're my rock, and I feel like I can do anything with you at my back, including writing from the comfort of your porches. Love y'all.

Mary, my sista from another mista, thank you for making this book be all it can be and for being a part of the tribe that put Bryant and Zhanna back together again. You've been on this crazy ride with me for so long that I can't remember a time when you weren't on it. I admire how strong, hard-working, and kind you are. I want to be you when I grow up. Love you.

Lee, my feisty, Scrappy Doo, none of this would be possible without you and your faith in me. I thank my lucky stars that you agreed to be my right hand, and at times, sanity. It's often a huge undertaking, but you do it with such grace. LOL I love you.

Mia, Nadine, Dee, and Tianna, I cannot thank you girls enough for combing through this book and agreeing to beta read False Start. This book was pieced together with your hands, and I can never truly show my gratitude for y'all being willing to read for an author you didn't know.

To my readers and the Goddesses, you are the reason I write. You are the reason I wake up and smile when I go to work each day. Thank

False Start

you for reading, purchasing, supporting, and reviewing my books. You have no idea how grateful I am to each of you for your love and faith in me.

ABOUT THE AUTHOR

Award-winning and best-selling author SASHA MARSHALL is devoted to giving her readers humorous adventures with a love story sure to melt their hearts— and their minds. She wants you to laugh, cry, get angry, and sigh when you find redemption in a story, because that's the roller coaster of real life. Her knowledge of the music industry comes from being a touring concert photographer with legendary bands such as The Allman Brothers Band and others she met along the way. A self-proclaimed free spirit, she's most often found outdoors, capturing a photograph, people watching, or reading a book. Sasha makes her home in the beautiful state of Georgia and loves to hear from her readers. Visit her website at SashaMarshall.com

False Start

Made in the USA
Monee, IL
26 April 2025